GUILTY CREATURES

GUILTY CREATURES

A MENAGERIE OF MYSTERIES

Edited and Introduced by
Martin Edwards

Poisoned Pen
PRESS

Published by Poisoned Pen Press, an imprint of Sourcebooks, in association with the
British Library
P.O. Box 4410, Naperville, Illinois 60567-4410
(630) 961-3900
sourcebooks.com

Library of Congress Cataloging-in-Publication Data

Names: Edwards, Martin, editor.
Title: Guilty creatures : a menagerie of mysteries / edited and introduced
   by Martin Edwards.
Description: Naperville, Illinois : Poisoned Pen Press, [2022] | Series:
   British Library crime classics
Identifiers: LCCN 2021042285 (print) | LCCN 2021042286 (ebook) | (trade paperback) |
(epub)
Subjects: LCSH: Detective and mystery stories, English. | Animals--Fiction.
   | Animals in literature. | LCGFT: Detective and mystery fiction. | Short
   stories.
Classification: LCC PR1309.D4 G85 2022 (print) | LCC PR1309.D4 (ebook) |
   DDC 823/.087208--dc23/eng/20210927
LC record available at https://lccn.loc.gov/2021042285
LC ebook record available at https://lccn.loc.gov/2021042286

Printed and bound in the United States of America.
SB 10 9 8 7 6 5 4 3 2 1

Contents

Introduction   vii

The Adventure of the Lion's Mane   1
Arthur Conan Doyle

The Case of Janissary   26
Arthur Morrison

The Sapient Monkey   56
Headon Hill

The Green Parrakeet   68
F. Tennyson Jesse

The Oracle of the Dog   96
G. K. Chesterton

The Man Who Hated Earthworms   125
Edgar Wallace

The Courtyard of the Fly   142
Vincent Cornier

The Yellow Slugs   152
H. C. Bailey

Pit of Screams   199
Garnett Radcliffe

Hanging by a Hair   213
Clifford Witting

The Man Who Shot Birds   223
Mary Fitt

Death in a Cage   243
Josephine Bell

The Man Who Loved Animals   259
Penelope Wallace

The Hornet's Nest   268
Christianna Brand

Introduction

FROM THE FIRST DETECTIVE STORY, EDGAR ALLAN Poe's locked room puzzle "The Murders in the Rue Morgue" onwards, animals, birds, and insects have played a memorable part in countless mysteries, and in a wide variety of ways. Count Fosco, the brilliantly characterised villain in Wilkie Collins's *The Woman in White* was surrounded by "a cockatoo, two canary-birds and a whole family of white mice," while the hound of the Baskervilles famously terrorised Dartmoor in Arthur Conan Doyle's superb Sherlock Holmes novel. Since then, many crime writers have written about members of the animal kingdom. This anthology celebrates an often-overlooked species of classic crime fiction.

Doyle was a man who loved sport and the outdoors, and his interest in animals is reflected in a few of his finest pieces of fiction, although it must be said that the guilty creature in "The Speckled Band," one of the finest entries in the Holmes case-book, does not actually exist.

Apart from *The Hound of the Baskervilles*, there is "Silver Blaze," one of the most popular short stories to feature animals. Holmes investigates the disappearance of a prize-winning racehorse, which is favourite for the Wessex Cup, and the death of its trainer owner. His inquiries give rise to a celebrated exchange with the competent but unimaginative Devonshire police officer Inspector Gregory:

> *Gregory: Is there any other point to which you would wish to draw my attention?*
> *Holmes: To the curious incident of the dog in the night-time.*
> *Gregory: The dog did nothing in the night-time.*
> *Holmes: That was the curious incident.*

The patterns of animal behaviour are central to the story, which was first published in 1892. Four years later, Doyle took up riding during a trip to Egypt. He soon received a reminder of the unpredictability of animals: on one occasion a frisky black stallion sent him flying and kicked him on the head with such force that he was lucky not to lose an eye.

By that time, the literary career of Nat Gould was already under way. His first book, *The Double Life: a Tale of the Melbourne Cup*, appeared in 1891, and he proceeded to turn out more than a hundred thrillers, generally with a horse racing theme. The *Morning Post* described him, with a touch of hyperbole, as: "the most widely read of all modern storytellers, and a genius in his down-right way." His successes were later eclipsed by those of the high-profile former jockey Dick Francis, whose crime writing career began in 1962 with *Dead Cert*. No fewer than three of his thrillers, which invariably drew on his knowledge of horse racing, won Edgar awards from the Mystery Writers of America.

Animals play an extraordinarily wide variety of roles in

crime stories. They may be victims, witnesses, even detectives. Authors who are passionate animal lovers are especially inclined to make use of them in their fiction. A prime example is Agatha Christie. She said in *An Autobiography*: "On my fifth birthday, I was given a dog. It was the most shattering thing that ever happened to me; such unbelievable joy that I was unable to say a word." The new pet was a Yorkshire terrier puppy, and Christie's devotion to dogs became lifelong.

Christie wrote a short story, "The Incident of the Dog's Ball," in or around 1933, although it was not published for more than three-quarters of a century, when John Curran included it in *Agatha Christie's Secret Notebooks: Mysteries in the Making*. The reason for its non-appearance seems to be that Christie decided to rework the central idea into a full-length Hercule Poirot novel, *Dumb Witness*, aka *Poirot Loses a Client*, which first appeared in 1937. Christie dedicated the book to her wire-haired terrier, Peter, who is fictionalised in the story as Bob, and whose picture took pride of place on the dust jacket of the first edition. She also has Poirot say approvingly: "The dog, he argues from reason. He is intelligent, he makes his deductions according to his point of view. There are people who may enter a house and there are people who may not—that a dog soon learns."

Stella Tower's *Dumb Vengeance*, published four years before Christie's book appeared, is a rare mystery by a talented but little-known writer (she also published under the name Faith Wolseley), but is even more striking. The story is told in the first person; the narrator is Miss Jenkins, who lives at Houghton, the home of well-to-do John Vine and his wife, Gloria. Vine is an amiable fellow, and Miss Jenkins is devoted to him. But the first twist in this interesting story comes when we discover that Miss Jenkins is a dog...

It is more than likely that *Dumb Vengeance* was the first crime novel to be narrated by an animal—I haven't yet found an earlier example—but it was not the last. *Felidae*, published in 1999 by the Turkish-German writer Akif Pirinçci, is an especially striking piece of work. Narrated by Francis, a cat, the book was subsequently filmed, and launched a series which has so far run to eight books.

Felidae is a dark story, in marked contrast to many of the so-called "cosy crime" mysteries which focus on animals and which have enjoyed considerable success right up to the present day. The American Clea Simon has become a prolific author of light-hearted pet mysteries such as *Probable Claws, Cries and Whiskers, Parrots Prove Deadly*, and *When Bunnies Go Bad*. Cats are especially popular protagonists in detective stories, and the long-running series by Lillian Jackson Braun which began in 1966 with *The Cat Who Could Read Backwards* (the cat in question is a Siamese called Koko) yielded many bestsellers.

Writers often find their imagination liberated by a storyline about an animal, bird, or insect. The British philosopher and mystic Gerald Heard made an unexpected splash with *A Taste for Honey*, a curiosity of a crime novel published in 1941 under the name H. F. Heard. The story featured an enigmatic beekeeper who calls himself Mr. Mycroft; it was filmed (not very successfully) in 1966 as *The Deadly Bees*, with a script co-written by Robert Bloch, and gave rise to a movie subgenre jokily dubbed as "beesploitation" and featuring legendary flops such as *The Swarm*.

A much more effective thriller film was Alfred Hitchcock's *The Birds*, based on a short story by Daphne du Maurier, and with a screenplay written by Evan Hunter, who was perhaps better known as Ed McBain, the master of the American police procedural novel. Ann Cleeves won a CWA Gold Dagger for *Raven Black*, published in 2006, and ornithology features in many of her books, above all her first series of eight novels featuring George and Molly Palmer-Jones. Birds continue to feature in interesting crime novels, including *Out of a Clear Sky*, a story of psychological suspense by Sally Hinchcliffe, and a first novel which seems, surprisingly, to have had no successors.

Guilty Creatures gathers together a wide range of stories illustrating some of the endless possibilities of this branch of mystery fiction. I'm grateful to the staff of the publishing department at the British Library for their work on the book, to Nigel Moss, John Cooper, and Jamie Sturgeon for their constructive suggestions about stories which might fit the brief, and to Doug Greene for his help as regards the story by F. Tennyson Jesse.

And now it just remains for me to express the hope that readers, whether animal lovers or not, will find plenty of entertainment in these pages. It's just possible you may never look at your much loved pet in quite the same way again…

—Martin Edwards
www.martinedwardsbooks.com

The Adventure of the Lion's Mane

Arthur Conan Doyle

THE EDINBURGH-BORN WRITER AND PHYSICIAN
Arthur Ignatius Conan Doyle (1859–1930) created, in
Sherlock Holmes, the most renowned character in the history of fiction. Detection was only one of his many literary interests. *Rodney Stone* was a novel about boxing, *The Tragedy of the Korosko* was a thriller set in Egypt, and *The Lost World*, a work of science fiction. His historical novels include *Sir Nigel*, set in the fourteenth century, and the Brigadier Gerard books looked back to Napoleonic times. Doyle's interest in the macabre surfaced in memorable short horror tales such as "The Leather Funnel," "The Terror of Blue John Gap," and "Lot No. 249."

"The Lion's Mane" was one of the last stories that Doyle wrote about Holmes, and its merits are often underestimated, although Doyle himself thought it one of the best of his stories in terms of plot. First published in *The Strand Magazine* in December 1926, although possibly written five or six years earlier, it presents an unusual mystery and is especially notable for its account of Holmes's activities during his retirement. The great detective himself, rather than Dr. Watson, narrates. The story features an intriguing "dying message clue" and the tragic death of a dog, as well as an extraordinary explanation for the mystery. Holmes's use of photography in his detective work is mentioned (for the first time in the canon), and the story illustrates the benefit to a sleuth of being exceptionally well read.

IT IS A MOST SINGULAR THING THAT A PROBLEM WHICH was certainly as abstruse and unusual as any which I have faced in my long professional career should have come to me after my retirement, and be brought, as it were, to my very door. It occurred after my withdrawal to my little Sussex home, when I had given myself up entirely to that soothing life of Nature for which I had so often yearned during the long years spent amid the gloom of London. At this period of my life the good Watson had passed almost beyond my ken. An occasional week-end visit was the most I ever saw of him. Thus I must act as my own chronicler. Ah! had he but been with me, how much he might have made of so wonderful a happening and of my eventual triumph against every difficulty! As it is, however, I must needs tell my tale in my own plain way, showing by my words each step upon the difficult road which lay before me as I searched for the mystery of the Lion's Mane.

My villa is situated upon the southern slope of the Downs, commanding a great view of the Channel. At this point the coast line is entirely of chalk cliffs, which can only be descended by a single, long, tortuous path, which is steep and slippery. At the bottom of the path lie a hundred yards of pebbles and shingle, even when the tide is at full. Here and there, however, there are curves and hollows which make splendid swimming pools filled afresh with each flow. This admirable beach extends for some miles in each direction, save only at one point where the little cove and village of Fulworth break the line.

My house is lonely. I, my old housekeeper, and my bees have the estate all to ourselves. Half a mile off, however, is Harold Stackhurst's well-known coaching establishment, The Gables—quite a large place, which contains some score of young fellows preparing for various professions, with a staff of several masters. Stackhurst himself was a well-known rowing Blue in his day, and an excellent all-round scholar. He and I were always friendly from the day I came to the coast, and he was the one man who was on such terms with me that we could drop in on each other in the evenings without an invitation.

Towards the end of July 1907, there was a severe gale, the wind blowing up-Channel, heaping the seas to the base of the cliffs, and leaving a lagoon at the turn of the tide. On the morning of which I speak the wind had abated, and all Nature was newly washed and fresh. It was impossible to work upon so delightful a day, and I strolled out before breakfast to enjoy the exquisite air. I walked along the cliff path which led to the steep descent to the beach. As I walked I heard a shout behind me, and there was Harold Stackhurst waving his hand in cheery greeting.

"What a morning, Mr. Holmes! I thought I should see you out."

"Going for a swim, I see."

"At your old tricks again," he laughed, patting his bulging

pocket. "Yes, McPherson started early, and I expect I may find him there."

Fitzroy McPherson was the science master, a fine upstanding young fellow whose life had been crippled by heart trouble following rheumatic fever. He was a natural athlete, however, and excelled in every game which did not throw too great a strain upon him. Summer and winter he went for his swim, and, as I am a swimmer myself, I have often joined him.

At this moment we saw the man himself. His head showed above the edge of the cliff where the path ends. Then his whole figure appeared at the top, staggering like a drunken man. The next instant he threw up his hands, and, with a terrible cry, fell upon his face. Stackhurst and I rushed forward—it may have been fifty yards—and turned him on his back. He was obviously dying. Those glazed sunken eyes and dreadful livid cheeks could mean nothing else. One glimmer of life came into his face for an instant, and he uttered two or three words with an eager air of warning. They were slurred and indistinct, but to my ear the last of them, which burst in a shriek from his lips, were "the lion's mane." It was utterly irrelevant and unintelligible, and yet I could twist the sound into no other sense. Then he half raised himself from the ground, threw his arms into the air and fell forward on his side. He was dead.

My companion was paralysed by the sudden horror of it, but I, as may well be imagined, had every sense on the alert. And I had need, for it was speedily evident that we were in the presence of an extraordinary case. The man was dressed only in his Burberry overcoat, his trousers, and an unlaced pair of canvas shoes. As he fell over, his Burberry, which had been simply thrown round his shoulders, slipped off, exposing his trunk. We stared at it in amazement. His back was covered with dark red lines as though he had been terribly flogged by a thin wire scourge. The instrument with which this punishment had been inflicted was clearly flexible, for the long, angry weals curved round his shoulders and ribs. There was blood dripping down his chin, for he had bitten through his lower lip in the paroxysm of his agony. His drawn and distorted face told how terrible that agony had been.

I was kneeling and Stackhurst standing by the body when a shadow fell across us, and we found that Ian Murdoch was by our side. Murdoch was the mathematical coach at the establishment, a tall, dark, thin man, so taciturn and aloof that none can be said to have been his friend. He seemed to live in some high abstract region of surds and conic sections with little to connect him with ordinary life. He was looked upon as an oddity by the students, and would have been their butt, but there was some strange outlandish blood in the man which showed itself not only in his coal-black eyes and swarthy face, but also in occasional outbreaks of temper, which could only be described as ferocious. On one occasion, being plagued by a little dog belonging to McPherson, he had caught the creature up and hurled it through the plate-glass window—an action for which Stackhurst would certainly have given him his dismissal had he not been a very valuable teacher. Such was the strange, complex man who now appeared beside us. He seemed to be honestly shocked at the sight before him, though the incident of the dog may show that there was no great sympathy between the dead man and himself.

"Poor fellow! Poor fellow! What can I do? How can I help?"

"Were you with him? Can you tell us what has happened?"

"No, no, I was late this morning. I was not on the beach at all. I have come straight from The Gables. What can I do?"

"You can hurry to the police station at Fulworth. Report the matter at once."

Without a word he made off at top speed, and I proceeded to take the matter in hand, while Stackhurst, dazed at this tragedy, remained by the body. My first task naturally was to note who was on the beach. From the top of the path I could see the whole sweep of it, and it was absolutely deserted save that two or three dark figures could be seen far away moving towards the village of Fulworth. Having satisfied myself upon this point, I walked slowly down the path. There was clay or soft marl mixed with the chalk, and every here and there I saw the same footstep, both ascending and descending. No one else had gone down to the beach by this track that morning. At one place I observed the print of an open hand with the fingers towards the incline. This could only mean that poor McPherson had fallen as he ascended. There were rounded depressions, too, which suggested that he had come down upon his knees more than once. At the bottom of the path was the considerable lagoon left by the retreating tide. At the side of it McPherson had undressed, for there lay his towel on a rock. It was folded and dry, so that it would seem that after all he had never entered the water. Once or twice as I hunted round amid the hard shingle I came on little patches of sand where the print of his canvas shoe, and also of his naked foot, could be seen. The latter fact proved that he had made all ready to bathe, though the towel indicated that he had not actually done so.

And here was the problem clearly defined—as strange a one as had ever confronted me. The man had not been on the beach more than a quarter of an hour at the most.

Stackhurst had followed him from The Gables, so there could be no doubt about that. He had gone to bathe and had stripped, as the naked footsteps showed. Then he had suddenly huddled on his clothes again—they were all dishevelled and unfastened—and he had returned without bathing, or at any rate without drying himself. And the reason for his change of purpose had been that he had been scourged in some savage, inhuman fashion, tortured until he bit his lip through in his agony, and was left with only strength enough to crawl away and to die. Who had done this barbarous deed? There were, it is true, small grottoes and caves in the base of the cliffs, but the low sun shone directly into them, and there was no place for concealment. Then, again, there were those distant figures on the beach. They seemed too far away to have been connected with the crime, and the broad lagoon in which McPherson had intended to bathe lay between him and them, lapping up to the rocks. On the sea two or three fishing boats were at no great distance. Their occupants might be examined at our leisure. There were several roads for inquiry, but none which led to any very obvious goal.

When I at last returned to the body I found that a little group of wandering folk had gathered round it. Stackhurst was, of course, still there, and Ian Murdoch had just arrived with Anderson, the village constable, a big, ginger-moustached man of the slow solid Sussex breed—a breed which covers much good sense under a heavy, silent exterior. He listened to everything, took note of all we said, and finally drew me aside.

"I'd be glad of your advice, Mr. Holmes. This is a big thing for me to handle, and I'll hear of it from Lewes if I go wrong."

I advised him to send for his immediate superior, and for a doctor, also to allow nothing to be removed, and as few fresh footmarks as possible to be made, until they came. In the mean time I searched the dead man's pockets. There were his handkerchief, a large knife, and a small folding card-case. From this projected a slip of paper, which I unfolded and handed to the constable. There was written on it in a scrawling feminine hand: *"I will be there you may be sure. Maudie."* It read like a love affair, an assignation, though when and where were a blank. The constable replaced it in the card-case and returned it with the other things to the pockets of the Burberry. Then, as nothing more suggested itself, I walked back to my house for breakfast, having first arranged that the base of the cliffs should be thoroughly searched.

Stackhurst was round in an hour or two to tell me that the body had been removed to The Gables, where the inquest would be held. He brought with him some serious and definite news. As I expected, nothing had been found in the small caves below the cliff, but he had examined the papers in McPherson's desk, and there were several which showed an intimate correspondence with a certain Miss Maud Bellamy, of Fulworth. We had then established the identity of the writer of the note.

"The police have the letters," he explained. "I could not bring them. But there is no doubt that it was a serious love affair. I see no reason, however, to connect it with that horrible happening save, indeed, that the lady had made an appointment with him."

"But hardly at a bathing-pool which all of you were in the habit of using," I remarked.

"It is mere chance," said he, "that several of the students were not with McPherson."

"*Was* it mere chance?"

Stackhurst knit his brows in thought.

"Ian Murdoch held them back," said he, "he would insist upon some algebraic demonstration before breakfast. Poor chap, he is dreadfully cut up about it all."

"And yet I gather that they were not friends."

"At one time they were not. But for a year or more Murdoch has been as near to McPherson as he ever could be to anyone. He is not of a very sympathetic disposition by nature."

"So I understand. I seem to remember your telling me once about a quarrel over the ill-usage of a dog."

"That blew over all right."

"But left some vindictive feeling, perhaps."

"No, no, I am sure they were real friends."

"Well, then, we must explore the matter of the girl. Do you know her?"

"Everybody knows her. She is the beauty of the neighbourhood—a real beauty, Holmes, who would draw attention everywhere. I knew that McPherson was attracted by her, but I had no notion that it had gone so far as these letters would seem to indicate."

"But who is she?"

"She is the daughter of old Tom Bellamy, who owns all the boats and bathing-cots at Fulworth. He was a fisherman to start with, but is now a man of some substance. He and his son William run the business."

"Shall we walk into Fulworth and see them?"

"On what pretext?"

"Oh, we can easily find a pretext. After all, this poor man did not ill-use himself in this outrageous way. Some human hand was on the handle of that scourge, if indeed it was a scourge which inflicted the injuries. His circle of acquaintances in this lonely place was surely limited. Let us follow it up in every direction and we can hardly fail to come upon the motive, which in turn should lead us to the criminal."

It would have been a pleasant walk across the thyme-scented downs had our minds not been poisoned by the tragedy we had witnessed. The village of Fulworth lies in a hollow curving in a semicircle round the bay. Behind the old-fashioned hamlet several modern houses have been built upon the rising ground. It was to one of these that Stackhurst guided me.

"That's The Haven, as Bellamy called it. The one with the corner tower and slate roof. Not bad for a man who started with nothing but—By Jove, look at that!"

The garden gate of The Haven had opened and a man had emerged. There was no mistaking that tall, angular, straggling figure. It was Ian Murdoch, the mathematician. A moment later we confronted him upon the road.

"Hullo!" said Stackhurst. The man nodded, gave us a sideways glance from his curious dark eyes, and would have passed us, but his principal pulled him up.

"What were you doing there?" he asked.

Murdoch's face flushed with anger. "I am your subordinate, sir, under your roof. I am not aware that I owe you any account of my private actions."

Stackhurst's nerves were near the surface after all he had endured. Otherwise, perhaps, he would have waited. Now he lost his temper completely.

"In the circumstances your answer is pure impertinence, Mr. Murdoch."

"Your own question might perhaps come under the same heading."

"This is not the first time that I have had to overlook your insubordinate ways. It will certainly be the last. You will kindly make fresh arrangements for your future as speedily as you can."

"I had intended to do so. I have lost today the only person who made The Gables habitable."

He strode off upon his way, while Stackhurst, with angry eyes, stood glaring after him. "Is he not an impossible, intolerable man?" he cried.

The one thing that impressed itself forcibly upon my mind was that Mr. Ian Murdoch was taking the first chance to open a path of escape from the scene of the crime. Suspicion, vague and nebulous, was now beginning to take outline in my mind. Perhaps the visit to the Bellamys might throw some further light upon the matter. Stackhurst pulled himself together and we went forward to the house.

Mr. Bellamy proved to be a middle-aged man with a flaming red beard. He seemed to be in a very angry mood, and his face was soon as florid as his hair.

"No, sir, I do not desire any particulars. My son here"—indicating a powerful young man, with a heavy, sullen face, in the corner of the sitting-room—"is of one mind with me that Mr. McPherson's attentions to Maud were insulting. Yes, sir, the word 'marriage' was never mentioned, and yet there were letters and meetings, and a great deal more of which neither of us could approve. She has no mother, and we are her only guardians. We are determined—"

But the words were taken from his mouth by the appearance of the lady herself. There was no gainsaying that she would have graced any assembly in the world. Who could have imagined that so rare a flower would grow from such a root and in such an atmosphere? Women have seldom been an attraction to me, for my brain has always governed my heart, but I could not look upon her perfect clear-cut face, with all the soft freshness of the Downlands in her delicate colouring, without realising that no young man would cross her path unscathed. Such was the girl who had pushed open the door and stood now, wide-eyed and intense, in front of Harold Stackhurst.

"I know already that Fitzroy is dead," she said. "Do not be afraid to tell me the particulars."

"This other gentleman of yours let us know the news," explained the father.

"There is no reason why my sister should be brought into the matter," growled the younger man.

The sister turned a sharp, fierce look upon him. "This is my business, William. Kindly leave me to manage it in my own way. By all accounts there has been a crime committed. If I can help to show who did it, it is the least I can do for him who is gone."

She listened to a short account from my companion, with a composed concentration which showed me that she possessed strong character as well as great beauty. Maud Bellamy will always remain in my memory as a most complete and remarkable woman. It seems that she already knew me by sight, for she turned to me at the end.

"Bring them to justice, Mr. Holmes. You have my sympathy and my help, whoever they may be." It seemed to me that she glanced defiantly at her father and brother as she spoke.

"Thank you," said I. "I value a woman's instinct in such matters. You use the word 'they.' You think that more than one person was concerned?"

"I knew Mr. McPherson well enough to be aware that he

was a brave and a strong man. No single person could ever have inflicted such an outrage upon him."

"Might I have one word with you alone?"

"I tell you, Maud, not to mix yourself up in the matter," cried her father angrily.

She looked at me helplessly. "What can I do?"

"The whole world will know the facts presently, so there can be no harm if I discuss them here," said I. "I should have preferred privacy, but if your father will not allow it, he must share the deliberations." Then I spoke of the note which had been found in the dead man's pocket. "It is sure to be produced at the inquest. May I ask you to throw any light upon it that you can?"

"I see no reason for mystery," she answered. "We were engaged to be married, and we only kept it secret because Fitzroy's uncle, who is very old and said to be dying, might have disinherited him if he had married against his wish. There was no other reason."

"You could have told us," growled Mr. Bellamy.

"So I would, father, if you had ever shown sympathy."

"I object to my girl picking up with men outside her own station."

"It was your prejudice against him which prevented us from telling you. As to this appointment"—she fumbled in her dress and produced a crumpled note—"it was in answer to this."

DEAREST, [ran the message]
The old place on the beach just after sunset on Tuesday. It is the only time I can get away.—F.M.

"Tuesday was today, and I had meant to meet him tonight."

I turned over the paper. "This never came by post. How did you get it?"

"I would rather not answer that question. It has really nothing to do with the matter which you are investigating. But anything which bears upon that I will most freely answer."

She was as good as her word, but there was nothing which was helpful in our investigation. She had no reason to think that her fiancé had any hidden enemy, but she admitted that she had had several warm admirers.

"May I ask if Mr. Ian Murdoch was one of them?"

She blushed and seemed confused.

"There was a time when I thought he was. But that was all changed when he understood the relations between Fitzroy and myself."

Again the shadow round this strange man seemed to me to be taking more definite shape. His record must be examined. His rooms must be privately searched. Stackhurst was a willing collaborator, for in his mind also suspicions were forming. We returned from our visit to The Haven with the hope that one free end of this tangled skein was already in our hands.

A week passed. The inquest had thrown no light upon the matter and had been adjourned for further evidence. Stackhurst had made discreet inquiry about his subordinate, and there had been a superficial search of his room, but without result. Personally, I had gone over the whole ground again, both physically and mentally, but with no new conclusions. In all my chronicles the reader will find no case which brought me so completely to the limit of my powers. Even my imagination could conceive no solution to the mystery. And then there came the incident of the dog.

It was my old housekeeper who heard of it first by that strange wireless by which such people collect the news of the countryside.

"Sad story this, sir, about Mr. McPherson's dog," said she one evening.

I do not encourage such conversations, but the words arrested my attention.

"What of Mr. McPherson's dog?"

"Dead, sir. Died of grief for its master."

"Who told you this?"

"Why, sir, everyone is talking of it. It took on terrible, and has eaten nothing for a week. Then today two of the young gentlemen from The Gables found it dead—down on the beach, sir, at the very place where its master met his end."

"At the very place." The words stood out clear in my memory. Some dim perception that the matter was vital rose in my mind. That the dog should die was after the beautiful, faithful nature of dogs. But "in the very place"! Why should this lonely beach be fatal to it? Was it possible that it also, had been sacrificed to some revengeful feud? Was it possible—? Yes, the perception was dim, but already something was building up in my mind. In a few minutes I was on my way to The Gables, where I found Stackhurst in his study. At my request he sent for Sudbury and Blount, the two students who had found the dog.

"Yes, it lay on the very edge of the pool," said one of them. "It must have followed the trail of its dead master."

I saw the faithful little creature, an Airedale terrier, laid out upon the mat in the hall. The body was stiff and rigid, the eyes projecting, and the limbs contorted. There was agony in every line of it.

From The Gables I walked down to the bathing pool.

The sun had sunk and the shadow of the great cliff lay black across the water, which glimmered dully like a sheet of lead. The place was deserted and there was no sign of life save for two sea-birds circling and screaming overhead. In the fading light I could dimly make out the little dog's spoor upon the sand round the very rock on which his master's towel had been laid. For a long time I stood in deep meditation while the shadows grew darker around me. My mind was filled with racing thoughts. You have known what it was to be in a nightmare in which you feel that there is some all-important thing for which you search and which you know is there, though it remains for ever just beyond your reach. That was how I felt that evening as I stood alone by that place of death. Then at last I turned and walked slowly homewards.

I had just reached the top of the path when it came to me. Like a flash, I remembered the thing for which I had so eagerly and vainly grasped. You will know, or Watson has written in vain, that I hold a vast store of out-of-the-way knowledge, without scientific system, but very available for the needs of my work. My mind is like a crowded boxroom with packets of all sorts stowed away therein—so many that I may well have but a vague perception of what was there. I had known that there was something which might bear upon this matter. It was still vague, but at least I knew how I could make it clear. It was monstrous, incredible, and yet it was always a possibility. I would test it to the full.

There is a great garret in my little house which is stuffed with books. It was into this that I plunged and rummaged for an hour. At the end of that time I emerged with a little chocolate and silver volume. Eagerly I turned up the chapter of which I had a dim remembrance. Yes, it was indeed a far-fetched and unlikely proposition, and yet I could not be at rest until I had made sure if it might, indeed, be so. It was late when I retired, with my mind eagerly awaiting the work of the morrow.

But that work met with an annoying interruption. I had hardly swallowed my early cup of tea and was starting for the beach when I had a call from Inspector Bardle of the Sussex Constabulary—a steady, solid, bovine man with thoughtful eyes, which looked at me now with a very troubled expression.

"I know your immense experience sir," said he. "This is quite unofficial, of course, and need go no farther. But I am fairly up against it in this McPherson case. The question is, shall I make an arrest, or shall I not?"

"Meaning Mr. Ian Murdoch?"

"Yes, sir. There is really no one else when you come to think of it. That's the advantage of this solitude. We narrow it down to a very small compass. If he did not do it, then who did?"

"What have you against him?"

He had gleaned along the same furrows as I had. There was Murdoch's character and the mystery which seemed to hang round the man. His furious bursts of temper, as shown in the incident of the dog. The fact that he had quarrelled with McPherson in the past, and that there was some reason to think that he might have resented his attentions to Miss Bellamy. He had all my points, but no fresh ones, save that Murdoch seemed to be making every preparation for departure.

"What would my position be if I let him slip away with all this evidence against him?" The burly, phlegmatic man was sorely troubled in his mind.

"Consider," I said, "all the essential gaps in your case.

On the morning of the crime he can surely prove an alibi. He had been with his scholars till the last moment, and within a few minutes of McPherson's appearance he came upon us from behind. Then bear in mind the absolute impossibility that he could single-handed have inflicted this outrage upon a man quite as strong as himself. Finally there is the question of the instrument with which these injuries were inflicted."

"What could it be but a scourge or flexible whip of some sort?"

"Have you examined the marks?" I asked.

"I have seen them. So has the doctor."

"But I have examined them very carefully with a lens. They have peculiarities."

"What are they, Mr. Holmes?"

I stepped to my bureau and brought out an enlarged photograph. "This is my method in such cases," I explained.

"You certainly do things thoroughly, Mr. Holmes."

"I should hardly be what I am if I did not. Now let us consider this weal which extends round the right shoulder. Do you observe nothing remarkable?"

"I can't say I do."

"Surely it is evident that it is unequal in its intensity. There is a dot of extravasated blood here, and another there. There are similar indications in this other weal down here. What can that mean?"

"I have no idea. Have you?"

"Perhaps I have. Perhaps I haven't. I may be able to say more soon. Anything which will define what made that mark will bring us a long way towards the criminal."

"It is, of course, an absurd idea," said the policeman, "but if a red-hot net of wire had been laid across the back, then these better-marked points would represent where the meshes crossed each other."

"A most ingenious comparison. Or shall we say a very stiff cat-o'-nine-tails with small hard knots upon it?"

"By jove, Mr. Holmes, I think you have hit it."

"Or there may be some very different cause, Mr. Bardle. But your case is far too weak for an arrest. Besides, we have those last words—'Lion's Mane.'"

"I have wondered whether Ian—"

"Yes, I have considered that. If the second word had any resemblance to Murdoch—but it did not. He gave it almost in a shriek. I am sure that it was 'Mane.'"

"Have you no alternative, Mr. Holmes?"

"Perhaps I have. But I do not care to discuss it until there is something solid to discuss."

"And when will that be?"

"In an hour—possibly less."

The Inspector rubbed his chin and looked at me with dubious eyes.

"I wish I could see what was in your mind, Mr. Holmes. Perhaps it's those fishing-boats."

"No, no, they were too far out."

"Well, then, is it Bellamy and that big son of his? They were not too sweet upon Mr. McPherson. Could they have done him a mischief?"

"No, no, you won't draw me until I am ready," said I with a smile. "Now, Inspector, we each have our own work to do. Perhaps if you were to meet me here at midday—?"

So far we had got when there came the tremendous interruption which was the beginning of the end.

My outer door was flung open, there were blundering footsteps in the passage, and Ian Murdoch staggered into the room, pallid, dishevelled, his clothes in wild disorder, clawing with his bony hands at the furniture to hold himself erect. "Brandy! Brandy!" he gasped, and fell groaning upon the sofa.

He was not alone. Behind him came Stackhurst, hatless and panting, almost as *distrait* as his companion.

"Yes, yes, brandy!" he cried. "The man is at his last gasp. It was all I could do to bring him here. He fainted twice upon the way."

Half a tumbler of the raw spirit brought about a wondrous change. He pushed himself up on one arm and swung his coat off his shoulders. "For God's sake! oil, opium, morphia!" he cried. "Anything to ease this infernal agony!"

The Inspector and I cried out at the sight. There, crisscrossed upon the man's naked shoulder, was the same strange reticulated pattern of red, inflamed lines which had been the death-mark of Fitzroy McPherson.

The pain was evidently terrible and was more than local, for the sufferer's breathing would stop for a time, his face would turn black, and then with loud gasps he would clap his hand to his heart, while his brow dropped beads of sweat. At any moment he might die. More and more brandy was poured down his throat, each fresh dose bringing him back to life. Pads of cotton wool soaked in salad oil seemed to take the agony from the strange wounds. At last his head fell heavily upon the cushion. Exhausted Nature had taken refuge in its last storehouse of vitality. It was half a sleep and half a faint, but at least it was ease from pain.

To question him had been impossible, but the moment we were assured of his condition Stackhurst turned upon me.

"My God!" he cried, "what is it, Holmes? What is it?"

"Where did you find him?"

"Down on the beach. Exactly where poor McPherson met his end. If this man's heart had been weak as McPherson's was, he would not be here now. More than once I thought he was gone as I brought him up. It was too far to The Gables, so I made for you."

"Did you see him on the beach?"

"I was walking on the cliff when I heard his cry. He was at the edge of the water, reeling about like a drunken man. I ran down, threw some clothes over him and brought him up. For heaven's sake, Holmes, use all the powers you have and spare no pains to lift the curse from this place, for life is becoming unendurable. Can you, with all your worldwide reputation, do nothing for us?"

"I think I can, Stackhurst. Come with me now! And you, Inspector, come along! We will see if we cannot deliver this murderer into your hands."

Leaving the unconscious man in the charge of my housekeeper, we all three went down to the deadly lagoon. On the shingle there was piled a little heap of towels and clothes, left by the stricken man. Slowly I walked round the edge of the water, my comrades in Indian file behind me. Most of the pool was quite shallow, but under the cliff where the beach was hollowed out it was four or five feet deep. It was to this part that a swimmer would naturally go, for it formed a beautiful pellucid green pool as clear as crystal. A line of rocks lay above it at the base of the cliff, and along this I led the way, peering eagerly into the depths beneath me. I had reached the deepest and stillest pool when my eyes caught that for which they were searching, and I burst into a shout of triumph.

"*Cyanea!*" I cried. "*Cyanea!* Behold the Lion's Mane!"

The strange object at which I pointed did indeed look

like a tangled mass torn from the mane of a lion. It lay upon a rocky shelf some three feet under the water, a curious waving, vibrating, hairy creature with streaks of silver among its yellow tresses. It pulsated with a slow, heavy dilation and contraction.

"It has done mischief enough. Its day is over!" I cried. "Help me, Stackhurst! Let us end the murderer for ever."

There was a big boulder just above the ledge, and we pushed it until it fell with a tremendous splash into the water. When the ripples had cleared we saw that it had settled upon the ledge below. One flapping edge of yellow membrane showed that our victim was beneath it. A thick oily scum oozed out from below the stone and stained the water round, rising slowly to the surface.

"Well, this gets me!" cried the Inspector. "What was it, Mr. Holmes? I'm born and bred in these parts, but I never saw such a thing. It don't belong to Sussex."

"Just as well for Sussex," I remarked. "It may have been the south-west gale that brought it up. Come back to my house, both of you, and I will give you the terrible experience of one who had good reason to remember his own meeting with the same peril of the seas."

When we reached my study, we found that Murdoch was so far recovered that he could sit up. He was dazed in mind, and every now and then was shaken by a paroxysm of pain. In broken words he explained that he had no notion what had occurred to him, save that terrific pangs had suddenly shot through him, and that it had taken all his fortitude to reach the bank.

"Here is a book," I said, taking up the little volume, "which first brought light into what might have been for ever dark. It is *Out of Doors*, by the famous observer J. G. Wood.

Wood himself very nearly perished from contact with this vile creature, so he wrote with a very full knowledge. *Cyanea capillata* is the miscreant's full name, and he can be as dangerous to life as, and far more painful than, the bite of the cobra. Let me briefly give this extract.

"'If the bather should see a loose roundish mass of tawny membranes and fibres, something like very large handfuls of lion's mane and silver paper, let him beware, for this is the fearful stinger, *Cyanea capillata*.' Could our sinister acquaintance be more clearly described?

"He goes on to tell his own encounter with one when swimming off the coast of Kent. He found that the creature radiated almost invisible filaments to the distance of fifty feet, and that anyone within that circumference from the deadly centre was in danger of death. Even at a distance the effect upon Wood was almost fatal. 'The multitudinous threads caused light scarlet lines upon the skin which on closer examination resolved into minute dots or pustules, each dot charged as it were with a red-hot needle making its way through the nerves.'

"The local pain was, as he explains, the least part of the exquisite torment. 'Pangs shot through the chest, causing me to fall if as struck by a bullet. The pulsation would cease, and then the heart would give six or seven leaps as if it would force its way through the chest.'

"It nearly killed him, although he had only been exposed to it in the disturbed ocean and not in the narrow calm waters of a bathing pool. He says that he could hardly recognise himself afterwards, so white, wrinkled and shrivelled was his face. He gulped down brandy, a whole bottleful, and it seems to have saved his life. There is the book, Inspector. I leave it with you, and you cannot doubt that it contains a full explanation of the tragedy of poor McPherson."

"And incidentally exonerates me," remarked Ian Murdoch with a wry smile. "I do not blame you, Inspector, nor you, Mr. Holmes, for your suspicions were natural. I feel that on the very eve of my arrest I have only cleared myself by sharing the fate of my poor friend."

"No, Mr. Murdoch. I was already upon the track, and had I been out as early as I intended I might well have saved you from this terrific experience."

"But how did you know, Mr. Holmes?"

"I am an omnivorous reader with a strangely retentive memory for trifles. That phrase 'Lion's Mane' haunted my mind. I knew that I had seen it somewhere in an unexpected context. You have seen that it does describe the creature. I have no doubt that it was floating on the water when McPherson saw it, and that this phrase was the only one by which he could convey to us a warning as to the creature which had been his death."

"Then I, at least, am cleared," said Murdoch, rising slowly to his feet. "There are one or two words of explanation which I should give, for I know the direction in which your inquiries have run. It is true that I loved this lady, but from the day when she chose my friend McPherson my one desire was to help her to happiness. I was well content to stand aside and act as their go-between. Often I carried their messages, and it was because I was in their confidence and because she was so dear to me that I hastened to tell her of my friend's death, lest someone should forestall me in a more sudden and heartless manner. She would not tell you, sir, of our relations lest you would disapprove and I might suffer. But with your leave I must try to get back to The Gables, for my bed will be very welcome."

Stackhurst held out his hand. "Our nerves have all been at concert pitch," said he. "Forgive what is past, Murdoch. We shall understand each other better in the future." They passed out together with their arms linked in friendly fashion. The Inspector remained, staring at me in silence with his ox-like eyes.

"Well, you've done it!" he cried at last. "I had read of you, but I never believed it. It's wonderful!"

I was forced to shake my head. To accept such praise was to lower one's own standards.

"I was slow at the outset—culpably slow. Had the body been found in the water I could hardly have missed it. It was the towel which misled me. The poor fellow had never thought to dry himself, and so I in turn was led to believe that he had never been in the water. Why, then, should the attack of any water creature suggest itself to me? That was where I went astray. Well, well, Inspector, I often ventured to chaff you gentlemen of the police force, but *Cyanea capillata* very nearly avenged Scotland Yard."

The Case of Janissary

Arthur Morrison

ARTHUR MORRISON (1863–1945) ROSE FROM HUMBLE beginnings to become a skilled and highly successful author. He grew up in London's East End, which supplied the background for books such as *Tales of Mean Streets* (1894) and *A Child of the Jago* (1906). When Arthur Conan Doyle appeared to kill off Sherlock Holmes at the Reichenbach Falls, Morrison became, in effect, the leader of the pack of writers who sought to fill the gap with detectives of their own. Morrison's Martin Hewitt was conceived as the antithesis of Holmes, a straightforward individual who was highly competent rather than a maverick genius. The stories were appealing, but Hewitt's ordinariness ultimately counted against him: crime readers tend to like a touch of the exotic in their protagonists.

More remarkable was Horace Dorrington, whose creation was influenced by another vogue for characters who combined detection with villainy; the leading example was A. J. Raffles, created by Doyle's brother-in-law, E. W.

Hornung. One drawback of the literary anti-hero is that his career tends to be short-lived, and Dorrington featured in a mere half dozen stories, collected in *The Dorrington Deed-Box*. The book has a distinctive flavour and is examined in depth in a chapter in Clare Clarke's *Late Victorian Crime Fiction in the Shadow of Sherlock*, an academic text that is both readable and insightful. Two of the stories were televised in 1971 in the anthology series *The Rivals of Sherlock Holmes*, with Peter Vaughan well cast as Dorrington. This story, which like Doyle's "Silver Blaze" concerns an attempt to nobble a racehorse, first appeared in *The Windsor Magazine* in February 1897.

———————

I

IN THIS CASE (AND INDEED IN MOST OF THE OTHERS) the notes and other documents found in the dockets would, by themselves, give but a faint outline of the facts, and, indeed, might easily be unintelligible to many people, especially as for much of my information I have been indebted to outside inquiries. Therefore I offer no excuse for presenting the whole thing digested into plain narrative form, with little reference to my authorities. Though I knew none of the actors in it, with the exception of the astute Dorrington, the case was especially interesting to me, as will be gathered from the narrative itself.

The only paper in the bundle which I shall particularly allude to was a newspaper cutting, of a date anterior by nine or ten months to the events I am to write of. It had evidently been cut at the time it appeared, and saved, in case it might be useful, in a box in the form of a book, containing many hundreds of others. From this receptacle it had been taken, and attached to the bundle during the progress of the case. I may say at once that the facts recorded had no direct concern with the case of the horse Janissary, but had been useful in affording a suggestion to Dorrington in connection therewith. The matter is the short report of an ordinary sort of inquest, and I here transcribe it.

"Dr. McCulloch held an inquest yesterday on the body of Mr. Henry Lawrence, whose body was found on Tuesday morning last in the river near Vauxhall Bridge. The deceased was well known in certain sporting circles. Sophia Lawrence, the widow, said that deceased had left home on Monday afternoon at about five, in his usual health, saying that he was to dine at a friend's, and she saw nothing more of him till called upon to identify the body. He had no reason for suicide, and so far as witness knew, was free from pecuniary embarrassments. He had, indeed, been very successful in betting recently. He habitually carried a large pocket-book, with papers in it. Mr. Robert Naylor, commission agent, said that deceased dined with him that evening at his house in Gold Street, Chelsea, and left for home at about half-past eleven. He had at the time a sum of nearly four hundred pounds upon him, chiefly in notes, which had been paid him by witness in settlement of a bet. It was a fine night, and deceased walked in the direction of Chelsea Embankment. That was the last witness saw of him. He might not have been perfectly sober, but he was not drunk, and was capable of taking care of himself. The evidence of the Thames police went to show that no money was on the body when found, except a few coppers, and no pocket-book. Dr. William Hodgetts said that death was due to drowning. There were some bruises on the arms and head which might have been caused before death. The body was a very healthy one. The coroner said that there seemed to be a very strong suspicion of foul play, unless the pocket-book of the deceased had got out of his pocket in the water; but the evidence was very meagre, although the police appeared to have made every possible inquiry. The jury returned a verdict of 'Found Drowned, though how the deceased came into the water there was no evidence to show.'"

I know no more of the unfortunate man Lawrence than this, and I have only printed the cutting here because it probably induced Dorrington to take certain steps in the case I am dealing with. With that case the fate of the man Lawrence has nothing whatever to do. He passes out of the story entirely.

II

MR. WARREN TELFER WAS A GENTLEMAN OF MEANS, and the owner of a few—very few—racehorses. But he had a great knack of buying hidden prizes in yearlings, and what his stable lacked in quantity it often more than made up for in quality. Thus he had once bought a St. Leger winner for as little as a hundred and fifty pounds. Many will remember his bitter disappointment of ten or a dozen years back, when his horse, Matfelon, starting an odds-on favourite for the Two Thousand, never even got among the crowd, and ambled in streets behind everything. It was freely rumoured (and no doubt with cause) that Matfelon had been "got at" and in some way "nobbled." There were hints of a certain bucket of water administered just before the race—a bucket of water observed in the hands, some said of one, some said

of another person connected with Ritter's training establishment. There was no suspicion of pulling, for plainly the
jockey was doing his best with the animal all the way along,
and never had a tight rein. So a nobbling it must have been,
said the knowing ones, and Mr. Warren Telfer said so too,
with much bitterness. More, he immediately removed his
horses from Ritter's stables, and started a small training
place of his own for his own horses merely; putting an old
steeplechase jockey in charge, who had come out of a bad
accident permanently lame, and had fallen on evil days.

The owner was an impulsive and violent-tempered
man, who, once a notion was in his head, held to it through
everything, and in spite of everything. His misfortune with
Matfelon made him the most insanely distrustful man alive.
In everything he fancied he saw a trick, and to him every
man seemed a scoundrel. He could scarce bear to let the very
stable-boys touch his horses, and although for years all went
as well as could be expected in his stables, his suspicious
distrust lost nothing of its virulence. He was perpetually
fussing about the stables, making surprise visits, and laying futile traps that convicted nobody. The sole tangible
result of this behaviour was a violent quarrel between Mr.
Warren Telfer and his nephew Richard, who had been making a lengthened stay with his uncle. Young Telfer, to tell the
truth, was neither so discreet nor so exemplary in behaviour
as he might have been, but his temper was that characteris-
tic of the family, and when he conceived that his uncle had
an idea that he was communicating stable secrets to friends
outside, there was an animated row, and the nephew betook
himself and his luggage somewhere else. Young Telfer
always insisted, however, that his uncle was not a bad fellow
on the whole, though he had habits of thought and conduct

that made him altogether intolerable at times. But the uncle had no good word for his graceless nephew; and indeed Richard Telfer betted more than he could afford, and was not so particular in his choice of sporting acquaintances as a gentleman should have been.

Mr. Warren Telfer's house, "Blackhall," and his stables were little more than two miles from Redbury, in Hampshire; and after the quarrel Mr. Richard Telfer was not seen near the place for many months—not, indeed, till excitement was high over the forthcoming race for the Redbury Stakes, for which there was an entry from the stable—Janissary, for long ranked second favourite; and then the owner's nephew did not enter the premises, and, in fact, made his visit as secret as possible.

I have said that Janissary was long ranked second favourite for the Redbury Stakes, but a little more than a week before the race he became first favourite, owing to a training mishap to the horse fancied first, which made its chances so poor that it might have been scratched at any moment. And so far was Janissary above the class of the field (though it was a two-year-old race, and there might be a surprise) that it at once went to far shorter odds than the previous favourite, which, indeed, had it run fit and well, would have found Janissary no easy colt to beat.

Mr. Telfer's nephew was seen near the stables but two or three days before the race, and that day the owner despatched a telegram to the firm of Dorrington & Hicks. In response to this telegram, Dorrington caught the first available train for Redbury, and was with Mr. Warren Telfer in his library by five in the afternoon.

"It is about my horse Janissary that I want to consult you, Mr. Dorrington," said Mr. Telfer. "It's right enough now—or at least was right at exercise this morning—but I feel certain that there's some diabolical plot on hand somewhere to interfere with the horse before the Redbury Stakes day, and I'm sorry to have to say that I suspect my own nephew to be mixed up in it in some way. In the first place I may tell you that there is no doubt whatever that the colt, if let alone, and bar accident, can win in a canter. He could have won even if Herald, the late favourite, had kept well, for I can tell you that Janissary is a far greater horse than anybody is aware of outside my establishment—or at any rate, than anybody ought to be aware of, if the stable secrets are properly kept. His pedigree is nothing very great, and he never showed his quality till quite lately, in private trials. Of course it has leaked out somehow that the colt is exceptionally good—I don't believe I can trust a soul in the place. How should the price have gone up to five to four unless somebody had been telling what he's paid not to tell? But that isn't all, as I have said. I've a conviction that something's on foot—somebody wants to interfere with the horse. Of course we get a tout about now and again, but the downs are pretty big, and we generally manage to dodge them if we want to. On the last three or four mornings, however, wherever Janissary might be taking his gallop, there was a big, hulking fellow, with a red beard and spectacles—not so much watching the horse as trying to get hold of the lad. I am always up and out at five, for I've found to my cost—you remember about Matfelon—that if a man doesn't want to be ramped he must never take his eye off things. Well, I have scarcely seen the lad ease the colt once on the last three or four mornings without that red-bearded fellow bobbing up from a knoll, or a clump of bushes, or something, close by—especially if Janissary was a bit away from the other horses, and not under my nose, or the head lad's, for a moment. I rode at the fellow, of course, when I saw what he was after, but he was artful as a cartload of monkeys, and vanished somehow before I could get near him. The head lad believes he has seen him about just after dark, too; but I am keeping the stable-lads in when they're not riding, and I suppose he finds he has no chance of getting at them except when they're out with the horses. This morning, not only did I see this fellow about, as usual, but, I am ashamed to say, I observed my own nephew acting the part of a common tout. He certainly had the decency to avoid me and clear out, but that was not all, as you shall see. This morning, happening to approach the stables from the back, I suddenly came upon the red-bearded man—giving money to a groom of mine! He ran off at once, as you may guess, and I discharged the groom where he stood, and would not allow him into the stables again. He offered no explanation or excuse, but took himself off, and half an hour afterward I almost sent away my head boy too. For when I told him of the dismissal, he admitted that he had seen that same groom taking money of my nephew at the back of the stables, an hour before, and had not informed me! He said that he thought that as it was 'only Mr. Richard' it didn't matter. Fool! Anyway, the groom has gone, and, so far as I can tell as yet, the colt is all right. I examined him at once, of course; and I also turned over a box that Weeks, the groom, used to keep brushes and odd things in. There I found this paper full of powder. I don't yet know what it is, but it's certainly nothing he had any business with in the stable. Will you take it?

"And now," Mr. Telfer went on, "I'm in such an uneasy state that I want your advice and assistance. Quite apart from the suspicious—more than suspicious—circumstances I have informed you of, I am *certain*—I know it without being able to give precise reasons—I am *certain* that some attempt is being made at disabling Janissary before Thursday's race. I feel it in my bones, so to speak. I had the same suspicion just before that Two Thousand, when Matfelon was got at. The thing was in the air, as it is now. Perhaps it's a sort of instinct; but I rather think it is the result of an unconscious absorption of a number of little indications about me. Be it as it may, I am resolved to leave no opening to the enemy if I can help it, and I want you to see if you can suggest any further precautions beyond those I am taking. Come and look at the stables."

Dorrington could see no opening for any piece of rascality by which he might make more of the case than by serving his client loyally, so he resolved to do the latter. He followed Mr. Telfer through the training stables, where eight or nine thoroughbreds stood, and could suggest no improvement upon the exceptional precautions that already existed.

"No," said Dorrington, "I don't think you can do any better than this—at least on this, the inner line of defence. But it is best to make the outer lines secure first. By the way, *this* isn't Janissary, is it? We saw him farther up the row, didn't we?"

"Oh no, that's a very different sort of colt, though he does look like, doesn't he? People who've been up and down the stables once or twice often confuse them. They're both bays, much of a build, and about the same height, and both have a bit of stocking on the same leg, though Janissary's is bigger, and this animal has a white star. But you never saw two creatures look so like and run so differently. This is a dead loss—not worth his feed. If I can manage to wind him up to something like a gallop I shall try to work him off in a selling plate somewhere; but as far as I can see he isn't good enough even for that. He's a disappointment. And his stock's far better than Janissary's too, and he cost half as

much again! Yearlings are a lottery. Still, I've drawn a prize
or two among them, at one time or another."

"Ah yes, so I've heard. But now as to the outer defences
I was speaking of. Let us find out *who* is trying to interfere
with your horse. Do you mind letting me into the secrets of
the stable commissions?"

"Oh no. We're talking in confidence, of course. I've backed
the colt pretty heavily all round, but not too much anywhere.
There's a good slice with Barker—you know Barker, of
course; Mullins has a thousand down for him, and that was at
five to one, before Herald went amiss. Then there's Ford and
Lascelles—both good men, and Naylor—he's the smallest
man of them all, and there's only a hundred or two with him,
though he's been laying the horse pretty freely everywhere, at
least until Herald went wrong. And there's Pedder. But there
must have been a deal of money laid to outside backers, and
there's no telling who may contemplate a ramp."

"Just so. Now as to your nephew. What of your suspicions in that direction?"

"Perhaps I'm a little hasty as to that," Mr. Telfer answered,
a little ashamed of what he had previously said. "But I'm
worried and mystified, as you see, and hardly know what
to think. My nephew Richard is a little erratic, and he has
a foolish habit of betting more than he can afford. He and
I quarrelled some time back, while he was staying here,
because I had an idea that he had been talking too freely
outside. He had, in fact; and I regarded it as a breach of confidence. So there was a quarrel and he went away."

"Very well. I wonder if I can get a bed at the 'Crown,' at
Redbury? I'm afraid it'll be crowded, but I'll try."

"But why trouble? Why not stay with me, and be near
the stables?"

"Because then I should be of no more use to you than one of your lads. People who come out here every morning are probably staying at Redbury, and I must go there after them."

III

THE "CROWN" AT REDBURY WAS FULL IN ANTICIPA-tion of the races, but Dorrington managed to get a room ordinarily occupied by one of the landlord's family, who undertook to sleep at a friend's for a night or two. This settled, he strolled into the yard, and soon fell into animated talk with the hostler on the subject of the forthcoming races. All the town was backing Janissary for the Stakes, the hostler said, and he advised Dorrington to do the same.

During this conversation two men stopped in the street, just outside the yard gate, talking. One was a big, heavy, vulgar-looking fellow in a box-cloth coat, and with a shaven face and hoarse voice; the other was a slighter, slimmer, younger and more gentlemanlike man, though there was a certain patchy colour about his face that seemed to hint of anything but teetotalism.

"There," said the hostler, indicating the younger of these two men, "that's young Mr. Telfer, him as whose uncle's owner o' Janissary. He's a young plunger, he is, and he's on Janissary too. He give me the tip, straight, this mornin'. 'You put your little bit on my uncle's colt,' he said. 'It's all right. I ain't such pals with the old man as I was, but I've got the tip that *his* money's down on it. So don't neglect your opportunities, Thomas,' he says; and I haven't. He's stoppin' in our house, is young Mr. Richard."

"And who is that he is talking to? A bookmaker?"

"Yes, sir, that's Naylor—Bob Naylor. He's got Mr. Richard's bets. P'raps he's puttin' on a bit more now."

The men at the gate separated, and the bookmaker walked off down the street in the fast gathering dusk. Richard Telfer, however, entered the house, and Dorrington followed him. Telfer mounted the stairs and went into his room. Dorrington lingered a moment on the stairs and then went and knocked at Telfer's door.

"Hullo!" cried Telfer, coming to the door and peering out into the gloomy corridor.

"I beg pardon," Dorrington replied courteously. "I thought this was Naylor's room."

"No—it's No. 23, by the end. But I believe he's just gone down the street."

Dorrington expressed his thanks and went to his own room. He took one or two small instruments from his bag and hurried stealthily to the door of No. 23.

All was quiet, and the door opened at once to Dorrington's picklock, for there was nothing but the common tumbler rim-lock to secure it. Dorrington, being altogether an unscrupulous scoundrel, would have thought nothing of entering a man's room thus for purposes of mere robbery. Much less scruple had he in doing so in the present circumstances. He lit the candle in a little pocket lantern, and, having secured the door, looked quickly about the room. There was nothing unusual to attract his attention, and he turned to two bags lying near the dressing-table. One was the usual bookmaker's satchel, and the other was a leather travelling-bag; both were locked. Dorrington unbuckled the straps of the large bag, and produced a slender picklock of steel wire, with a sliding joint, which, with a little skilful "humouring," turned the lock in the course of a minute or two. One glance inside was enough. There on the top lay a large false beard of strong red, and upon the shirts below was a pair of spectacles. But

Dorrington went farther, and felt carefully below the linen till his hand met a small, flat, mahogany box. This he withdrew and opened. Within, on a velvet lining, lay a small silver instrument resembling a syringe. He shut and replaced the box, and, having rearranged the contents of the bag, shut, locked, and strapped it, and blew out his light. He had found what he came to look for. In another minute Mr. Bob Naylor's door was locked behind him, and Dorrington took his picklocks to his own room.

It was a noisy evening in the Commercial Room at the "Crown." Chaff and laughter flew thick, and Richard Telfer threatened Naylor with a terrible settling day. More was drunk than thirst strictly justified, and everybody grew friendly with everybody else. Dorrington, sober and keenly alert, affected the reverse, and exhibited especial and extreme affection for Mr. Bob Naylor. His advances were unsuccessful at first, but Dorrington's manner and the "Crown" whisky overcame the bookmaker's reserve, and at about eleven o'clock the two left the house arm in arm for a cooling stroll in the High Street. Dorrington blabbed and chattered with great success, and soon began about Janissary.

"So you've pretty well done all you want with Janissary, eh? Book full? Ah! nothing like keeping a book even all round—it's the safest way—'specially with such a colt as Janissary about. Eh, my boy?" He nudged Naylor genially. "Ah! no doubt it's a good colt, but old Telfer has rum notions about preparation, hasn't he?"

"I dunno," replied Naylor. "How do you mean?"

"Why, what does he have the horse led up and down behind the stable for, half an hour every afternoon?"

"Didn't know he did."

"Ah! but he does. I came across it only this afternoon. I was coming over the downs, and just as I got round behind Telfer's stables there I saw a fine bay colt, with a white stocking on the off hind leg, well covered up in a suit of clothes, being led up and down by a lad, like a sentry—up and down, up and down—about twenty yards each way, and nobody else about. 'Hullo!' says I to the lad, 'hullo! what horse is this?' 'Janissary,' says the boy—pretty free for a stable-lad. 'Ah!' says I. 'And what are you walking him like that for?' 'Dunno,' says the boy, 'but it's guv'nor's orders. Every afternoon, at two to the minute, I have to bring him out here and walk him like this for half an hour exactly, neither more nor less, and then he goes in and has a handful of malt. But I dunno why.' 'Well,' says I, 'I never heard of that being done before. But he's a fine colt,' and I put my hand under the cloth and felt him—hard as nails and smooth as silk."

"And the boy let you touch him?"

"Yes; he struck me as a bit easy for a stable-boy. But it's an odd trick, isn't it, that of the half-hour's walk and the handful of malt? Never hear of anybody else doing it, did you?"

"No, I never did."

They talked and strolled for another quarter of an hour, and then finished up with one more drink.

IV

THE NEXT WAS THE DAY BEFORE THE RACE, AND IN THE morning Dorrington, making a circuit, came to Mr. Warren Telfer's from the farther side. As soon as they were assured of privacy: "Have you seen the man with the red beard this morning?" asked Dorrington.

"No; I looked out pretty sharply, too."

"That's right. If you like to fall in with my suggestions, however, you shall see him at about two o'clock, and take a handsome rise out of him."

"Very well," Mr. Telfer replied. "What's your suggestion?"

"I'll tell you. In the first place, what's the value of that other horse that looks so like Janissary?"

"Hamid is his name. He's worth—well, what he will fetch. I'll sell him for fifty and be glad of the chance."

"Very good. Then you'll no doubt be glad to risk his health temporarily to make sure of the Redbury Stakes, and to get longer prices for anything you may like to put on between now and tomorrow afternoon. Come to the stables and I'll tell you. But first, is there a place where we may command a view of the ground behind the stables without being seen?"

"Yes, there's a ventilation grating at the back of each stall."

"Good! Then we'll watch from Hamid's stall, which will be empty. Select your most wooden-faced and most careful boy, and send him out behind the stable with Hamid at two o'clock to the moment. Put the horse in a full suit of clothes—it is necessary to cover up that white star—and tell the lad he must *lead* it up and down slowly for twenty yards or so. I rather expect the red-bearded man will be coming along between two o'clock and half-past two. You will understand that Hamid is to be Janissary for the occasion. You must drill your boy to appear a bit of a fool, and to overcome his stable education sufficiently to chatter freely—so long as it is the proper chatter. The man may ask the horse's name, or he may not. Any way, the boy mustn't forget it is Janissary he is leading. You have an odd fad, you must know (and the boy must know it too) in the matter of training. This ridiculous fad is to have your colt walked up and down for half an hour exactly at two o'clock every afternoon, and then given a handful of malt as he comes in. The boy can talk as freely about this as he pleases, and also about the colt's chances, and anything else he likes; and he is to let the stranger come up, talk to the horse, pat him—in short, to do as he pleases. Is that plain?"

"Perfectly. You have found out something about this red-bearded chap then?"

"Oh, yes—it's Naylor the bookmaker, as a matter of fact, with a false beard."

"What! Naylor?"

"Yes. You see the idea, of course. Once Naylor thinks he has nobbled the favourite he will lay it to any extent, and the odds will get longer. Then you can make him pay for his little games."

"Well, yes, of course. Though I wouldn't put too much with Naylor in any case. He's not a big man, and he might break and lose me the lot. But I can get it out of the others."

"Just so. You'd better see about schooling your boy now, I think. I'll tell you more presently."

A minute or two before two o'clock Dorrington and Telfer, mounted on a pair of steps, were gazing through the ventilation grating of Hamid's stall, while the colt, clothed completely, was led round. Then Dorrington described his operations of the previous evening.

"No matter what he may think of my tale," he said, "Naylor will be pretty sure to come. He has tried to bribe your stablemen, and has been baffled. Every attempt to get hold of the boy in charge of Janissary has failed, and he will be glad to clutch at any shadow of a chance to save his money now. Once he is here, and the favourite apparently at his mercy, the thing is done. By the way, I expect your nephew's little present to the man you sacked was a fairly innocent one. No doubt he merely asked the man whether Janissary was keeping well, and was thought good enough to win, for I find he is backing it pretty heavily. Naylor came afterwards, with much less innocent intentions, but fortunately you were down on him in time. Several considerations induced me to go to Naylor's room. In the first place, I have heard rather shady tales of his doings on one or two occasions, and he did not seem a sufficiently big man to stand to lose a great deal over your horse. Then, when I saw him, I observed that his figure bore a considerable resemblance to that of the man you had described, except as regards the red beard and the spectacles—articles easily enough assumed, and, indeed, often enough used by the scum of the ring whose trade is welshing. And, apart from these considerations, here, at any rate, was one man who had an interest in keeping your colt from winning, and here was his room waiting for me to explore. So I explored it, and the card turned up trumps."

As he was speaking, the stable-boy, a stolid-looking youngster, was leading Hamid back and forth on the turf before their eyes.

"There's somebody," said Dorrington suddenly, "over in that clump of trees. Yes—our man, sure enough. I felt pretty sure of him after you had told me that he hadn't thought it worth while to turn up this morning. Here he comes."

Naylor, with his red beard sticking out over the collar of his big coat, came slouching along with an awkwardly assumed air of carelessness and absence of mind.

"Hullo!" he said suddenly, as he came abreast of the horse, turning as though but now aware of its presence, "that's a valuable sort of horse, ain't it, my lad?"

"Yes," said the boy, "it is. He's goin' to win the Redbury Stakes tomorrow. It's Janissary."

"Oh! Janey Sairey, is it?" Naylor answered, with a quaint affectation of gaping ignorance. "Janey Sairey, eh? Well, she do look a fine 'orse, what I can see of 'er. What a suit o' clo'es! An' so she's one o' the 'orses that runs in races, is she? Well, I never! Pretty much like other 'orses, too, to look at, ain't she? Only a bit thin in the legs."

The boy stood carelessly by the colt's side, and the man approached. His hand came quickly from an inner pocket, and then he passed it under Hamid's cloths, near the shoulder. "Ah, it do feel a lovely skin, to be sure!" he said. "An' so there's goin' to be races at Redbury tomorrow, is there? I dunno anythin' about races myself, an'—Oo my!"

Naylor sprang back as the horse, flinging back its ears, started suddenly, swung round, and reared. "Lor," he said, "what a vicious brute! Jist because I stroked her! I'll be careful about touching racehorses again." His hand passed stealthily to the pocket again, and he hurried on his way, while the stable-boy steadied and soothed Hamid.

Telfer and Dorrington sniggered quietly in their concealment. "He's taken a deal of trouble, hasn't he?" Dorrington remarked. "It's a sad case of the biter bit for Mr. Naylor, I'm afraid. That was a prick the colt felt—hypodermic injection with the syringe I saw in the bag, no doubt. The boy won't be such a fool as to come in again at once, will he? If Naylor's taking a look back from anywhere, that may make him suspicious."

"No fear. I've told him to keep out for the half-hour, and he'll do it. Dear, dear, what an innocent person Mr. Bob Naylor is! 'Well, I never! Pretty much like other horses!' He didn't know there were to be races at Redbury! 'Janey Sairey,' too—it's really very funny!"

Ere the half-hour was quite over, Hamid came stumbling

and dragging into the stable yard, plainly all amiss, and collapsed on his litter as soon as he gained his stall. There he lay, shivering and drowsy.

"I expect he'll get over it in a day or two," Dorrington remarked. "I don't suppose a vet. could do much for him just now, except, perhaps, give him a drench and let him take a rest. Certainly, the effect will last over tomorrow. That's what it is calculated for."

V

THE REDBURY STAKES WERE RUN AT THREE IN THE AFTERnoon, after two or three minor events had been disposed of. The betting had undergone considerable fluctuations during the morning, but in general it ruled heavily against Janissary. The story had got about, too, that Mr. Warren Telfer's colt would not start. So that when the numbers went up, and it was seen that Janissary was starting after all, there was much astonishment, and a good deal of uneasiness in the ring.

"It's a pity we can't see our friend Naylor's face just now, isn't it?" Dorrington remarked to his client, as they looked on from Mr. Telfer's drag.

"Yes; it would be interesting," Telfer replied. "He was quite confident last night, you say."

"Quite. I tested him by an offer of a small bet on your colt, asking some points over the odds, and he took it at once. Indeed, I believe he has been going about gathering up all the wagers he could about Janissary, and the market has felt it. Your nephew has risked some more with him, I believe, and altogether it looks as though the town would spoil the 'bookies' badly."

As the horses came from the weighing enclosure,

Janissary was seen conspicuous among them, bright, clean, and firm, and a good many faces lengthened at the sight. The start was not so good as it might have been, but the favourite (the starting-price had gone to evens) was not left, and got away well in the crowd of ten starters. There he lay till rounding the bend, when the Telfer blue and chocolate was seen among the foremost, and near the rails. Mr. Telfer almost trembled as he watched through his glasses.

"Hang that Willett!" he said, almost to himself. "He's *too* clever against those rails before getting clear. All right, though, all right! He's coming!"

Janissary, indeed, was showing in front, and as the horses came along the straight it was plain that Mr. Telfer's colt was holding the field comfortably. There were changes in the crowd; some dropped away, some came out and attempted to challenge for the lead, but the favourite, striding easily, was never seriously threatened, and in the end, being a little let out, came in a three-lengths winner, never once having been made to show his best.

"I congratulate you, Mr. Telfer," said Dorrington, "and you may congratulate me."

"Certainly, certainly," said Mr. Telfer hastily, hurrying off to lead in the winner.

It was a bad race for the ring, and in the open parts of the course many a humble fielder grabbed his satchel ere the shouting was over, and made his best pace for the horizon; and more than one pair of false whiskers, as red as Naylor's, came off suddenly while the owner betook himself to a fresh stand. Unless a good many outsiders sailed home before the end of the week there would be a bad Monday for layers. But all sporting Redbury was jubilant. They had all been "on" the local favourite for the local race, and it had won.

VI

MR. BOB NAYLOR "GOT A BIT BACK," IN HIS OWN phrase, on other races by the end of the week, but all the same he saw a black settling day ahead. He had been done—done for a certainty. He had realised this as soon as he saw the numbers go up for the Redbury Stakes. Janissary had not been drugged after all. That meant that another horse had been substituted for him, and that the whole thing was an elaborate plant. He thought he knew Janissary pretty well by sight, too, and rather prided himself on having an eye for a horse. But clearly it was a plant—a complete do. Telfer was in it, and so of course was that gentlemanly stranger who had strolled along Redbury High Street with him that night, telling that cock-and-bull story about the afternoon walks and the handful of malt. There was a nice schoolboy tale to take in a man who thought himself broad as Cheapside! He cursed himself high and low. To be done, and to know it, was a galling thing, but this would be worse. The tale would get about. They would boast of a clever stroke like that, and that would injure him with everybody; with honest men, because his reputation, as it was, would bear no worsening, and with knaves like himself, because they would laugh at him, and leave him out when any little co-operative swindle was in contemplation. But though the chagrin of the defeat was bitter bad enough, his losses were worse. He had taken everything offered on Janissary after he had nobbled the wrong horse, and had given almost any odds demanded. Do as he might, he could see nothing but a balance against him on Monday, which, though he might pay out his last cent, he could not cover by several hundred pounds.

But on the day he met his customers at his club, as usual, and paid out freely. Young Richard Telfer, however, with whom he was heavily "in," he put off till the evening. "I've been a bit disappointed this morning over some ready that was to be paid over," he said, "and I've used the last cheque-form in my book. You might come and have a bit of dinner with me tonight, Mr. Telfer, and take it then."

Telfer assented without difficulty.

"All right, then, that's settled. You know the place—Gold Street. Seven sharp. The missis'll be pleased to see you, I'm sure, Mr. Telfer. Let's see—it's fifteen hundred and thirty altogether, isn't it?"

"Yes, that's it. I'll come."

Young Telfer left the club, and at the corner of the street ran against Dorrington. Telfer, of course, knew him but as his late fellow-guest at the "Crown" at Redbury, and this was their first meeting in London after their return from the races.

"Ah!" said Telfer. "Going to draw a bit of Janissary money, eh?"

"Oh, I haven't much to draw," Dorrington answered. "But I expect your pockets are pretty heavy, if you've just come from Naylor."

"Yes, I've just come from Naylor, but I haven't touched the merry sovs. just yet," replied Telfer cheerfully. "There's been a run on Naylor, and I'm going to dine with him and his respectable missis this evening, and draw the plunder then. I feel rather curious to see what sort of establishment a man like Naylor keeps going. His place is in Gold Street, Chelsea."

"Yes, I believe so. Anyhow, I congratulate you on your haul, and wish you a merry evening." And the two men parted.

Dorrington had, indeed, a few pounds to draw as the result of his "fishing" bet with Naylor, but now he resolved to ask for the money at his own time. This invitation to Telfer took his attention, and it reminded him oddly of the circumstances detailed in the report of the inquest on Lawrence, transcribed at the beginning of this paper. He had cut out this report at the time it appeared, because he saw certain singularities about the case, and he had filed it, as he had done hundreds of other such cuttings. And now certain things led him to fancy that he might be much interested to observe the proceedings at Naylor's house on the evening after a bad settling-day. He resolved to gratify himself with a strict professional watch in Gold Street that evening, on chance of something coming of it. For it was an important thing in Dorrington's rascally trade to get hold of as much of other people's private business as possible, and to know exactly in what cupboard to find every man's skeleton. For there was no knowing but it might be turned into money sooner or later. So he found the number of Naylor's house from the handiest directory, and at six o'clock, a little disguised by a humbler style of dress than usual, he began his watch.

Naylor's house was at the corner of a turning, with the flank wall blank of windows, except for one at the top; and a public-house stood at the opposite corner. Dorrington, skilled in watching without attracting attention to himself, now lounged in the public-house bar, now stood at the street corner, and now sauntered along the street, a picture of vacancy of mind, and looking, apparently, at everything in turn, except the house at the corner. The first thing he noted was the issuing forth from the area steps of a healthy-looking girl in much gaily beribboned finery. Plainly a servant taking an evening out. This was an odd thing, that a servant should be allowed out on an evening when a guest was expected to dinner; and the house looked like one where it was more likely that one servant would be kept than two. Dorrington hurried after the girl, and, changing his manner of address to that of a civil labourer, said—

"Beg pardon, Miss, but is Mary Walker still in service at your 'ouse?"

"Mary Walker?" said the girl. "Why, no. I never 'eard the name. And there ain't nobody in service there but me."

"Beg pardon—it must be the wrong 'ouse. It's my cousin, Miss, that's all."

Dorrington left the girl and returned to the public-house. As he reached it he perceived a second noticeable thing. Although it was broad daylight, there was now a light behind the solitary window at the top of the side-wall of Naylor's house. Dorrington slipped through the swing-doors of the public-house and watched through the glass.

It was a bare room behind the high window—it might have been a bathroom—and its interior was made but dimly visible from outside by the light. A tall, thin woman was setting up an ordinary pair of house-steps in the middle of the room. This done, she turned to the window and pulled down the blind, and as she did so Dorrington noted her very extreme thinness, both of face and body. When the blind was down the light still remained within. Again there seemed some significance in this. It appeared that the thin woman had waited until her servant had gone before doing whatever she had to do in that room. Presently the watcher came again into Gold Street, and from there caught a passing glimpse of the thin woman as she moved busily about the front room over the breakfast parlour.

Clearly, then, the light above had been left for future use.

Dorrington thought for a minute, and then suddenly stopped, with a snap of the fingers. He saw it all now. Here was something altogether in his way. He would take a daring course.

He withdrew once more to the public-house, and ordering another drink, took up a position in a compartment from which he could command a view both of Gold Street and the side turning. The time now, he saw by his watch, was ten minutes to seven. He had to wait rather more than a quarter of an hour before seeing Richard Telfer come walking jauntily down Gold Street, mount the steps, and knock at Naylor's door. There was a momentary glimpse of the thin woman's face at the door, and then Telfer entered.

It now began to grow dusk, and in about twenty minutes more Dorrington took to the street again. The room over the breakfast-parlour was clearly the dining-room. It was lighted brightly, and by intent listening the watcher could distinguish, now and again, a sudden burst of laughter from Telfer, followed by the deeper grunts of Naylor's voice, and once by sharp tones that it seemed natural to suppose were the thin woman's.

Dorrington waited no longer, but slipped a pair of thick sock-feet over his shoes, and, after a quick look along the two streets, to make sure nobody was near, he descended the area steps. There was no light in the breakfast-parlour. With his knife he opened the window-catch, raised the sash quietly and stepped over the sill, and stood in the dark room within.

All was quiet, except for the talking in the room above. He had done but what many thieves—"parlour-jumpers"—do every day; but there was more ahead. He made his way silently to the basement passage, and passed into the kitchen. The room was lighted, and cookery utensils were scattered about, but nobody was there. He waited till he heard a request in Naylor's gruff voice for "another slice" of something, and noiselessly mounted the stairs. He noticed that the dining-room door was ajar, but passed quickly on to the second flight, and rested on the landing above. Mrs. Naylor would probably have to go downstairs once or twice again, but he did not expect anybody in the upper part of the house just yet. There was a small flight of stairs above the landing whereon he stood, leading to the servant's bed-room and the bathroom. He took a glance at the bathroom with its feeble lamp, its steps, and its open ceiling-trap, and returned again to the bedroom landing. There he stood, waiting watchfully.

Twice the thin woman emerged from the dining-room, went downstairs and came up again, each time with food and plates. Then she went down once more, and was longer gone. Meantime Naylor and Telfer were talking and joking loudly at the table.

When once again Dorrington saw the crown of the thin woman's head rising over the bottom stair, he perceived that she bore a tray set with cups already filled with coffee. These she carried into the dining-room, whence presently came the sound of striking matches. After this the conversation seemed to flag, and Telfer's part in it grew less and less, till it ceased altogether, and the house was silent, except for a sound of heavy breathing. Soon this became almost a snore, and then there was a sudden noisy tumble, as of a drunken man; but still the snoring went on, and the Naylors were talking in whispers.

There was a shuffling and heaving sound, and a chair was knocked over. Then at the dining-room door appeared Naylor, walking backward, and carrying the inert form of

Telfer by the shoulders, while the thin woman followed, supporting the feet. Dorrington retreated up the small stair-flight, cocking a pocket revolver as he went.

Up the stairs they came, Naylor puffing and grunting with the exertion, and Telfer still snoring soundly on, till at last, having mounted the top flight, they came in at the bathroom door, where Dorrington stood to receive them, smiling and bowing pleasantly, with his hat in one hand and his revolver in the other.

The woman, from her position, saw him first, and dropped Telfer's legs with a scream. Naylor turned his head and then also dropped his end. The drugged man fell in a heap, snoring still.

Naylor, astounded and choking, made as if to rush at the interloper, but Dorrington thrust the revolver into his face, and exclaimed, still smiling courteously, "Mind, mind! It's a dangerous thing, is a revolver, and apt to go off if you run against it!"

He stood thus for a second, and then stepped forward and took the woman—who seemed like to swoon—by the arm, and pulled her into the room. "Come, Mrs. Naylor," he said, "you're not one of the fainting sort, and I think I'd better keep two such clever people as you under my eye, or one of you may get into mischief. Come now, Naylor, we'll talk business."

Naylor, now white as a ghost, sat on the edge of the bath, and stared at Dorrington as though in a fascination of terror. His hands rested on the bath at each side, and an odd sound of gurgling came from his thick throat.

"We will talk business," Dorrington resumed. "Come, you've met me before now, you know—at Redbury. You can't have forgotten Janissary, and the walking exercise and the handful of malt. I'm afraid you're a clumsy sort of rascal, Naylor, though you do your best. I'm a rascal myself (though I don't often confess it), and I assure you that your conceptions are crude as yet. Still, that isn't a bad notion in its way, that of drugging a man and drowning him in your cistern up there in the roof, when you prefer not to pay him his winnings. It has the very considerable merit that, after the body has been fished out of any river you may choose to fling it into, the stupid coroner's jury will never suspect that it was drowned in any other water but that. Just as happened in the Lawrence case, for instance. You remember that, eh? So do I, very well, and it was because I remembered that I paid you this visit tonight. But you do the thing much too clumsily, really. When I saw a light up here in broad daylight I knew at once it must be left for some purpose to be executed later in the evening; and when I saw the steps carefully placed at the same time, after the servant had been sent out, why the thing was plain, remembering, as I did, the curious coincidence that Mr. Lawrence was drowned the very evening he had been here to take away his winnings. The steps *must* be intended to give access to the roof, where there was probably a tank to feed the bath, and what more secret place to drown a man than there? And what easier place, so long as the man was well drugged, and there was a strong lid to the tank? As I say, Naylor, your notion was meritorious, but your execution was wretched—perhaps because you had no notion that I was watching you."

He paused, and then went on. "Come," he said, "collect your scattered faculties, both of you. I shan't hand you over to the police for this little invention of yours; it's too useful an invention to give away to the police. I shan't hand you over, that is to say, as long as you do as I tell you. If you get mutinous, you shall hang, both of you, for the Lawrence business. I may as well tell you that I'm a bit of a scoundrel myself, by way of profession. I don't boast about it, but it's well to be frank in making arrangements of this sort. I'm going to take you into my service. I employ a few agents, and you and your tank may come in very handy from time to time. But we must set it up, with a few improvements, in another house—a house which hasn't quite such an awkward window. And we mustn't execute our little suppressions so regularly on settling-day; it looks suspicious. So as soon as you can get your faculties together we'll talk over this thing."

The man and the woman had exchanged glances during this speech, and now Naylor asked, huskily, jerking his thumb toward the man on the floor, "An'—an' what about 'im?"

"What about him? Why, get rid of him as soon as you like. Not that way, though." (He pointed toward the ceiling-trap.) "It doesn't pay *me*, and I'm master now. Besides, what will people say when you tell the same tale at his inquest that you told at Lawrence's? No, my friend, bookmaking and murder don't assort together, profitable as the combination may seem. Settling-days are too regular. And I'm not going to be your accomplice, mind. You are going to be mine. Do what you please with Telfer. Leave him on somebody's doorstep if you like."

"But I owe him fifteen hundred, and I ain't got more than half of it! I'll be ruined!"

"Very likely," Dorrington returned placidly. "Be ruined as soon as possible, then, and devote all your time to my business. You're not to ornament the ring any longer, remember—you're to assist a private inquiry agent, you and your wife and your charming tank. Repudiate the debt if you like—it's a mere gaming transaction, and there is no legal claim—or leave him in the street and tell him he's been robbed. Please yourself as to this little roguery—you may as well, for it's the last you will do on your own account. For the future your respectable talents will be devoted to the service of Dorrington & Hicks, private inquiry agents; and if you don't give satisfaction, that eminent firm will hang you, with the assistance of the judge at the Old Bailey. So settle your business yourselves, and quickly, for I've a good many things to arrange with you."

And, Dorrington watching them continually, they took Telfer out by the side gate in the garden wall and left him in a dark corner.

Thus I learnt the history of the horrible tank that had so nearly ended my own life, as I have already related. Clearly the Naylors had changed their name to Crofting on taking compulsory service with Dorrington, and Mrs. Naylor was the repulsively thin woman who had drugged me with her coffee in the house at Highgate. The events I have just recorded took place about three years before I came to England. In the meantime how many people, whose deaths might be turned to profit, had fallen victims to the murderous cunning of Dorrington and his tools?

The Sapient Monkey

Headon Hill

FRANCIS EDWARD GRAINGER (1857–1927), BORN IN Lowestoft and educated at Eton, was a journalist who married in his twenties and moved to the Isle of Wight. He took his pen-name, Headon Hill, from a coastal landmark between Alum Bay and Totland; *The Spies of the Wight* (1899), an "invasion thriller" of the type popular in its day, and *The Cottage in the Chine* (1913), benefit from his knowledge of the island. He was a highly prolific author, concentrating on short stories in the early years of his career and subsequently producing a long run of novels. His books are often dismissed as potboilers, but although he wrote too much to achieve sustained excellence, the best of his stories display a lively imagination and touches of flair and Hitchcockian suspense.

He created a number of rivals to Sherlock Holmes, including the parodic Radford Shone, and the rather more interesting Kala Persad, a wizened Hindu seer who assists the British detective Mark Poignard in *The Divinations of Kala Persad and other stories* (1895). This story features his principal detective, Sebastian Zambra, whose cases he recorded in short stories and novels starting with *Clues from a Detective's Camera* in 1893 and concluding more than thirty years later with *The Narrowing Circle* (a title later used by Julian Symons for a novel of psychological suspense). Zambra may have been inspired by Holmes, but he was quicker to make use of photography in his detective work. This story was originally published in *The Million* in October 1892.

I WOULD ADVISE EVERY PERSON WHOSE DUTIES TAKE him into the field of "private enquiry" to go steadily through the daily papers the first thing every morning. Personally I have found the practice most useful, for there are not many *causes célèbres* in which my services are not enlisted on one side or the other, and by this method I am always up in my main facts before I am summoned to assist. When I read the account of the proceedings at Bow Street against Franklin Gale in connection with the Tudways' bank robbery, I remember thinking that on the face of it there never was a clearer case against a misguided young man.

Condensed for the sake of brevity, the police-court report disclosed the following state of things:

Franklin Gale, clerk, aged twenty-three, in the employment of Messrs. Tudways, the well-known private bankers of the Strand, was brought up on a warrant charged with stealing the sum of £500—being the moneys of his employers. Mr. James Spruce, assistant cashier at the bank, gave evidence to the effect that he missed the money from his till on the afternoon of July 22. On making up his cash for the day he discovered that he was short of £300 worth of notes and £200 in gold. He had no idea how the amount had been abstracted. The prisoner was an assistant bookkeeper at the bank, and had access behind the counter. Detective-sergeant Simmons said that the case had been placed in his hands for the purpose of tracing the stolen notes. He had ascertained that one of them—of the value of £5—had been paid to Messrs. Crosthwaite & Co., tailors, of New Bond Street, on July 27th, by Franklin Gale. As a result, he had applied for a warrant, and had arrested the prisoner. The latter was remanded for a week, at the end of which period it was expected that further evidence would be forthcoming.

I had hardly finished reading the report when a telegram was put into my hands demanding my immediate presence at "Rosemount," Twickenham. From the address given, and from the name of "Gale" appended to the despatch, I concluded that the affair at Tudways' Bank was the cause of the summons. I had little doubt that I was to be retained in the interests of the prisoner, and my surmise proved correct.

"Rosemount" was by no means the usual kind of abode from which the ordinary run of bank clerks come gaily trooping into the great City in shoals by the early trains. There was nothing of cheap gentility about the "pleasant suburban residence standing in its own grounds of an acre," as the house-agent would say—with its lawns sloping down to the river, shaded by mulberry and chestnut trees, and plentifully garnished with the noble flower which gave it half its name. "Rosemount" was assuredly the home either of some prosperous merchant or of a private gentleman, and when I crossed its threshold I did so quite prepared for the fuller enlightenment which was to follow. Mr. Franklin Gale was evidently not one of the struggling genus bank clerk, but must be the son of well-to-do people, and not yet flown from the parent nest. When I left my office I had thought that I was bound on a forlorn hope, but at the sight of "Rosemount"—my first real "touch" of the case—my spirits revived. Why should a young man living amid such signs of wealth want to rob his employers? Of course I recognised that the youth of the prisoner precluded the probability of the place being his own. Had he been older, I should have reversed the argument. "Rosemount" in the actual occupation of a middle-aged bank clerk would have been prima-facie evidence of a tendency to outrun the constable.

I was shown into a well-appointed library, where I was received by a tall, silver-haired old gentleman of ruddy complexion, who had apparently been pacing the floor in a state of agitation. His warm greeting towards me—a perfect stranger—had the air of one who clutches at a straw.

"I have sent for you to prove my son's innocence, Mr. Zambra," he said. "Franklin no more stole that money than I did. In the first place, he didn't want it; and, secondly, if he had been ever so pushed for cash, he would rather have cut off his right hand than put it into his employer's till. Besides, if these thick-headed policemen were bound to lock one of us up, it ought to have been me. The five-pound note with which Franklin paid his tailor was one—so he assures me, and I believe him—which I gave him myself."

"Perhaps you would give me the facts in detail?" I replied.

"As to the robbery, both my son and I are as much in the dark as old Tudway himself," Mr. Gale proceeded. "Franklin tells me that Spruce, the cashier, is accredited to be a most careful man, and the very last to leave his till to take care of itself. The facts that came out in evidence are perfectly true.

Franklin's desk is close to the counter, and the note identified as one of the missing ones was certainly paid by him to Crosthwaite & Co., of New Bond Street, a few days after the robbery. It bears his endorsement, so there can be no doubt about that.

"So much for their side of the case. Ours is, I must confess, from a legal point of view, much weaker, and lies in my son's assertion of innocence, coupled with the knowledge of myself and his mother and his sisters that he is incapable of such a crime. Franklin insists that the note he paid to Crosthwaite & Co., the tailors, was one that I gave him on the morning of the 22nd. I remember perfectly well giving him a five-pound note at breakfast on that day, just before he left for town, so that he must have had it several hours before the robbery was committed. Franklin says that he had no other banknotes between the 22nd and 27th, and that he cannot, therefore, be mistaken. The note which I gave him I got fresh from my own bankers a day or two before, together with some others; and here is the most unfortunate point in the case. The solicitor whom I have engaged to defend Franklin has made the necessary enquiries at my bankers, and finds that the note paid to the tailors is *not* one of those which I drew from the bank."

"Did not your son take notice of the number of the note you gave him?" I asked.

"Unfortunately, no. He is too much worried about the numbers of notes at his business, he says, to note those which are his own property. He simply sticks to it that he knows it must be the same note because he had no other."

In the slang of the day, Mr. Franklin Gale's story seemed a little too thin. There was the evidence of Tudways that the note paid to the tailor was one of those stolen from them, and there was the evidence of Mr. Gale, senior's, bankers that it was not one of those handed to their client. What was the use of the prisoner protesting in the face of this that he had paid his tailor with his father's present? The notes stolen from Tudways were, I remembered reading, consecutive ones of a series, so that the possibility of young Gale having at the bank changed his father's gift for another note, which was subsequently stolen, was knocked on the head. Besides, he maintained that it was the *same* note.

"I should like to know something of your son's circumstances and position," I said, trying to divest the question of any air of suspicion it might have implied.

"I am glad you asked me that," returned Mr. Gale, "for it touches the very essence of the whole case. My son's circumstances and position are such that were he the most unprincipled scoundrel in creation he would have been nothing less than an idiot to have done this thing. Franklin is not on the footing of an ordinary bank clerk, Mr. Zambra. I am a rich man, and can afford to give him anything in reason, though he is too good a lad ever to have taken advantage of me. Tudway is an old friend of mine, and I got him to take Franklin into the bank with a view to a partnership. Everything was going on swimmingly towards that end: the boy had perfected himself in his duties, and made himself valuable; I was prepared to invest a certain amount of capital on his behalf; and, lastly, Tudway, who lives next door to me here, got so fond of him that he allowed Franklin to become engaged to his daughter Maud. Would any young man in his senses go and steal a paltry £500 under such circumstances as that?"

I thought not, but I did not say so yet.

"What are Mr. Tudway's views about the robbery?" I asked.

"Tudway is an old fool," replied Mr. Gale. "He believes what the police tell him, and the police tell him that Franklin is guilty. I have no patience with him. I ordered him out of this house last night. He had the audacity to come and offer not to press the charge if the boy would confess."

"And Miss Tudway?"

"Ah! she's a brick. Maud sticks to him like a true woman. But what is the use of our sticking to him against such evidence?" broke down poor Mr. Gale, impotently. "Can you, Mr. Zambra, give us a crumb of hope?"

Before I could reply there was a knock at the library door, and a tall, graceful girl entered the room. Her face bore traces of weeping, and she looked anxious and dejected; but I could see that she was naturally quick and intelligent.

"I have just run over to see if there is any fresh news this morning," she said, with an enquiring glance at me.

"This is Mr. Zambra, my dear, come to help us," said Mr. Gale; "and this," he continued, turning to me, "is Miss Maud Tudway. We are all enlisted in the same cause."

"You will be able to prove Mr. Franklin Gale's innocence, sir?" she exclaimed.

"I hope so," I said; "and the best way to do it will be to trace the robbery to its real author. Has Mr. Franklin any suspicions on that head?"

"He is as much puzzled as we are," said Miss Tudway. "I went with Mr. Gale here to see him in that horrible place yesterday, and he said there was absolutely no one in the bank he cared to suspect. But he *must* get off the next time he appears. My evidence ought to do that. I saw with my own eyes that he had only one £5 note in his purse on the 25th—that is two days before he paid the tailor, and three days after the robbery."

"I am afraid that won't help us much," I said. "You see, he might easily have had the missing notes elsewhere. But tell me, under what circumstances did you see the £5 note?"

"There was a garden party at our house," replied Miss Tudway, "and Franklin was there. During the afternoon a man came to the gate with an accordion and a performing monkey, and asked permission to show the monkey's tricks. We had the man in, and after the monkey had done a lot of clever things the man said that the animal could tell a good banknote from a 'flash' one. He was provided with spurious notes for the purpose; would any gentlemen lend him a good note for a minute, just to show the trick? The man was quite close to Franklin, who was sitting next to me. Franklin, seeing the man's hand held out towards him, took out his purse and handed him a note, at the same time calling my attention to the fact that it was his only one, and laughingly saying that he hoped the man was honest. The sham note and the good one were placed before the monkey, who at once tore up the bad note and handed the good one back to Franklin."

"This is more important than it seems," I said, after a moment's review of the whole case. "I must find that man with the monkey, but it bids fair to be difficult. There are so many of them in that line of business."

Miss Tudway smiled for the first time during the interview.

"It is possible that I may be of use to you there," she said. "I go in for amateur photography, and I thought that the man and his monkey made so good a 'subject' that I insisted on taking him before he left. Shall I fetch the photograph?"

"By all means," I said. "Photography is of the greatest use to me in my work. I generally arrange it myself, but if you have chanced to take the right picture for me in this case so much the better."

Miss Tudway hurried across to her father's house and quickly returned with the photograph. It was a fair effort for an amateur, and portrayed an individual of the usual seedy stamp, equipped with a huge accordion and a small monkey secured by a string. With this in my hand it would only be a matter of time before I found the itinerant juggler who had presented himself at the Tudways' garden party, and I took my leave of old Mr. Gale and Miss Maud in a much more hopeful frame of mind. Every circumstance outside the terrible array of actual evidence pointed to my client's innocence, and if this evidence had been manufactured for the purpose, I felt certain that the "monkey man" had had a hand in it.

On arriving at my office I summoned one of my assistants—a veteran of doubtful antecedents—who owns to no other name than "Old Jemmy." Old Jemmy's particular line of business is a thorough knowledge of the slums and the folk who dwell there; and I knew that after an hour or two on Saffron Hill my ferret, armed with the photograph, would bring me the information I wanted. Towards evening Old Jemmy came in with his report, to the effect that the "party" I was after was to be found in the top attic of 7 Little Didman's Fields, Hatton Garden, just recovering from the effects of a prolonged spree.

"He's been drunk for three or four days, the landlord told me," Old Jemmy said. "Had a stroke of luck, it seems, but he is expected to go on tramp tomorrow, now his coin has given out. His name is Pietro Schilizzi."

I knew I was on the right scent now, and that the "monkey man" had been made the instrument of *changing* the note which Franklin Gale had lent him for one of the stolen ones. A quick cab took me to Little Didman's Fields in a quarter of an hour, and I was soon standing inside the doorway of a pestilential apartment on the top floor of No. 7, which had been pointed out to me as the abode of Pietro Schilizzi. A succession of snores from a heap of rags in a corner told me the whereabouts of the occupier. I went over, and shaking him roughly by the shoulder, said in Italian:

"Pietro, I want you to tell me about that little juggle with a banknote at Twickenham the other day. You will be well rewarded."

The fellow rubbed his eyes in half-drunken astonishment, but there certainly was no guilty fear about him as he replied:

"Certainly, signor; anything for money. There was nothing wrong about the note, was there? Anyhow, I acted innocently in the matter."

"No one finds fault with you," I said; "but see, here is a five-pound note. It shall be yours if you will tell me exactly what happened."

"I was with my monkey up at Highgate the other evening," Mr. Schilizzi began, "and was showing Jacko's trick of telling a good note from a bad one. It was a small house in the Napier Road. After I had finished, the gentleman took me into a public house and stood me a drink. He wanted me to do something for him, he said. He had a young friend who was careless, and never took the number of notes, and he wanted to teach him a lesson. He had a bet about the number of a note, he said. Would I go down to Twickenham next day to a house he described, where there was to be a party, and do my trick with the monkey? I was to borrow a note from the young gentleman, and then, instead of giving him back his own note after the performance, I was to substitute one which the Highgate gentleman gave me for the purpose. He met me at Twickenham next day, and came behind the garden wall to point out the young gentleman to me. I managed it just as the Highgate gentleman wanted, and he gave me a couple of pounds for my pains. I have done no wrong; the note I gave back was a good one."

"Yes," I said, "but it happens to have been stolen. Put on your hat and show me where this man lives in Highgate."

The Napier Road was a shabby street of dingy houses, with a public house at the corner. Pietro stopped about half-way down the row and pointed out No. 21.

"That is where the gentleman lives," he said.

We retraced our steps to the corner public house.

"Can you tell me who lives at No. 21?" I asked of the landlord, who happened to be in the bar.

"Certainly," was the answer; "it is Mr. James Spruce—a good customer of mine, and the best billiard player hereabouts. He is a cashier at Messrs. Tudways' bank, in the Strand, I believe."

It all came out at the trial—not of Franklin Gale, but of James Spruce, the fraudulent cashier. Spruce had himself abstracted the notes and gold entrusted to him, and his guilty conscience telling him that he might be suspected, he had cast about for a means of throwing suspicion on some other person. Chancing to witness the performance of Pietro's monkey, he had grasped the opportunity for foisting one of the stolen notes on Franklin Gale, knowing that sooner or later it would be traced to him. The other notes he had intended to hold over till it was safe to send them out of the country; but the gold was the principal object of his theft.

Mr. Tudway, the banker, was, I hear, so cut up about the false accusation that he had made against his favourite that he insisted on Franklin joining him as a partner at once, and the marriage is to take place before very long. I am also told that the photograph of the "monkey man," handsomely enlarged and mounted, will form one of the mural decorations of the young couple.

The Green Parrakeet

F. Tennyson Jesse

WYNIFRED MARGARET JESSE (1888–1958) AMENDED her first name to Fryniwid, which was in turn shortened to "Fryn." Her father was a vicar whose uncle was Alfred, Lord Tennyson, and she married the dramatist H. M. Harwood. Rebecca West described her as "one of the loveliest girls of her time," but although she achieved considerable success with a wide variety of literary endeavours, she suffered from mental health problems for much of her life. She was an influential writer on criminology and an occasional novelist, as well as a poet and author of short stories and war correspondent for the *Daily Mail*.

Solange Fontaine, an amateur detective blessed with an invaluable ability to sense the presence of evil, first appeared in "Mademoiselle Lamont of the Mantles" in the August 1918 issue of *The Metropolitan Magazine*; a series of stories featuring the same character then appeared in *The Premier Magazine*; "The Green Parrakeet" was published in December 1918. A subsequent series of stories about Solange began in 1929, resulting in a collection two years later, but this story was not collected until 1994. Twenty years after that, an American scholar of the genre, Douglas Greene, introduced a comprehensive volume of Solange's cases, *The Compleat Adventures of Solange Fontaine*.

MONSIEUR AND MADAME PASTRE AND THEIR ADOPTED daughter Leonie had only been a week at the charming little villa, Mon Repos, when Solange took Terence Corkery and his young American friend to call. Both Corkery and Raymond Ker found the villa as delicious as their peep at it from the road had led them to expect, and to Raymond the whole visit came as a refreshment after his ears and mind had been filled with the story of Solange's tracking-down of the train murderers. This villa, these two kindly, middle-aged French people, with their perhaps exaggerated care of the pretty girl who lived with them—just a sweet, ordinary, rather stupid girl—all came to him as a welcome relief.

Mon Repos looked like a house out of a fairy story. Its whitewashed walls were decorated, just below the overhanging red roof, with a painted frieze of flowers and fruit; its shutters, that flanked each large window, were bright green, and on either side of the front door was one of those ridiculous dragons in turquoise-blue china which you find adorning these little modern *bonbonnières* in the Maritime Alps. The garden had an attempt at regularity in two beds filled with ugly carpet bedding and tufted with palms; but beyond these it was delightful, a wild mingling of lawn and trees, and a little olive grove where, under the silver foliage, the earth was cut into rough, grassy terraces, where stocks and violets grew.

Below the terrace was an ornamental, paved pool, only about six inches in depth, with a marble rim, overhung in places by straggling roses. Altogether, it only needed some money spent on it to make Mon Repos a perfect little place of its kind. But money, apparently, was what Monsieur and Madame Pastre had not too much of, since madame did all of the work herself.

It made it all the odder, thought Raymond, though in a way all the nicer, of the couple to spoil their adopted daughter so, and allow her to lead such an indolent life. So far as he could make out, all Leonie did was to clean out the cage of the new parrakeet.

"That is all her own, that dear bird," explained madame. "No one is to touch it but herself, apparently!"

And she shrugged her shoulders the least little bit in the world, as at a child's pardonable caprice.

After going round the garden, they all sat in the simply furnished drawing-room, for the swift sunset of the south was nearly upon them, when the air would grow so suddenly chill. Leonie, as daughter of the house, served them with little glasses of wine, and Raymond, who was observant where young women were concerned, noticed that her hands, though beautifully manicured, were large and roughened.

He had an idle moment of thinking that odd, since the girl was not made to do any of the housework, both on her own statement and on that of her adopted mother.

"I suppose we spoil the child," the lady had said to him, within about five minutes of his having been introduced to her, as she and he had lagged behind a trifle in going over the garden. "But what would you do? She is all we have, and my husband and myself wish her to marry well. So why should we let her make herself look old and tired with working about the house? No, no; I like the young to enjoy themselves. Why knows, they may not have long to do it in?"

And later, when Solange asked the girl whether the cake they were eating had been made by her, Leonie had replied:

"No, no, mam'selle. Maman does not like me to do anything in the kitchen. But I used to make very good cakes before I—"

"Leonie, do not be such a little chatterbox," interrupted M. Pastre, a silent man who had not spoken much. "See if you cannot make yourself useful for once, and find the cigarettes to offer these gentlemen."

He had spoken a little sharply, and Leonie was heard to mutter under her breath something to the effect that she was always perfectly willing to make herself useful, that she never thought—But the words trailed off into silence as M. Pastre rose to help her in the search for cigarettes. He patted her hand kindly as she found the box on a side-table.

"There, *petite*," he said, "did I wound thy little heart. Thou shalt be as useful as I wish thee to be, and mend thy papa's cravat for him this evening. It has been torn a long while now."

Leonie cheered up at once, the cloud passed from her pink and white face and large blue eyes. Intelligent or not, she certainly was astoundingly pretty, and not in the least like either of her adoptive parents.

Raymond made up his mind she was no relation until Madame Pastre volunteered the statement that she was a cousin of theirs. Madame Pastre added, in a moment while Leonie was out of the room, that it would be better for the child if people took her to be actually her daughter.

Leonie herself had let out the fact that she was an "adopted" to Solange when she first met her, but greater worldly wisdom had been impressed on her since.

"People are so uncharitably apt to discuss the origin of an adopted child," madame added, with a shake of the head.

Solange hastened to promise discretion for herself and her party.

Madame Pastre was a heavy, burnt-out-looking woman with eyes that had once been very handsome, though they were haggard now at times, when she was tired, for instance. Poor woman, she probably had enough to do in that house, and M. Pastre did not seem too easy to manage.

Irritable, very likely, thought Raymond, noting, according to the useful habit of his profession, the quick, dark eyes, the slightly bilious skin, and the rather hairy, constantly moving hands of the master of the house.

"Younger by a good deal than his wife," thought Raymond. "I wonder she consented to the adoption of the girl. But I suppose it was long ago, when Leonie was only a child."

Indeed, Madame Pastre seemed well over fifty, while M. Pastre might easily have been only forty-five or thereabouts; but his manner to the girl was strikingly paternal, and she, on her side, seemed to cling more to madame than to him.

But they all seemed very united, very happy together, and there was something inexpressibly delightful to Raymond in the simplicity of it all, in the beauty of the garden, and the quiet charm of the little villa, and the eager friendliness of the people themselves, these good *bourgeois*, probably retired on a modest income saved from some business, and only occupying themselves now in schemes for the future of the young girl in their charge.

M. Pastre spoke chiefly—when he spoke at all, which was

not often—to Corkery, but Madame Pastre devoted herself entirely to Raymond, and, though the young man was very far from being a coxcomb, he asked himself if perhaps she were not, in her busy brain of the planning *bourgeoise*, thinking of him as a possible husband for the pretty, sweetly stupid Leonie.

He laughed a little at the notion of a young journalist with all his way to make saddling himself with a French girl, who, unlike most of her nation, apparently was not even any good about a house. But he liked her and he liked the kindly, voluble madame, whatever her notions, and he was sorry when Solange, who had been very pale and silent, rose and made her farewells.

"You must let Mademoiselle Leonie come and see me," she said. "I am afraid I am a good deal older than she is, but perhaps I can find some nice girls of her own age for her to meet."

"Oh, I should love—" began Leonie, but M. Pastre interrupted.

"You are too amiable, mademoiselle, but Leonie is still so young—she has only just left school—that we do not like her to go anywhere without us. I am sure you will understand."

Solange spoke again, and only Corkery, who knew her so well, detected any effort in her voice.

"Of course, you must all come and see us," she said. "I only thought you and madame would probably be too busy. You know where we live, the little yellow house with the outside gallery. Perhaps you will come and take tea with us, English fashion, tomorrow?"

"Tomorrow? Is it not tomorrow you are expecting the gentleman on that little matter of business, Marc?" observed Madame Pastre rapidly to her husband.

"We cannot come tomorrow, I fear, mademoiselle, but perhaps some other day," said M. Pastre.

Solange nodded.

"Certainly, monsieur; any day that suits you. We will arrange it another time." And, with much handshaking, the three visitors got away.

"What jolly people," said Raymond, and Corkery echoed him. Solange, it appeared, had had a headache, and was only dying to get out into the air all the time. Nevertheless, she was herself again at dinner, to which she and Dr. Fontaine insisted both the visitors should stay.

"The inn is clean enough, you will sleep there," observed Dr. Fontaine. "But if you are taking a badly-needed holiday, Mr. Ker, you must use this house for your meals as much as you like. You must forgive us if you sometimes are left to eat alone, because when Solange and I are very busy in the laboratory we don't emerge for meals."

Raymond decided to linger on in the mountains, partly because he really was in need of a holiday, partly because he had fallen in love with the place, and partly because, deprecate as his sentimental side might the unwomanly nature of Solange's avocations, his own quick, sensitive brain could not but rejoice in the intelligence both of her and her father. He saw nothing of them the next morning. They were occupied in compiling a treatise upon the relative amount of convolutions in the brains of apes, of moral imbeciles, and in normal human brains, and after one peep into the laboratory and the sight of a small, faintly greenish sponge-like object floating in liquid, which Doctor Fontaine had told him was the brain of a murderer, pointing out its likeness to that, hardly more simple, of an ape, which reposed alongside, he felt he had seen enough.

He gave one look at Solange, grave and pale in her white overall, her eyes shining with the intentness of her concentration on her work, and went out into the garden where Corkery, with a broad smile on his face, was awaiting him under the plane-tree.

Corkery had to go back to Nice, where he was British consul, that afternoon, and he asked Raymond to walk part of the way back with him. Raymond agreed, and Solange opened the door of the laboratory to call goodbye to Corkery.

"Come again soon, Terence," she called in the friendly fashion she seemed to keep for the little grey Irishman, and Corkery blew her a kiss.

"Come, too, and see me off," he said. "A walk would do you good, and Raymond here wouldn't have to find his way back alone."

But Solange shook her fair head.

"I shall have to be busy all the afternoon," she said. "Take Mr. Ker as far as you can. I shall feel less guilty at neglecting him."

She waved her hand to them both, and vanished into the laboratory again, and Corkery and Raymond set off down the winding white road that led to Nice.

In spite of Miss Fontaine's advice, Raymond said he did not think he would come very far. He had rather thought of going over to Mon Repos and seeing if he could help Mademoiselle Leonie to make new perches for her parrakeet. He had pointed out to her yesterday that those already in the cage were too small and rounded, and would cause the bird's toes to contract.

Terence laughed at him.

"Oh, youth—youth," he said. "So a pair of big, blue eyes

has only to look at you, and you desert the finest soul and the best brain the good God ever put in a woman to go and make perches for a parrot. Well, peace go with you."

"When the finest soul and the best brain is shut up in a laboratory and poring over other brains floating about in a green juice," retorted Raymond, "I don't see what else there is for me to do."

"Don't you?" said Terence Corkery. "Well, I think I'll go back to Nice by the *petit train,* so just see me as far as the station, and then you can skedaddle to the arms of your blue-eyed charmer."

At the little station they found a train had just come in from Nice, and a couple of men had alighted from it. Terence waited till the train had gone on to cross the line to his own train, which had come in a minute later. He hung out of the window to talk to Raymond.

"By the way," he said, "did you see those two men? I expect they are the 'messieurs' Madame Pastre said they were expecting on business. I'd forgotten that. You'll be rather *de trop.*"

"Oh, I hadn't forgotten, but I don't suppose they want to talk to the girl on business," said Raymond. "See you before long, old man. And, I say, thanks awfully for introducing me to the Fontaines. I shouldn't have had much of a holiday alone."

"Oh, that's all right. They're always glad to do anything for anyone. Don't let Solange work too hard. It's not like her to be so pale and silent as she was at the Pastres' yesterday."

The train whistled hysterically and began to creak out of the station, and Raymond set off down the road towards Mon Repos, in the wake of the two men.

They certainly were the visitors Madame Pastre was

expecting, for they glanced in at the wrought iron gates, and Raymond decided he had better give them time to get their arrival over before he too put in an appearance, so after all he went on for a walk, down the road he and Corkery had come up yesterday, past the turning whence they had first sighted the red-fluted roof of Mon Repos.

Then he threw himself down on a grassy slope beneath an olive tree, and lay there, half-drowsy, in the warmth of the sun, though in the valley at his feet the ice still held on the shadowed stream, and half-thinking over the events of yesterday. Of what Corkery had told him of Solange and her "gift," that queer "feeling" she registered, as a seismograph registers earth-waves, when she was in the presence of evil, hidden evil less finely strung folk did not discover till too late.

She was a theorist, that must be it, and sometimes her theories came off. That was bound to happen sometimes. He wondered what failures she had had—and if she had had any. He would try and make her talk more about herself after dinner, he decided.

Then the warmth and the scented air overcame him, and he slept, till the passing of a flock of sheep, their hundreds of little pattering hoofs making a sound like a heavy rainstorm upon the road, awoke him. He sat up and looked at his watch. It was four o'clock, and he had been asleep half an hour. He scrambled to his feet and brushed the bits of grass off his suit, for he was a particular young man, and turned to go up the road towards the villa.

There was no one in sight in the garden as he went along the gravel-path to the absurd turquoise-blue dragons. He knocked at the door, but as no one answered his knock, and as he heard voices from within, he ventured to push the door open a little way, then stood hesitating as he realised that the two visitors were still there, and that it was one of them he heard speaking.

Now, Raymond was a Southerner. He came from New Orleans, and had as a child attended a French school there; consequently, though a little out of practice, his French was correct, and he understood it perfectly, which was why his paper had sent him to France to do a series of special articles. Before he knew what he was doing he heard the stranger say:

"That is understood, then. For a sum of one hundred thousand francs, monsieur."

"Made payable to M. Fouroux, Mademoiselle Pastre's former guardian."

Raymond drew back hastily, and was just on the steps again when the three men, Pastre and his two visitors, came out into the little hall and saw him. There was nothing for it but to advance boldly, and Raymond did so, taking off his hat.

"Good-afternoon, M. Pastre," he said. "I hope I'm not disturbing a business conference. I ventured to come over to help Mademoiselle Leonie make the new perches."

M. Pastre stood quite still, staring at him without speaking for a moment, and Raymond thinking he was not understood, added:

"The new perches for the parrakeet."

"The parrakeet," M. Pastre repeated, and it suddenly struck Raymond that the man looked rather pale. "Of course, the new perches for the parrakeet. I hope you have not been waiting long at the door, monsieur?"

"I've only just this minute arrived," said Raymond, who saw no need to enter upon long explanations. "Have I the good fortune to find madame and mademoiselle at home?"

M. Pastre seemed to come to a sudden decision.

"Come in, come in," he said; "and allow me to introduce you to my old friend M. Fouroux, and to M. Baillet."

Raymond bowed, and noticed that M. Fouroux, the old friend, and the erstwhile guardian of Leonie, was a heavy-featured, red-bearded man, rather shabbily dressed, while M. Baillet was a smart-looking, little businesslike person, with a portfolio under his arm.

M. Pastre insisted on drinks of vermouth all round, and for a few minutes they chatted of nothing in particular in the little dining-room.

There were no signs of Leonie. The parrakeet was clambering about on the wires of his cage, cocking its green head sideways on his snaky neck, and fluttering its wings. Raymond went over to the cage and began scratching the proffered poll.

"Excuse me, monsieur," said the voice of little M. Baillet behind him, "but in case you should wish to do any business of the kind while you are in France—the profession of journalist is sometimes dangerous, I understand—perhaps you will allow me to present you with my card."

"Certainly, monsieur," said Raymond, amused, and he took the card the little man importantly presented him with. He glanced at it, saw that it stated Monsieur Baillet to be the agent at Nice for an insurance company, and slipped it into his pocket. The other two men had their backs turned, and were speaking in low tones by the sideboard.

Now the man called Fouroux turned round, and catching sight of M. Baillet chatting to Raymond, called to him rather ungraciously that they would miss their train. Raymond watched them down the path, smiling a little at the business-like methods of the dapper M. Baillet, who evidently let no chance slip to advantage his company and incidentally himself.

M. Pastre, after seeing off his guests, took Raymond through to the garden at the back of the house, and there, to his intense surprise, Raymond saw, sitting talking with Madame Pastre and Leonie, no other than Solange— Solange who had said she would have to be busy all the afternoon. Yet she must have changed her frock as soon as he and Corkery had left the house, for here she was, evidently having had tea—the empty cups were on the garden-table—and not the severely plain Solange of the laboratory, but a charmingly dressed, gloved Solange. With her was Doctor Fontaine, also attired for paying a visit.

Raymond felt rather hurt. They might have let him know instead of having obviously got rid of him under pretence of work.

Solange gave him a quick, searching glance, then motioned him to take an empty chair beside her, and there was nothing for him to do but obey.

"It occurred to me," said Solange cheerfully, "that I had better bring papa to call for the sake of my character. Do you realise that it was a dreadfully unconventional thing of me to do, especially in France, and considering I had only met the Pastres once before, bringing you two men to call with me? I've lived so much in England as well as in the waste places of the earth where the white people all cling together, that I am stupidly apt to forget these things."

She seemed so unconscious of offence as she sat there, she smiled at him so kindly, that Raymond began to feel his resentment fading.

Besides, it was such a lovely evening, and Solange, though not pretty, looked so somehow "nice," and Leonie—Leonie looked as though she were made of roses and cream, as she sat there in a pink silk *peignour*, eating little cakes with the frank enjoyment of a child. Raymond had a passing thought that it was surely a queer hour of the day to be in a morning wrapper but how pretty she looked in it!

He got no chance to be alone with her, and, indeed, he was not sure he wanted one. Her conversation was not inspired, and all he asked was to be allowed to look at her, which he was able to do as much as he liked.

Solange soon made a move, and Raymond asked madame if he might come another day about the perches. He would be making some, he said, and when they were done he would bring them and fix them in for Mademoiselle Leonie.

Madame Pastre murmured something rather vague, but Leonie, with a distinct blush mounting in her usually tranquil pink-and-white, seemed shyly pleased at the notion.

That night, after dinner, the professor went to the laboratory, but Solange, who said she was tired, stayed and talked to Raymond in the sitting-room. It was a very plain apartment, for they had taken the house furnished, and then banished everything except the bare necessities to the attics. Solange was not one of those women who trail nicknacks about with them, and so, beyond great branches of mimosa in earthenware jugs, there were no individual touches about the long, low room. Yet it occurred to Raymond, as he saw the thin, graceful body of Solange lying opposite him in a long chair, that her personality in itself filled a room; there was no need of a "background" to enhance her.

It was odd, for she was in no way striking at first sight, and only a connoisseur would have appreciated her big, straight brow and delicately curved jaw, and her pallor tonight was more pronounced than usual.

"I wish you'd tell me something," said Raymond suddenly.

"Certainly, if I can. What is it?"

"How did you first find out your—your 'feeling'? What I want to know is whether you acquired it, because, being so interested in psychology, particularly criminal psychology, much studying of these things has made you expert, or whether it was your gift for seeing crime that made you study it?"

"Neither, I think. They are quite independent. My gift, as you call it, I suppose I've always had, though naturally it had to be exercised a lot of times before we thought it was anything more than coincidence. It's a purely spiritual thing—by that I mean that the feeling itself is quite independent of reasoning. But I became interested in criminology because that is papa's work—the trying to throw light on the causes and cure of crime. And, of course, strict scientific study is a great help to me. Imagine a very musical person who is yet quite ignorant of the technique of music. He loves it, his ear makes him recognise what he has heard before, but not till he has studied does he get the full understanding of what he hears, not till then does he recognise the technique, the construction, the art of the way in which effects are achieved. So it has been with me. I would know that someone I met was bad, I would feel that overpowering miasma of evil, the horror of which I can't describe to you, but I couldn't classify it, couldn't see where and to whom the danger lay, or argue out a certain course of action from what I felt."

"And now, when you feel it, you look for the formation of the person's skull or the length of his thumbs?" asked Raymond flippantly.

"Roughly speaking, that is part of the proceeding," said Solange, laughing; "but don't run away with the idea that

I'm an ardent follower of Lombroso, because I'm not. I think he goes further than is justifiable, and I dispute many of his premises. But there are certain signs that are fairly unfailing, though not by any means invariably so. It is as well to be able to note them, though it is equally well to learn not to attach undue importance to them. The real importance of my scientific education, such as it is, has been to teach me to classify crime. To enable me to reduce motives, methods, types, both of crime and criminals, to certain essentials for classification. But, of course, all that is mere criminology. If it wasn't for the 'feeling' I should be nothing of a detective, but a mere studio performer."

"So you do call yourself a detective? Corkery scouted the notion."

"He's right. I only used the word because I have occasionally been enabled to track out a crime, as that affair of the railway murder you were asking about yesterday. But I am a coward about it. I never go out of my way to look for cases. I sometimes feel I ought to, if that is the way I am meant to help. I tell myself that papa would miss me so in the laboratory, but in my heart I know it is my own dread that stops me. You can't think what it is like the 'feeling,' I told you it reminded me of nothing so much as the smell of musk in an alligator swamp. My soul sickens when it smells it."

She spoke with unusual passion, then, checking herself, she smiled.

"But what a gruesome conversation for a man on his holiday. It is really all your fault for having come here in the first place with the idea of getting 'copy' about the railway murder. Tell me, how far did you go with Terence today?"

"Only to the station. He wanted to go back by train."

"The station? Did you happen to see anyone?"

"No one in particular. Oh, yes, we saw the two men who were going to the Pastres on business. They were still there when I arrived at the villa, so I saw them again. I rather gathered that one of them—the chap with a red beard called Fouroux—had been Leonie's guardian, which rather surprised me. I thought somehow the Pastres had had her from a child."

"And the other man was the doctor, I suppose?" asked Solange carelessly.

"The doctor? No, he was an insurance agent. What made you think he was a doctor?"

"Oh, only because when papa and I arrived Leonie was closeted in with them, and we had to sit and wait in the garden till they had finished with her, when Madame Pastre brought her out to us. But how do you know he was an insurance agent?"

"Why," said Raymond, smiling at the recollection of the eager little M. Baillet, "he gave me his card. I've got it somewhere." And he began searching in his pockets.

Solange held out her hand, and he passed her the bit of pasteboard. She glanced at it before slipping it into the little bag she carried.

"I'll keep it, if you don't mind," she said. "We haven't insured against fire or burglary yet, and it's really very silly of us. Did M. Fouroux tell you he had been Leonie's guardian?"

"Well, not exactly," said Raymond, and then he told her how he had inadvertently overheard some of the conversation between the men as he stood at the door. "To tell you the truth," he added, "I rather wondered if the Pastres weren't arranging to pay Fouroux something for giving up the girl. They evidently adore her, and would do anything for her."

"The Pastres couldn't pay a hundred thousand francs for anything," replied Solange. "However, it very likely wasn't that at all, and, anyway, their business is their own affair. Oh, I'm so sleepy. Shall you think me very rude if I slip away to bed?"

She had stood up, and Raymond saw a great shudder pass over her. He looked at her in concern.

"You're tired out," he exclaimed. "I am a brute to have kept you up like this."

"Come tomorrow, if you like," said Solange, as she stood at the front door to see him off. And Raymond, who no longer felt, after this evening, the aversion that had taken him by the throat in the laboratory, replied eagerly:

"You bet I'll like."

He spent a week longer in the mountains, seeing Solange every day, but he only managed to see Leonie Pastre once again, and then only for a few minutes. Smiling, amiable as they were, the two Pastres certainly watched over the girl as though they had been the turquoise dragons come to life. At the end of the week Raymond felt bound to get to work again, but it was with many promises of return that he said goodbye to the Fontaines, and went down to Nice.

A bare fortnight later he was back, and Corkery was with him, and this time owing to a special invitation from Solange. Corkery shook his head over her letter when it arrived.

"It's not like Solange to be so emphatic about wanting anyone," he said. "And as I don't flatter myself that it's because she's pining for either of us, I can't help being afraid something is wrong."

"Oh, I don't suppose so," said Raymond. "What should there be?"

The two men arrived at the yellow house on just such an evening as they had three weeks earlier, except that now it was distinctly warmer. As before, Dr. Fontaine was awaiting them under the plane-tree, and this time Solange was with him, in her pale green frock that made her look like a wood nymph. She gave them tea, and then she said:

"By the way, if you've sent your bags to the inn you must fetch them back again. Papa and I are going to give ourselves the pleasure of putting you up here this time. We haven't nearly so much work on hand; at least, not in the laboratory."

"You're an angel. We'll go right away and get the bags before you change your mind," said Corkery, standing up. But Solange stood up also.

"You can do that later on," she said. "I thought first we'd all go and call on the Pastres. Leonie has asked several times after the '*beau monsieur Americain.*'" And Solange twinkled mischievously at Raymond.

"How are the Pastres? All right?" asked Corkery, as they all, except Dr. Fontaine, made their way towards Mon Repos. "D'you know, I half thought something must be wrong, you sending for us like that, and you and the professor look all right."

"The Pastres are very well," said Solange, "especially Leonie, who I should think is splendidly healthy, though Madame Pastre tells me she is liable to fainting fits."

"Goodness, she certainly doesn't look as though she ever fainted," observed Corkery. And when they saw Leonie, looking more blooming than ever, he thought it all the more emphatically. Madame Pastre, whose colour looked less high and fixed than before, seemed a more likely subject for a bad heart.

M. Pastre was out, and somehow it happened that Raymond wandered round the garden with Madame Pastre, as Solange had captured Leonie. Once or twice Madame Pastre looked back at the others, as though wondering whether she ought not to join them, but every fragment of their harmless conversation floated to her ears as she listened, so she resigned herself and chatted to Raymond.

She asked him a few idle questions about the Fontaines. The *demoiselle* was a *savante*, was she not? Spent her time in dissecting, and in suchlike nastiness?

In arms for Solange, Raymond gave a sketch of her activities before it occurred to him to wonder whether he had not been indiscreet. He remembered too late Solange was apt to be sensitive over what she called her "nose for crime," and he was relieved when they all turned to go back.

As they were going down the path Solange stopped and asked after the parrakeet, and Leonie ran to fetch it. She came out and stood on the top of the steps between the turquoise dragons, with the bird in her hands, holding it up against her cheek. The three involuntarily stood still a moment at the gate, to look at the pretty picture she made as she stood there, the bright green bird pressed to her rosy face. Neither of the two men ever forgot it, for it was the last time either of them saw Leonie alive.

After dinner that night Raymond mentioned apologetically to Solange that he was afraid he had rather boasted about her powers to Madame Pastre. He was quite prepared for her to be annoyed, but he was not prepared for the look of utter dismay that dawned on her face or for her sudden paling.

"You—you didn't say, I hope, that I had anything to do with the discovering of the railway murderer?" she asked.

And when Raymond ruefully admitted that he had said something about it, she made a little gesture of despair.

"Why, does it matter so awfully?" he asked anxiously, and Solange only repeated: "Matter so awfully! So awfully! Oh, well, I can only trust not. But we shall have to act at once—tomorrow, if only it is in time—"

She finished the sentence to herself, and Raymond did not like to press her to explain; he was feeling too guilty. But the expression that seemed to be on Solange had communicated itself to him, and he tossed restlessly half the night beneath his stout crimson *duvet* before he could fall into a troubled sleep.

It was late when he awoke, and dressing and taking his towel, he descended the stairs on his way for a bathe in the stream, when the door of Solange's room opened and she came out, fully dressed. She smiled at him.

"I have been before you," she said. "I have my cold bath in the stream every morning. And today I came back by the Pastres' house and got a glimpse of Leonie cleaning the bird's cage on the lawn."

Raymond could not have told why he felt such a sudden lightening of the heart, such a relief from strain. He went whistling to his bathe, and he, too, came back by Mon Repos, but caught no glimpse of Leonie, only of a strange man with a black bag hastening up the path to the front door.

The Fontaines breakfasted downstairs, English fashion, and the party of four were just finishing, when Marie, the woman who did the menage, came bursting into the room, her rubicund face pale and her eyes wide with excitement.

"It has happened! I am too late!"

The words fell from Solange, but everyone was too intent on the agitated woman to heed them.

"Oh, monsieur, oh, mademoiselle, such a dreadful thing has happened at Mon Repos!" cried Marie. "The young lady, Mam'zelle Leonie, has been found dead."

Gradually they got the story from her. Leonie had been found dead, drowned in six inches of water, in the little ornamental pond, clutching the parrot in one hand. M. Pastre had found her, and sent at once for the doctor in the town, though why he passed Dr. Fontaine's very door to do so, Marie was indignantly anxious to be told. However, M. Blanchard, the only doctor in the little hill town, had gone at once, and he stated that the poor girl must have tripped and fallen into the pond while chasing the parrakeet, that had escaped from the cage which she had been cleaning on the lawn. She must have fainted, and so was drowned in the shallow water of the basin, and the bird was drowned in her hand.

Marie had been in the town doing the shopping when the doctor got back with the news, and she had heard him telling the mayor, who was in the square, all about it.

It was very dreadful, and everyone was very agitated about it. Poor Madame Pastre was broken-hearted, and did nothing but shriek, and M. Pastre was beside himself.

Solange listened to it all, standing erect, clutching the edge of the table, but when Marie had made an end, and Dr. Fontaine had got her out of the room, all Solange said was:

"So that was what the parrakeet was for. I had wondered and wondered. I knew it would be something to do with the parrakeet, and I couldn't see—I couldn't see!"

She turned a blank, white face and blind eyes towards Corkery and Raymond, and went from the room. Dr. Fontaine hurried after her.

"Good Heavens! It isn't possible!" stammered Raymond.

"Those kind, devoted people! It can't be true what she thinks."

"It is true, or she wouldn't have thought it," said Corkery heavily.

Later in the day they heard more. The little Dr. Blanchard, very fluttered by the case, called on his distinguished *confrère* to tell him all about it. He said the grief of the mother was terrible, the father seemed more stunned with sorrow. As an example of maternal instinct he related how Madame Pastre had said to him:

"I always thought something like that would happen. I had a presentiment about that bird. It had a habit, whenever it escaped from the cage, of flying to the rose bushes round the basin, and Leonie used to run after it. I always thought some day she would catch her foot in the root of a tree and fall headlong, and now it has happened."

Dr. Blanchard was very touched by this proof of a mother's heart, and Dr. Fontaine sat and smoked and listened to him.

"Was there no blow to the head that would account for her having become unconscious?" he asked at last, and little Blanchard told him there was a contusion on one side of the head, doubtless where it had struck on the marble edge of the basin when she fell.

That afternoon Solange told Raymond and Corkery they must come to the villa with her and offer their condolences. She allowed of no refusal, and impressed on them that they must not say she had come with them, and must keep both the Pastres occupied while she was busied at the back of the house. She would tell them why after, but it was of vital importance.

Thus it came about that two very reluctant, sick-feeling

men dragged themselves to Mon Repos, and having parted with Solange in the road, went up to the house and knocked. Solange waited till she had seen them disappear inside and the door shut, then she ran swiftly round to the back of the house, crept to the corner where, standing under the drawing-room window, she could hear the voices of the two Pastres in conversation with the visitors, then turned and went to the back door.

A big tin for holding rubbish stood there, and Solange plunged her white, fastidious fingers boldly into the garbage, thrusting her arm down this way and that. Then, with a glance round, she tipped the heavy tin over and shook the contents out upon the path.

From among the scraps of torn paper, the bits of cabbage, the dust, the whole unsavoury mess, fell the damp, green body of the parrakeet.

Solange picked it up, and for a moment stood stroking the limp, pathetic little body very tenderly. Then she thrust it into the front of her loose blouse, and began stuffing the rubbish into the tin again. She was back at the yellow house before the two men, and when they arrived she was waiting for them in the cool, darkened sitting-room, the green parrakeet lying on the table before her.

"So that was what you were after!" observed Corkery.

Raymond, who was looking ghastly—he was younger than Corkery, and never before had he had to take two murderers by the hand in simulated friendship—stared dully at it.

"What are you going to do with that?" he asked.

Solange showed a stern face over the dead bird.

"With that I am going to send Pastre to the guillotine," she answered. "That bird's neck was wrung before it was put into the water."

"By the way, Solange," said Corkery, after a minute's silence, "I noticed Pastre's hands were covered with scratches."

"Oh, thank you; that's important," said Solange.

It was not till some time after, when Pastre and the woman Amelie Fouroux, who was his mistress, and had passed as Madame Fouroux, had been tried, along with her brother Fouroux, and found guilty, that Solange could be brought to discuss it all. She and her father had had to be present at the assizes, and were now taking a holiday at a hotel in Nice, trying to recover from the effects of the sinister time behind them. Raymond and Corkery took them out to dinner, and at last the conversation turned inevitably on the drama of Mon Repos.

"Of course I knew, the first time I met the Pastres, when they were making inquiries about where the various shops in the town were. That was how I first spoke to them, you know. And there, in the marketplace, I got the 'feeling' unmistakably. I knew there was something sinister about that smiling couple, something that gave me gooseflesh. I knew I ought to go and see them, and try and find out and prevent whatever it was, and yet I felt such a repulsion that the first day you came, Mr. Ker, and suggested going there, I wanted to get out of it. But we went, and I set myself to notice things. I noticed, for instance, that though Leonie's hands were big and red, they were lately manicured."

"I noticed that," put in Raymond.

"I saw, too, what you probably didn't, that her eyelashes had been dyed, also that, though she was elaborately dressed, and her hair waved, there was a distinct 'high-water-mark' round the base of her neck. The Pastres had got her up to look like a fine lady, but they had not taught her to be really clean. It was like a servant being dressed up. Yet Leonie wasn't a servant, wasn't allowed to do anything in the house. And I noticed, as more curious than anything, that the Pastres never for a moment let her be alone with any one of us, and that she often looked nervously at them before she spoke."

"I can notice it all now, too," said Raymond wryly.

"Then the day the insurance agent came. Poor Leonie was actually in her rose peignoir to receive him. Don't you see the impression that was meant to convey? Not that she was the servant, but that she was the spoiled darling of the household. That, as you now know, was what the agent did think. Madame Pastre was known to him as the sister of Fouroux. Poor Leonie was tricked out that day to look as pampered, as luxurious, as fresh and strong and young as she possibly could, and surrounded with devotion. The agent was told she was the ward of Fouroux and his sister, and he had no idea of the truth, that she was a friendless servant girl from the Midi, come to a registry office in Nice to apply for a place, and taken by the Pastres."

Solange fell silent, as she went over in her mind the emotions the bewildered young girl must have experienced; being taken up by this strict but affectionate couple, spoilt, made much of, stuffed with cakes, manicured, shampooed, dressed in silken wrappers, and forced to spend her days in idleness save for the cleaning of a parrakeet's cage.

"The evidence of the keeper of the registry office would have been enough without anything else," Solange went on. "Think of what the Pastres required: 'A young girl, not more than twenty-five, pretty, submissive, discreet, *and knowing no one in Nice*'?"

"When did you first find that out, Solange?" asked Corkery.

"The day after Mr. Ker went away the first time. I went down to Nice and went round the registry offices, describing Leonie, and saying I was looking for her. Oh, Terence, I shall never, never forget that I delayed too long. But I knew they would have to allow a certain time to elapse. I knew they had taken the villa for a month, and that they would not want to take it on for another. Criminals are always economical about the expenses of their profession. Besides, they would not want to have to pay a second instalment on the policy. But they would want it to be as long after the first payment as they could to avoid suspicion of haste. Therefore I gave them at the least four weeks, though, to be on the safe side, I asked you two up a few days earlier. You see, there was nothing for it but to keep a strict watch, and try and catch him with all the evidence possible."

"And then I precipitated it," said Raymond bitterly.

"My poor friend, you could not help it. But I knew, directly you said you had told the woman that I found the train murderer, that she would hurry it on. They knew that I had only seen Leonie a few times, that I had been perfectly friendly, that they must all have produced the most favourable impression, and they would rush the thing before I had time to have any suspicions aroused or make inquiries. Well, I was too late. If only I could have guessed the part the parrakeet was to play—"

"How could you?" said Corkery soothingly.

"Just think of it," went on Solange, not heeding him, "think of the struggle that strong, healthy girl must have had for her life, think how she scratched his hands, how she must have fought till he hit her that great blow on the head. And though you'll think it absurd, exaggerated, I can't help thinking as well of the poor, little martyred parrakeet, spoilt, made a fuss of, too, and then to be snatched up and have its soft, green neck brutally wrung."

Solange shook herself, as though to shake away the thoughts that were depressing her.

"The poor little parrakeet," she repeated. "Do you know, I might have guessed what they meant to do from something Leonie said to me that first day when for one minute we were alone by the cage. She said, 'I can't say I care about the bird, but THEY'—she said 'they' in capital letters—'want me to love it. They say I must be devoted to it, so I suppose I shall be.' They had literally stupefied the child with their—their kindness, as she thought it."

"You know, it's been a wonderful story from my point of view," admitted Raymond to Corkery, as they went through the moonlit streets of Nice after seeing the Fontaines back to their hotel. "I'm as sorry and sick as possible over that poor kid, but it's been a wonderful story. I've written it up for my paper under the title of 'The Young Girl with the Parrakeet.' Don't you think that's telling? It's more like the title of a picture by Greuze than anything else."

Corkery, remembering Raymond's one-time strictures on the subject of Solange's work making her hard, hid a smile.

"A charming little murder," he said drily.

"Now you're laughing at me," said Raymond, "and thinking me a heartless beast, and I'm not. But it's the *decor* that's been so wonderful, like something in a ballet. That painted villa, and the turquoise dragons, and the marble basin, then the parrakeet—"

"And the young girl. Don't forget her," said Corkery.

The Oracle of the Dog

G. K. Chesterton

GILBERT KEITH CHESTERTON (1874–1936) WAS—
like Doyle—a man of many talents, but today he is most
widely remembered as a detective writer and as the creator
of Father Brown. Chesterton's love of paradox went hand in
hand with an enthusiasm for stories about seemingly impossible crimes. "The Oracle of the Dog" appeared in *Nash's
and Pall Mall Magazine* in December 1923 and was included
in *The Incredulity of Father Brown*, published in 1926. Many
Chesterton devotees regard it as one of his finest mysteries;
it certainly illustrates the flavour of his writing admirably.

The story combines an engaging premise for an impossible crime—how could Colonel Druce have been stabbed
to death while alone in a summer-house under constant
observation?—with a fine example of "armchair detection"
by the little priest. Although Father Brown is one hundred
miles away from the scene of the crime, he still manages
to solve it, with his own brand of human understanding.

We also see his understanding of the animal world, and Chesterton offers a stern rebuke to those who project their own assumptions onto animals, as well as other human beings. At the end of the story, the priest articulates the moral: "'The dog could almost have told you the story, if he could talk,' said the priest. 'All I complain of is that because he couldn't talk you made up his story for him... It's part of something I've noticed more and more in the modern world, appearing in all sorts of newspaper rumours and conversational catchwords; something that's arbitrary without being authoritative. People readily swallow the untested claims of this, that, or the other. It's drowning all your old rationalism and scepticism, it's coming in like a sea; and the name of it is superstition.'"

"YES," SAID FATHER BROWN, "I ALWAYS LIKE A DOG, SO long as he isn't spelt backwards."

Those who are quick in talking are not always quick in listening. Sometimes even their brilliancy produces a sort of stupidity. Father Brown's friend and companion was a young man with a stream of ideas and stories, an enthusiastic young man named Fiennes, with eager blue eyes and blond hair that seemed to be brushed back, not merely with a hair-brush but with the wind of the world as he rushed through it. But he stopped in the torrent of his talk in a momentary bewilderment before he saw the priest's very simple meaning.

"You mean that people make too much of them?" he said. "Well, I don't know. They're marvellous creatures. Sometimes I think they know a lot more than we do."

Father Brown said nothing, but continued to stroke the

head of the big retriever in a half-abstracted but apparently soothing fashion.

"Why," said Fiennes, warming again to his monologue, "there was a dog in the case I've come to see you about: what they call the 'Invisible Murder Case,' you know. It's a strange story, but from my point of view the dog is about the strangest thing in it. Of course, there's the mystery of the crime itself, and how old Druce can have been killed by somebody else when he was all alone in the summer-house—"

The hand stroking the dog stopped for a moment in its rhythmic movement, and Father Brown said calmly: "Oh, it was a summer-house, was it?"

"I thought you'd read all about it in the papers," answered Fiennes. "Stop a minute; I believe I've got a cutting that will give you all the particulars." He produced a strip of newspaper from his pocket and handed it to the priest, who began to read it, holding it close to his blinking eyes with one hand while the other continued its half-conscious caresses of the dog. It looked like the parable of a man not letting his right hand know what his left hand did.

Many mystery stories, about men murdered behind locked doors and windows, and murderers escaping without means of entrance and exit, have come true in the course of the extraordinary events at Cranston on the coast of Yorkshire, where Colonel Druce was found stabbed from behind by a dagger that has entirely disappeared from the scene, and apparently even from the neighbourhood.

The summer-house in which he died was indeed accessible at one entrance, the ordinary doorway which looked down the central walk of the garden towards the house. But, by a combination of events almost to be called a coincidence, it appears that both the path and the entrance were watched during the crucial time, and there is a chain of witnesses who confirm each other. The summer-house stands at the extreme end of the garden, where there is no exit or entrance of any kind. The central garden path is a lane between two ranks of tall delphiniums, planted so close that any stray step off the path would leave its traces; and both path and plants run right up to the very mouth of the summer-house, so that no straying from that straight path could fail to be observed, and no other mode of entrance can be imagined.

Patrick Floyd, secretary of the murdered man, testified that he had been in a position to overlook the whole garden from the time when Colonel Druce last appeared alive in the doorway to the time when he was found dead; as he, Floyd, had been on the top of a step-ladder clipping the garden hedge. Janet Druce, the dead man's daughter, confirmed this, saying that she had sat on the terrace of the house throughout that time and had seen Floyd at his work. Touching some part of the time, this is again supported by Donald Druce, her brother—who overlooked the garden—standing at his bedroom window in his dressing-gown, for he had risen late. Lastly, the account is consistent with that given by Dr. Valentine, a neighbour, who called for a time to talk with Miss Druce on the terrace, and by the Colonel's solicitor, Mr. Aubrey Traill, who was apparently the last to see the murdered man alive—presumably with the exception of the murderer.

All are agreed that the course of events was as follows: About half past three in the afternoon, Miss Druce went down the path to ask her father when he would like tea; but he said he did not want any and was waiting to see Traill, his lawyer, who was to be sent to him in the summer-house. The girl then came away and met Traill coming down the path; she directed him to her father and he went in as directed. About half an hour afterwards he came out again, the Colonel coming with him to the door and showing himself to all appearance in health and even high spirits. He had been somewhat annoyed earlier in the day by his son's irregular hours, but seemed to recover his temper in a perfectly normal fashion, and had been rather markedly genial in receiving other visitors, including two of his nephews, who came over for the day. But as these were out walking during the whole period of the tragedy, they had no evidence to give. It is said, indeed, that the Colonel was not on very good terms with Dr. Valentine, but that gentleman only had a brief interview with the daughter of the house, to whom he is supposed to be paying serious attentions.

Traill, the solicitor, says he left the Colonel entirely alone in the summer-house, and this is confirmed by Floyd's bird's-eye view of the garden, which showed nobody else passing the only entrance. Ten minutes later, Miss Druce again went down the garden and had not reached the end of the path when she saw her father, who was conspicuous by his white linen coat, lying in a heap on the floor. She uttered a scream which brought others to the spot, and on entering the place they found the Colonel lying dead beside his basket-chair, which was also upset. Dr. Valentine, who was still in the immediate neighbourhood, testified that the wound was made by some sort of stiletto, entering under the shoulder-blade and piercing the heart. The police have searched the neighbourhood for such a weapon, but no trace of it can be found.

"So Colonel Druce wore a white coat, did he?" said Father Brown as he put down the paper.

"Trick he learnt in the tropics," replied Fiennes, with some wonder. "He'd had some queer adventures there, by his own account; and I fancy his dislike of Valentine was connected with the doctor coming from the tropics, too. But it's all an infernal puzzle. The account there is pretty accurate; I didn't see the tragedy, in the sense of the discovery; I was out walking with the young nephews and the dog—the dog I wanted to tell you about. But I saw the stage set for it as described; the straight lane between the blue flowers right up to the dark entrance, and the lawyer going down it in his blacks and his silk hat, and the red head of the secretary showing high above the green hedge as he worked on it with his shears. Nobody could have mistaken that red head at any distance; and if people say they saw it there all the time, you may be sure they did. This red-haired secretary, Floyd, is quite a character; a breathless bounding sort of fellow, always doing everybody's work as he was doing the gardener's. I think he is an American; he's certainly got the American view of life—what they call the view-point, bless 'em."

"What about the lawyer?" asked Father Brown.

There was a silence and then Fiennes spoke quite slowly for him. "Traill struck me as a singular man. In his fine black clothes he was almost foppish, yet you can hardly call him fashionable. For he wore a pair of long, luxuriant black whiskers such as haven't been seen since Victorian times. He had rather a fine grave face and a fine grave manner, but every now and then he seemed to remember to smile. And when he showed his white teeth he seemed to lose a little of his dignity, and there was something faintly fawning about him. It may have been only embarrassment, for he would also fidget with his cravat and his tie-pin, which were at once handsome and unusual, like himself. If I could think of anybody—but what's the good, when the whole thing's impossible? Nobody knows who did it. Nobody knows how it could be done. At least there's only one exception I'd make, and that's why I really mentioned the whole thing. The dog knows."

Father Brown sighed and then said absently: "You were there as a friend of young Donald, weren't you? He didn't go on your walk with you?"

"No," replied Fiennes smiling. "The young scoundrel had gone to bed that morning and got up that afternoon. I went with his cousins, two young officers from India, and our conversation was trivial enough. I remember the elder, whose name I think is Herbert Druce and who is an authority on horse-breeding, talked about nothing but a mare he had bought and the moral character of the man who sold her; while his brother Harry seemed to be brooding on his bad luck at Monte Carlo. I only mention it to show you, in the light of what happened on our walk, that there was nothing psychic about us. The dog was the only mystic in our company."

"What sort of a dog was he?" asked the priest.

"Same breed as that one," answered Fiennes. "That's what started me off on the story, your saying you didn't believe in believing in a dog. He's a big black retriever, named Nox, and a suggestive name, too; for I think what he did a darker mystery than the murder. You know Druce's house and garden are by the sea; we walked about a mile from it along the sands and then turned back, going the other way. We passed a rather curious rock called the Rock of Fortune, famous in the neighbourhood because it's one of those examples of one stone barely balanced on another, so that a touch would knock it over. It is not really very high but the hanging outline of it makes it look a little wild and sinister; at least it made it look so to me, for I don't imagine my jolly young companions were afflicted with the picturesque. But it may be that I was beginning to feel an atmosphere; for just then the question arose of whether it was time to go back to tea, and even then I think I had a premonition that time counted for a good deal in the business. Neither Herbert Druce nor I had a watch, so we called out to his brother, who was some paces behind, having stopped to light his pipe under the hedge. Hence it happened that he shouted out the hour, which was twenty past four, in his big voice through the growing twilight; and somehow the loudness of it made it sound like the proclamation of something tremendous. His unconsciousness seemed to make it all the more so; but that was always the way with omens; and particular ticks of the clock were really very ominous things that afternoon. According to Dr. Valentine's testimony, poor Druce had actually died just about half past four.

"Well, they said we needn't go home for ten minutes, and we walked a little farther along the sands, doing nothing in particular—throwing stones for the dog and throwing sticks into the sea for him to swim after. But to me the twilight seemed to grow oddly oppressive, and the very shadow of the top-heavy Rock of Fortune lay on me like a load. And then the curious thing happened. Nox had just brought back Herbert's walking-stick out of the sea and his brother had thrown his in also. The dog swam out again, but just about what must have been the stroke of the half-hour, he stopped swimming. He came back again on to the shore and stood in front of us. Then he suddenly threw up his head and sent up a howl or wail of woe—if ever I heard one in the world.

"'What the devil's the matter with the dog?' asked Herbert; but none of us could answer. There was a long silence after the brute's wailing and whining died away on the desolate shore; and then the silence was broken. As I live, it was broken by a faint and far-off shriek, like the shriek of a woman from beyond the hedges inland. We didn't know what it was then; but we knew afterwards. It was the cry the girl gave when she first saw the body of her father."

"You went back, I suppose," said Father Brown patiently. "What happened then?"

"I'll tell you what happened then," said Fiennes with a grim emphasis. "When we got back into that garden the first thing we saw was Traill, the lawyer; I can see him now with his black hat and black whiskers relieved against the perspective of the blue flowers stretching down to the summer-house, with the sunset and the strange outline of the Rock of Fortune in the distance. His face and figure were in shadow against the sunset; but I swear the white teeth were showing in his head and he was smiling.

"The moment Nox saw that man the dog dashed forward and stood in the middle of the path barking at him madly, murderously, volleying out curses that were almost verbal in their dreadful distinctness of hatred. And the man doubled up and fled along the path between the flowers."

Father Brown sprang to his feet with a startling impatience.

"So the dog denounced him, did he?" he cried. "The oracle of the dog condemned him. Did you see what birds were flying, and are you sure whether they were on the right hand or the left? Did you consult the augurs about the sacrifices? Surely you didn't omit to cut open the dog and examine his entrails. That is the sort of scientific test you heathen humanitarians seem to trust when you are thinking of taking away the life and honour of a man."

Fiennes sat gaping for an instant before he found breath to say: "Why, what's the matter with you? What have I done now?"

A sort of anxiety came back into the priest's eyes—the anxiety of a man who has run against a post in the dark and wonders for a moment whether he has hurt it.

"I'm most awfully sorry," he said with sincere distress. "I beg your pardon for being so rude; pray forgive me."

Fiennes looked at him curiously. "I sometimes think you are more of a mystery than any of the mysteries," he said.

"But anyhow, if you don't believe in the mystery of the dog, at least you can't get over the mystery of the man. You can't deny that at the very moment when the beast came back from the sea and bellowed, his master's soul was driven out of his body by the blow of some unseen power that no mortal man can trace or even imagine. And as for the lawyer—I don't go only by the dog—there are other curious details, too. He struck me as a smooth, smiling, equivocal sort of person; and one of his tricks seemed like a sort of hint. You know the doctor and the police were on the spot very quickly; Valentine was brought back when walking away from the house, and he telephoned instantly. That, with the secluded house, small numbers, and enclosed space, made it pretty possible to search everybody who could have been near; and everybody was thoroughly searched—for a weapon. The whole house, garden, and shore were combed for a weapon. The disappearance of the dagger is almost as crazy as the disappearance of the man."

"The disappearance of the dagger," said Father Brown, nodding. He seemed to have become suddenly attentive.

"Well," continued Fiennes, "I told you that man Traill had a trick of fidgeting with his tie and tie-pin—especially his tie-pin. His pin, like himself, was at once showy and old-fashioned. It had one of those stones with concentric coloured rings that look like an eye; and his own concentration on it got on my nerves, as if he had been a Cyclops with one eye in the middle of his body. But the pin was not only large but long; and it occurred to me that his anxiety about its adjustment was because it was even longer than it looked; as long as a stiletto in fact."

Father Brown nodded thoughtfully. "Was any other instrument ever suggested?" he asked.

"There was another suggestion," answered Fiennes, "from one of the young Druces—the cousins, I mean. Neither Herbert nor Harry Druce would have struck one at first as likely to be of assistance in scientific detection; but while Herbert was really the traditional type of heavy Dragoon, caring for nothing but horses and being an ornament to the Horse Guards, his younger brother Harry had been in the Indian Police and knew something about such things. Indeed, in his own way he was quite clever; and I rather fancy he had been too clever; I mean he had left the police through breaking some red-tape regulations and taking some sort of risk and responsibility of his own. Anyhow, he was in some sense a detective out of work, and threw himself into this business with more than the ardour of an amateur. And it was with him that I had an argument about the weapon—an argument that led to something new. It began by his countering my description of the dog barking at Traill; and he said that a dog at his worst didn't bark, but growled."

"He was quite right there," observed the priest.

"This young fellow went on to say that, if it came to that, he'd heard Nox growling at other people before then; and among others at Floyd, the secretary. I retorted that his own argument answered itself; for the crime couldn't be brought home to two or three people, and least of all to Floyd, who was as innocent as a harum-scarum schoolboy, and had been seen by everybody all the time perched above the garden hedge with his fan of red hair as conspicuous as a scarlet cockatoo. 'I know there's difficulties anyhow,' said my colleague; 'but I wish you'd come with me down the garden a minute. I want to show you something I don't think any one else has seen.' This was on the very day of the discovery, and the garden was just as it had been. The step-ladder was still standing by the hedge, and just under the hedge my guide stopped and disentangled something from the deep grass. It was the shears used for clipping the hedge, and on the point of one of them was a smear of blood."

There was a short silence, and then Father Brown said suddenly, "What was the lawyer there for?"

"He told us the Colonel sent for him to alter his will," answered Fiennes. "And, by the way, there was another thing about the business of the will that I ought to mention. You see, the will wasn't actually signed in the summer-house that afternoon."

"I suppose not," said Father Brown; "there would have to be two witnesses."

"The lawyer actually came down the day before and it was signed then; but he was sent for again next day because the old man had a doubt about one of the witnesses and had to be reassured."

"Who were the witnesses?" asked Father Brown.

"That's just the point," replied his informant eagerly, "the witnesses were Floyd, the secretary, and this Dr. Valentine, the foreign sort of surgeon or whatever he is; and the two had a quarrel. Now I'm bound to say that the secretary is something of a busybody. He's one of those hot and headlong people whose warmth of temperament has unfortunately turned mostly to pugnacity and bristling suspicion; to distrusting people instead of to trusting them. That sort of red-haired red-hot fellow is always either universally credulous or universally incredulous; and sometimes both. He was not only a Jack-of-all-trades, but he knew better than all tradesmen. He not only knew everything, but he warned everybody against everybody. All that must be taken into account in his suspicions about Valentine; but in that particular case there seems to have been something behind it. He said the name of Valentine was not really Valentine. He said he had seen him elsewhere known by the name of De Villon. He said it would invalidate the will; of course he was kind enough to explain to the lawyer what the law was on that point. They were both in a frightful wax."

Father Brown laughed. "People often are when they are to witness a will," he said; "for one thing, it means that they can't have any legacy under it. But what did Dr. Valentine say? No doubt the universal secretary knew more about the doctor's name than the doctor did. But even the doctor might have some information about his own name."

Fiennes paused a moment before he replied.

"Dr. Valentine took it in a curious way. Dr. Valentine is a curious man. His appearance is rather striking but very foreign. He is young but wears a beard cut square; and his face is very pale, dreadfully pale and dreadfully serious. His eyes have a sort of ache in them, as if he ought to wear glasses, or had given himself a headache with thinking; but he is quite handsome and always very formally dressed, with a top hat and a dark coat and a little red rosette. His manner is rather cold and haughty, and he has a way of staring at you which is very disconcerting. When thus charged with having changed his name, he merely stared like a sphinx and then said with a little laugh that he supposed Americans had no names to change. At that I think the Colonel also got into a fuss and said all sorts of angry things to the doctor; all the more angry because of the doctor's pretensions to a future place in his family. But I shouldn't have thought much of that but for a few words that I happened to hear later, early in the afternoon of the tragedy. I don't want to make a lot of them, for they weren't the sort of words on which one would like, in the ordinary way, to play the eavesdropper. As I was passing out towards the front gate with my two companions and the dog, I heard voices which told me that Dr. Valentine and Miss Druce had withdrawn for a moment in the shadow of the house, in an angle behind a row of flowering plants, and were talking to each other in passionate whisperings— sometimes almost like hissings; for it was something of a lovers' quarrel as well as a lovers' tryst. Nobody repeats the sort of things they said for the most part; but in an unfortunate business like this I'm bound to say that there was repeated more than once a phrase about killing somebody. In fact, the girl seemed to be begging him not to kill somebody, or saying that no provocation could justify killing anybody; which seems an unusual sort of talk to address to a gentleman who has dropped in to tea."

"Do you know," asked the priest, "whether Dr. Valentine seemed to be very angry after the scene with the secretary and the Colonel—I mean about witnessing the will?"

"By all accounts," replied the other, "he wasn't half so angry as the secretary was. It was the secretary who went away raging after witnessing the will."

"And now," said Father Brown, "what about the will itself?"

"The Colonel was a very wealthy man, and his will was important. Traill wouldn't tell us the alteration at that stage, but I have since heard only this morning in fact—that most of the money was transferred from the son to the daughter. I told you that Druce was wild with my friend Donald over his dissipated hours."

"The question of motive has been rather over-shadowed by the question of method," observed Father Brown thoughtfully. "At that moment, apparently, Miss Druce was the immediate gainer by the death."

"Good God! What a cold-blooded way of talking," cried Fiennes, staring at him. "You don't really mean to hint that she—"

"Is she going to marry that Dr. Valentine?" asked the other.

"Some people are against it," answered his friend. "But he is liked and respected in the place and is a skilled and devoted surgeon."

"So devoted a surgeon," said Father Brown, "that he had surgical instruments with him when he went to call on the young lady at teatime. For he must have used a lancet or something, and he never seems to have gone home."

Fiennes sprang to his feet and looked at him in a heat of inquiry. "You suggest he might have used the very same lancet—"

Father Brown shook his head. "All these suggestions are fancies just now," he said. "The problem is not who did it or what did it, but how it was done. We might find many men and even many tools—pins and shears and lancets. But how did a man get into the room? How did even a pin get into it?"

He was staring reflectively at the ceiling as he spoke, but as he said the last words his eye cocked in an alert fashion as if he had suddenly seen a curious fly on the ceiling.

"Well, what would you do about it?" asked the young man. "You have a lot of experience; what would you advise now?"

"I'm afraid I'm not much use," said Father Brown with a sigh. "I can't suggest very much without having ever been near the place or the people. For the moment you can only go on with local inquiries. I gather that your friend from the Indian Police is more or less in charge of your inquiry down there. I should run down and see how he is getting on. See what he's been doing in the way of amateur detection. There may be news already."

As his guests, the biped and the quadruped, disappeared, Father Brown took up his pen and went back to his interrupted occupation of planning a course of lectures on the Encyclical *Rerum Novarum*. The subject was a large one and he had to recast it more than once, so that he was somewhat similarly employed some two days later when the big black dog again came bounding into the room and sprawled all over him with enthusiasm and excitement. The master who followed the dog shared the excitement if not the enthusiasm. He had been excited in a less pleasant fashion, for his blue eyes seemed to start from his head and his eager face was even a little pale.

"You told me," he said abruptly and without preface, "to find out what Harry Druce was doing. Do you know what he's done?"

The priest did not reply, and the young man went on in jerky tones:

"I'll tell you what he's done. He's killed himself."

Father Brown's lips moved only faintly, and there was nothing practical about what he was saying—nothing that has anything to do with this story or this world.

"You give me the creeps sometimes," said Fiennes. "Did you—did you expect this?"

"I thought it possible," said Father Brown; "that was why I asked you to go and see what he was doing. I hoped you might not be too late."

"It was I who found him," said Fiennes rather huskily. "It

was the ugliest and most uncanny thing I ever knew. I went down that old garden again, and I knew there was something new and unnatural about it besides the murder. The flowers still tossed about in blue masses on each side of the black entrance into the old grey summer-house; but to me the blue flowers looked like blue devils dancing before some dark cavern of the underworld. I looked all round, everything seemed to be in its ordinary place. But the queer notion grew on me that there was something wrong with the very shape of the sky. And then I saw what it was. The Rock of Fortune always rose in the background beyond the garden hedge and against the sea. The Rock of Fortune was gone."

Father Brown had lifted his head and was listening intently.

"It was as if a mountain had walked away out of a landscape or a moon fallen from the sky; though I knew, of course, that a touch at any time would have tipped the thing over. Something possessed me and I rushed down that garden path like the wind and went crashing through that hedge as if it were a spider's web. It was a thin hedge really, though its undisturbed trimness had made it serve all the purposes of a wall. On the shore I found the loose rock fallen from its pedestal; and poor Harry Druce lay like a wreck underneath it. One arm was thrown round it in a sort of embrace as if he had pulled it down on himself; and on the broad brown sands beside it, in large crazy lettering, he had scrawled the words: 'The Rock of Fortune falls on the Fool.'"

"It was the Colonel's will that did that," observed Father Brown. "The young man had staked everything on profiting himself by Donald's disgrace, especially when his uncle sent for him on the same day as the lawyer, and welcomed him with so much warmth. Otherwise he was done; he'd lost his police job; he was beggared at Monte Carlo. And he killed himself when he found he'd killed his kinsman for nothing."

"Here, stop a minute!" cried the staring Fiennes. "You're going too fast for me."

"Talking about the will, by the way," continued Father Brown calmly, "before I forget it, or we go on to bigger things, there was a simple explanation, I think, of all that business about the doctor's name. I rather fancy I have heard both names before somewhere. The doctor is really a French nobleman with the title of the Marquis de Villon. But he is also an ardent Republican and has abandoned his title and fallen back on the forgotten family surname. 'With your Citizen Riquetti you have puzzled Europe for ten days.'"

"What is that?" asked the young man blankly.

"Never mind," said the priest. "Nine times out of ten it is a rascally thing to change one's name; but this was a piece of fine fanaticism. That's the point of his sarcasm about Americans having no names—that is, no titles. Now in England the Marquis of Hartington is never called Mr. Hartington; but in France the Marquis de Villon is called M. de Villon. So it might well look like a change of name. As for the talk about killing, I fancy that also was a point of French etiquette. The doctor was talking about challenging Floyd to a duel, and the girl was trying to dissuade him."

"Oh, I *see*," cried Fiennes slowly. "Now I understand what she meant."

"And what is that about?" asked his companion, smiling.

"Well," said the young man, "it was something that happened to me just before I found that poor fellow's body; only the catastrophe drove it out of my head. I suppose it's hard to remember a little romantic idyll when you've just

come on top of a tragedy. But as I went down the lanes leading to the Colonel's old place I met his daughter walking
with Dr. Valentine. She was in mourning, of course, and
he always wore black as if he were going to a funeral; but
I can't say that their faces were very funereal. Never have
I seen two people looking in their own way more respect-
ably radiant and cheerful. They stopped and saluted me,
and then she told me they were married and living in a little
house on the outskirts of the town, where the doctor was
continuing his practice. This rather surprised me, because I
knew that her old father's will had left her his property; and
I hinted at it delicately by saying I was going along to her
father's old place and had half expected to meet her there.
But she only laughed and said: 'Oh, we've given up all that.
My husband doesn't like heiresses.' And I discovered with
some astonishment they really had insisted on restoring the
property to poor Donald; so I hope he's had a healthy shock
and will treat it sensibly. There was never much really the
matter with him; he was very young and his father was not
very wise. But it was in connexion with that that she said
something I didn't understand at the time; but now I'm sure
it must be as you say. She said with a sort of sudden and
splendid arrogance that was entirely altruistic:

"'I hope it'll stop that red-haired fool from fussing any
more about the will. Does he think my husband, who has
given up a crest and a coronet as old as the Crusades for
his principles, would kill an old man in a summer-house for
a legacy like that?' Then she laughed again and said, 'My
husband isn't killing anybody except in the way of business.
Why, he didn't even ask his friends to call on the secretary.'
Now, of course, I see what she meant."

"I see part of what she meant, of course," said Father

Brown. "What did she mean exactly by the secretary fussing about the will?"

Fiennes smiled as he answered, "I wish you knew the secretary, Father Brown. It would be a joy to you to watch him make things hum, as he calls it. He made the house of mourning hum. He filled the funeral with all the snap and zip of the brightest sporting event. There was no holding him, after something had really happened. I've told you how he used to oversee the gardener as he did the garden, and how he instructed the lawyer in the law. Needless to say, he also instructed the surgeon in the practice of surgery; and as the surgeon was Dr. Valentine, you may be sure it ended in accusing him of something worse than bad surgery. The secretary got it fixed in his red head that the doctor had committed the crime, and when the police arrived he was perfectly sublime. Need I say that he became, on the spot, the greatest of all amateur detectives? Sherlock Holmes never towered over Scotland Yard with more Titanic intellectual pride and scorn than Colonel Druce's private secretary over the police investigating Colonel Druce's death. I tell you it was a joy to see him. He strode about with an abstracted air, tossing his scarlet crest of hair and giving curt impatient replies. Of course it was his demeanour during these days that made Druce's daughter so wild with him. Of course he had a theory. It's just the sort of theory a man would have in a book; and Floyd is the sort of man who ought to be in a book. He'd be better fun and less bother in a book."

"What was his theory?" asked the other.

"Oh, it was full of pep," replied Fiennes gloomily. "It would have been glorious copy if it could have held together for ten minutes longer. He said the Colonel was still alive when they found him in the summer-house, and the doctor killed him with the surgical instrument on pretence of cutting the clothes."

"I see," said the priest. "I suppose he was lying flat on his face on the mud floor as a form of siesta."

"It's wonderful what hustle will do," continued his informant. "I believe Floyd would have got his great theory into the papers at any rate, and perhaps had the doctor attested, when all these things were blown sky high as if by dynamite by the discovery of that dead body lying under the Rock of Fortune. And that's what we come back to after all. I suppose the suicide is almost a confession. But nobody will ever know the whole story."

There was a silence, and then the priest said modestly: "I rather think I know the whole story."

Fiennes stared. "But look here," he cried; "how do you come to know the whole story, or to be sure it's the true story? You've been sitting here a hundred miles away writing a sermon; do you mean to tell me you really know what happened already? If you've really come to the end, where in the world do you begin? What started you off with your own story?"

Father Brown jumped up with a very unusual excitement and his first exclamation was like an explosion.

"The dog!" he cried. "The dog, of course! You had the whole story in your hands in the business of the dog on the beach, if you'd only noticed the dog properly."

Fiennes stared still more. "But you told me before that my feelings about the dog were all nonsense, and the dog had nothing to do with it."

"The dog had everything to do with it," said Father Brown, "as you'd have found out if you'd only treated the dog as a dog, and not as God Almighty judging the souls of men."

He paused in an embarrassed way for a moment, and then said, with a rather pathetic air of apology: "The truth is, I happen to be awfully fond of dogs. And it seemed to me that in all this lurid halo of dog superstitions nobody was really thinking about the poor dog at all. To begin with a small point, about his barking at the lawyer or growling at the secretary. You asked how I could guess things a hundred miles away; but honestly it's mostly to your credit, for you described people so well that I know the types. A man like Traill, who frowns usually and smiles suddenly, a man who fiddles with things, especially at his throat, is a nervous, easily embarrassed man. I shouldn't wonder if Floyd, the efficient secretary, is nervy and jumpy, too; those Yankee hustlers often are. Otherwise he wouldn't have cut his fingers on the shears and dropped them when he heard Janet Druce scream.

"Now dogs hate nervous people. I don't know whether they make the dog nervous, too; or whether, being after all a brute, he is a bit of a bully; or whether his canine vanity (which is colossal) is simply offended at not being liked. But anyhow there was nothing in poor Nox protesting against those people, except that he disliked them for being afraid of him. Now I know you're awfully clever, and nobody of sense sneers at cleverness. But I sometimes fancy, for instance, that you are too clever to understand animals. Sometimes you are too clever to understand men, especially when they act almost as simply as animals. Animals are very literal; they live in a world of truisms. Take this case: a dog barks at a man and a man runs away from a dog. Now you do not seem to be quite simple enough to see the fact: that the dog barked because he disliked the man and the man fled because he was frightened of the dog. They had no other motives and they needed none; but you must read psychological mysteries into it and suppose the dog had super-normal vision, and was a mysterious mouthpiece of doom. You must suppose the man was running away, not from the dog but from the hangman. And yet, if you come to think if it, all this deeper psychology is exceedingly improbable. If the dog really could completely and consciously realise the murderer of his master he wouldn't stand yapping as he might at a curate at a tea-party; he's much more likely to fly at his throat. And on the other hand, do you really think a man who had hardened his heart to murder an old friend and then walk about smiling at the old friend's family, under the eyes of his old friend's daughter and post-mortem doctor—do you think a man like that would be doubled up by mere remorse because a dog barked? He might feel the tragic irony of it; it might shake his soul, like any other tragic trifle. But he wouldn't rush madly the length of a garden to escape from the only witness whom he knew to be unable to talk. People have a panic like that when they are frightened, not of tragic ironies, but of teeth. The whole thing is simpler than you can understand.

"But when we come to that business by the seashore, things are much more interesting. As you stated them, they were much more puzzling. I didn't understand that tale of the dog going in and out of the water; it didn't seem to me a doggy thing to do. If Nox had been very much upset about something else, he might possibly have refused to go after the stick at all. He'd probably go off nosing in whatever direction he suspected the mischief. But when once a dog is actually chasing a thing, a stone or a stick or a rabbit, my experience is that he won't stop for anything but the most peremptory command, and not always for that. That he should turn round because his mood changed seems to me unthinkable."

"But he did turn round," insisted Fiennes; "and came back without the stick."

"He came back without the stick for the best reason in the world," replied the priest. "He came back because he couldn't find it. He whined because he couldn't find it. That's the sort of thing a dog really does whine about. A dog is a devil of a ritualist. He is as particular about the precise routine of a game as a child about the precise repetition of a fairy-tale. In this case something had gone wrong with the game. He came back to complain seriously of the conduct of the stick. Never had such a thing happened before. Never had an eminent and distinguished dog been so treated by a rotten old walking-stick."

"Why, what had the walking-stick done?" inquired the young man.

"It had sunk," said Father Brown.

Fiennes said nothing, but continued to stare; and it was the priest who continued:

"It had sunk because it was not really a stick, but a rod of steel with a very thin shell of cane and a sharp point. In other words, it was a sword-stick. I suppose a murderer never gets rid of a bloody weapon so oddly and yet so naturally as by throwing it into the sea for a retriever."

"I begin to see what you mean," admitted Fiennes; "but even if a sword-stick was used, I have no guess of how it was used."

"I had a sort of guess," said Father Brown, "right at the beginning when you said the word summer-house. And another when you said that Druce wore a white coat. As long as everybody was looking for a short dagger, nobody thought of it; but if we admit a rather long blade like a rapier, it's not so impossible."

He was leaning back, looking at the ceiling, and began like one going back to his own first thoughts and fundamentals.

"All that discussion about detective stories like the Yellow Room, about a man found dead in sealed chambers which no one could enter, does not apply to the present case, because it is a summer-house. When we talk of a Yellow Room, or any room, we imply walls that are really homogeneous and impenetrable. But a summer-house is not made like that; it is often made, as it was in this case, of closely interlaced but separate boughs and strips of wood, in which there are chinks here and there. There was one of them just behind Druce's back as he sat in his chair up against the wall. But just as the room was a summer-house, so the chair was a basket-chair. That also was a lattice of loopholes. Lastly, the summer-house was close up under the hedge; and you have just told me that it was really a thin hedge. A man standing outside it could easily see, amid a network of twigs and branches and canes, one white spot of the Colonel's coat as plain as the white of a target.

"Now, you left the geography a little vague; but it was possible to put two and two together. You said the Rock of Fortune was not really high; but you also said it could be seen dominating the garden like a mountain-peak. In other words, it was very near the end of the garden, though your walk had taken you a long way round to it. Also, it isn't likely the young lady really howled so as to be heard half a mile. She gave an ordinary involuntary cry, and yet you heard it on the shore. And among other interesting things that you told me, may I remind you that you said Harry Druce had fallen behind to light his pipe under a hedge."

Fiennes shuddered slightly. "You mean he drew his blade there and sent it through the hedge at the white spot. But surely it was a very odd chance and a very sudden choice. Besides, he couldn't be certain the old man's money had passed to him, and as a fact it hadn't."

Father Brown's face became animated.

"You misunderstand the man's character," he said, as if he himself had known the man all his life. "A curious but not unknown type of character. If he had really *known* the money would come to him, I seriously believe he wouldn't have done it. He would have seen it as the dirty thing it was."

"Isn't that rather paradoxical?" asked the other.

"This man was a gambler," said the priest, "and a man in disgrace for having taken risks and anticipated orders. It was probably for something pretty unscrupulous, for every imperial police is more like a Russian secret police than we like to think. But he had gone beyond the line and failed. Now, the temptation of that type of man is to do a mad thing precisely because the risk will be wonderful in retrospect. He wants to say, 'Nobody but I could have seized that chance or seen that it was then or never. What a wild and wonderful guess it was, when I put all those things together; Donald in disgrace; and the lawyer being sent for; and Herbert and I sent for at the same time—and then nothing more but the way the old man grinned at me and shook hands. Anybody would say I was mad to risk it; but that is how fortunes are made, by the man mad enough to have a little foresight.' In short, it is the vanity of guessing. It is the megalomania of the gambler. The more incongruous the coincidence, the more instantaneous the decision, the more likely he is to snatch the chance. The accident, the very triviality of the white speck and the hole in the hedge intoxicated him like a vision of the world's desire. Nobody clever enough to see such a combination of accidents could be cowardly enough not to use them! That is how the devil talks to the gambler. But the devil himself would hardly have induced that unhappy man to go down in a dull, deliberate way and kill an old uncle from whom he'd always had expectations. It would be too respectable."

He paused a moment, and then went on with a certain quiet emphasis.

"And now try to call up the scene, even as you saw it yourself. As he stood there, dizzy with his diabolical opportunity, he looked up and saw that strange outline that might have been the image of his own tottering soul; the one great crag poised perilously on the other like a pyramid on its point, and remembered that it was called the Rock of Fortune. Can you guess how such a man at such a moment would read such a signal? I think it strung him up to action and even to vigilance. He who would be a tower must not fear to be a toppling tower. Anyhow, he acted; his next difficulty was to cover his tracks. To be found with a sword-stick, let alone a blood-stained sword-stick, would be fatal in the search that was certain to follow. If he left it anywhere, it would be found and probably traced. Even if he threw it into the sea the action might be noticed, and thought noticeable—unless indeed he could think of some more natural way of covering the action. As you know, he did think of one, and a very good one. Being the only one of you with a watch, he told you it was not yet time to return, strolled a little farther, and started the game of throwing in sticks for the retriever. But how his eyes must have rolled darkly over all that desolate sea-shore before they alighted on the dog!"

Fiennes nodded, gazing thoughtfully into space. His mind seemed to have drifted back to a less practical part of the narrative.

"It's queer," he said, "that the dog really was in the story after all."

"The dog could almost have told you the story, if he could talk," said the priest. "All I complain of is that because he couldn't talk you made up his story for him, and made him talk with the tongues of men and angels. It's part of something I've noticed more and more in the modern world, appearing in all sorts of newspaper rumours and conversational catchwords; something that's arbitrary without being authoritative. People readily swallow the untested claims of this, that, or the other. It's drowning all your old rationalism and scepticism, it's coming in like a sea; and the name of it is superstition." He stood up abruptly, his face heavy with a sort of frown, and went on talking almost as if he were alone. "It's the first effect of not believing in God that you lose your common sense and can't see things as they are. Anything that anybody talks about, and says there's a good deal in it, extends itself indefinitely like a vista in a nightmare. And a dog is an omen, and a cat is a mystery, and a pig is a mascot, and a beetle is a scarab, calling up all the menagerie of polytheism from Egypt and old India; Dog Anubis and great green-eyed Pasht and all the holy howling Bulls of Bashan; reeling back to the bestial gods of the beginning, escaping into elephants and snakes and crocodiles; and all because you are frightened of four words: 'He was made Man.'"

The young man got up with a little embarrassment, almost as if he had overheard a soliloquy. He called to the dog and left the room with vague but breezy farewells. But he had to call the dog twice, for the dog had remained behind quite motionless for a moment, looking up steadily at Father Brown as the wolf looked at St. Francis.

The Man Who
Hated Earthworms

Edgar Wallace

THE FIRST BESTSELLING THRILLER WRITTEN BY
Richard Horatio Edgar Wallace (1875–1932) was an
"impossible crime" novel called *The Four Just Men*, which
began life as a competition mystery and made his name,
even though the cost of paying out the competition prize
money almost ruined him. The "four just men" were a quar-
tet of wealthy foreign vigilantes, and in the first book they
murder a stubborn but principled British politician. Wallace
brought the four just men back for further adventures, but
as time passed they aligned themselves increasingly with
the forces of law and order. This story does, however, give a
reminder of their ruthlessness in pursuit of an objective in
which they believe.

"The Man Who Hated Earthworms" appeared in *The
Strand Magazine* in July 1921 and is, like "The Lion's
Mane," set on England's south coast. Complete in itself,
this story was subsequently included in *The Law of the*

Four Just Men, also published in 1921. The man who hates earthworms is described as "of the new school, rather superior, rather immaculate, very Balliol." This could easily be a description of Lord Peter Wimsey, who made his debut in print a couple of years later. But Dr. Felix Viglow proves to be a very different character from Dorothy L. Sayers' Great Detective.

————

"The death has occurred at Staines of Mr. Falmouth, late Superintendent of the Criminal Investigation Department. Mr. Falmouth will best be remembered as the Officer who arrested George Manfred, the leader of the Four Just Men gang. The sensational escape of this notorious man is perhaps the most remarkable chapter in criminal history. The 'Four Just Men' was an organisation which set itself to right acts of injustice which the law left unpunished. It is believed that the members were exceedingly rich men who devoted their lives and fortunes to this quixotic but wholly unlawful purpose. The gang has not been heard of for many years."

Manfred read the paragraph from the *Morning Telegram* and Leon Gonsalez frowned.

"I have an absurd objection to being called a 'gang,'" he said, and Manfred smiled quietly.

"Poor old Falmouth," he reflected, "well, he knows! He was a nice fellow."

"I liked Falmouth," agreed Gonsalez. "He was a perfectly normal man except for a slight progenism—"

Manfred laughed.

"Forgive me if I appear dense, but I have never been able to keep up with you in this particular branch of science," he said, "what is a 'progenism'?"

"The unscientific call it an 'underhung jaw,'" explained Leon, "and it is mistaken for strength. It is only normal in Piedmont where the brachycephalic skull is so common. With such a skull, progenism is almost a natural condition."

"Progenism or not, he was a good fellow," insisted Manfred and Leon nodded. "With well-developed wisdom teeth," he added slyly, and Gonsalez went red, for teeth formed a delicate subject with him. Nevertheless he grinned.

"It will interest you to know, my dear George," he said triumphantly, "that when the famous Dr. Carrara examined the teeth of four hundred criminals and a like number of non-criminals—you will find his detailed narrative in the monograph 'Sullo Sviluppo Del Terzo Dente Morale Nei Criminali'—he found the wisdom tooth more frequently present in normal people."

"I grant you the wisdom tooth," said Manfred hastily. "Look at the bay! Did you ever see anything more perfect?"

They were sitting on a little green lawn overlooking Babbacombe Beach. The sun was going down and a perfect day was drawing to its close. High above the blue sea towered the crimson cliffs and green fields of Devon.

Manfred looked at his watch.

"Are we dressing for dinner?" he asked, "or has your professional friend Bohemian tastes?"

"He is of the new school," said Leon, "rather superior, rather immaculate, very Balliol. I am anxious that you should meet him, his hands are rather fascinating."

Manfred in his wisdom did not ask why.

"I met him at golf," Gonsalez went on, "and certain things happened which interested me. For example, every time he saw an earthworm he stopped to kill it and displayed such an extraordinary fury in the assassination that I was astounded. Prejudice has no place in the scientific mind. He is exceptionally wealthy. People at the club told me that his uncle left him close on a million, and the estate of his aunt or cousin who died last year was valued at another million and he was the sole legatee. Naturally a good catch. Whether Miss Moleneux thinks the same I have had no opportunity of gauging," he added after a pause.

"Good lord!" cried Manfred in consternation as he jumped up from his chair. "She is coming to dinner too, isn't she?"

"And her mamma," said Leon soberly. "Her mamma has learnt Spanish by correspondence lessons, and insists upon greeting me with *habla usted Espanol?*"

The two men had rented Cliff House for the spring. Manfred loved Devonshire in April when the slopes of the hills were yellow with primroses and daffodils made a golden path across the Devon lawns. "Senor Fuentes" had taken the house after one inspection and found the calm and the peace which only nature's treasury of colour and fragrance could bring to his active mind.

Manfred had dressed and was sitting by the wood fire in the drawing-room when the purr of a motor-car coming cautiously down the cliff road brought him to his feet and through the open French window.

Leon Gonsalez had joined him before the big limousine had come to a halt before the porch.

The first to alight was a man and George observed him closely. He was tall and thin. He was not bad looking, though the face was lined and the eyes deep set and level. He greeted Gonsalez with just a tiny hint of patronage in his tone.

"I hope we haven't kept you waiting, but my experiments

detained me. Nothing went right in the laboratory today. You know Miss Moleneux and Mrs. Moleneux?"

Manfred was introduced and found himself shaking hands with a grave-eyed girl of singular beauty.

Manfred was unusually sensitive to "atmosphere" and there was something about this girl which momentarily chilled him. Her frequent smile, sweet as it was and undoubtedly sincere, was as undoubtedly mechanical. Leon, who judged people by reason rather than instinct, reached his conclusion more surely and gave shape and definite description to what in Manfred's mind was merely a distressful impression. The girl was afraid! Of what? wondered Leon. Not of that stout, complacent little woman whom she called mother, and surely not of this thin-faced academic gentleman in pince-nez.

Gonsalez had introduced Dr. Viglow and whilst the ladies were taking off their cloaks in Manfred's room above, he had leisure to form a judgment. There was no need for him to entertain his guest. Dr. Viglow spoke fluently, entertainingly and all the time.

"Our friend here plays a good game of golf," he said, indicating Gonsalez, "a good game of golf indeed for a foreigner. You two are Spanish?"

Manfred nodded. He was more thoroughly English than the doctor, did that gentleman but know, but it was as a Spaniard and armed, moreover, with a Spanish passport that he was a visitor to Britain.

"I understood you to say that your investigations have taken rather a sensational turn, Doctor," said Leon and a light came into Dr. Viglow's eyes.

"Yes," he said complacently, and then quickly, "who told you that?"

"You told me yourself at the club this morning."

The doctor frowned.

"Did I?" he said and passed his hand across his forehead. "I can't recollect that. When was this?"

"This morning," said Leon, "but your mind was probably occupied with much more important matters."

The young professor bit his lip and frowned thoughtfully.

"I ought not to have forgotten what happened this morning," he said in a troubled tone.

He gave the impression to Manfred that one half of him was struggling desperately to overcome a something in the other half. Suddenly he laughed.

"A sensational turn!" he said. "Yes indeed, and I rather think that within a few months I shall not be without fame, even in my own country! It is, of course, terribly expensive. I was only reckoning up today that my typists' wages come to nearly £60 a week."

Manfred opened his eyes at this.

"Your typists' wages?" he repeated slowly. "Are you preparing a book?"

"Here are the ladies," said Dr. Felix.

His manner was abrupt to rudeness and later when they sat round the table in the little dining-room Manfred had further cause to wonder at the boorishness of this young scientist. He was seated next to Miss Moleneux and the meal was approaching its end when most unexpectedly he turned to the girl and in a loud voice said:

"You haven't kissed me today, Margaret."

The girl went red and white and the fingers that fidgeted with the table-ware before her were trembling when she faltered:

"Haven't—haven't I, Felix?"

The bright eyes of Gonsalez never left the doctor. The man's face had gone purple with rage.

"By God! This is a nice thing!" he almost shouted. "I'm engaged to you. I've left you everything in my will and I'm allowing your mother a thousand a year and you haven't kissed me today!"

"Doctor!" it was the mild but insistent voice of Gonsalez that broke the tension. "I wonder whether you would tell me what chemical is represented by the formula Cl_2O_5."

The doctor had turned his head slowly at the sound of Leon's voice and now was staring at him. Slowly the strange look passed from his face and it became normal.

"Cl_2O_5 is Oxide of Chlorine," he said in an even voice, and from thenceforward the conversation passed by way of acid reactions into a scientific channel.

The only person at the table who had not been perturbed by Viglow's outburst had been the dumpy complacent lady on Manfred's right. She had tittered audibly at the reference to her allowance, and when the hum of conversation became general she lowered her voice and leant toward Manfred.

"Dear Felix is so eccentric," she said, "but he is quite the nicest, kindest soul. One must look after one's girls, don't you agree, senor?"

She asked this latter question in very bad Spanish and Manfred nodded. He shot a glance at the girl. She was still deathly pale.

"And I am perfectly certain she will be happy, much happier than she would have been with that impossible person."

She did not specify who the "impossible person" was, but Manfred sensed a whole world of tragedy. He was not romantic, but one look at the girl had convinced him that there was something wrong in this engagement. Now it was that he came to a conclusion which Leon had reached an hour before, that the emotion which dominated the girl was fear. And he pretty well knew of whom she was afraid.

Half an hour later when the tail light of Dr. Viglow's limousine had disappeared round a corner of the drive the two men went back to the drawing-room and Manfred threw a handful of kindling to bring the fire to a blaze.

"Well, what do you think?" said Gonsalez, rubbing his hands together with evidence of some enjoyment.

"I think it's rather horrible," replied Manfred, settling himself in his chair. "I thought the days when wicked mothers forced their daughters into unwholesome marriages were passed and done with. One hears so much about the modern girl."

"Human nature isn't modern," said Gonsalez briskly, "and most mothers are fools where their daughters are concerned. I know you won't agree but I speak with authority. Mantegazza collected statistics of 843 families—"

Manfred chuckled.

"You and your Mantegazza!" he laughed. "Did that infernal man know everything?"

"Almost everything," said Leon. "As to the girl," he became suddenly grave. "She will not marry him of course."

"What is the matter with him?" asked Manfred. "He seems to have an ungovernable temper."

"He is mad," replied Leon calmly and Manfred looked at him.

"Mad?" he repeated incredulously. "Do you mean to say that he is a lunatic?"

"I never use the word in a spectacular or even in a vulgar sense," said Gonsalez, lighting a cigarette carefully. "The man is undoubtedly mad. I thought so a few days ago and

I am certain of it now. The most ominous test is the test of memory. People who are on the verge of madness or entering its early stages do not remember what happened a short time before. Did you notice how worried he was when I told him of the conversation we had this morning?"

"That struck me as peculiar," agreed Manfred.

"He was fighting," said Leon, "the sane half of his brain against the insane half. The doctor against the irresponsible animal. The doctor told him that if he had suddenly lost his memory for incidents which had occurred only a few hours before, he was on the high way to lunacy. The crazy half of the brain told him that he was such a wonderful fellow that the rules applying to ordinary human beings did not apply to him. We will call upon him tomorrow to see his laboratory and discover why he is paying £60 a week for typists," he said. "And now, my dear George, you can go to bed. I am going to read the excellent but often misguided Lombroso on the male delinquent."

Dr. Viglow's laboratory was a new red building on the edge of Dartmoor. To be exact, it consisted of two buildings, one of which was a large army hut which had been recently erected for the accommodation of the doctor's clerical staff.

"I haven't met a professor for two or three years," said Manfred as they were driving across the moor, en route to pay their call, "nor have I been in a laboratory for five. And yet within the space of a few weeks I have met two extraordinary professors, one of whom I admit was dead. Also I have visited two laboratories."

Leon nodded.

"Some day I will make a very complete examination of the phenomena of coincidence," he said.

When they reached the laboratory they found a

post-office van, backed up against the main entrance and three assistants in white overalls were carrying post bags and depositing them in the van.

"He must have a pretty large correspondence," said Manfred in wonder.

The doctor, in a long white overall, was standing at the door as they alighted from their car and greeted them warmly.

"Come into my office," he said, and led the way to a large airy room which was singularly free from the paraphernalia which Gonsalez usually associated with such work-rooms.

"You have a heavy post," said Leon and the doctor laughed quietly.

"They are merely going to the Torquay post office," he said. "I have arranged for them to be despatched when—" he hesitated, "when I am sure. You see," he said, speaking with great earnestness, "a scientist has to be so careful. Every minute after he has announced a discovery he is tortured with the fear that he has forgotten something, some essential, or has reached a too hasty conclusion. But I think I'm right," he said, speaking half to himself. "I'm sure I'm right, but I must be even more sure!"

He showed them round the large room, but there was little which Manfred had not seen in the laboratory of the late Professor Tableman. Viglow had greeted them genially, indeed expansively, and yet within five minutes of their arrival he was taciturn, almost silent, and did not volunteer information about any of the instruments in which Leon showed so much interest, unless he was asked.

They came back to his room and again his mood changed and he became almost gay.

"I'll tell you," he said, "by Jove, I'll tell you! And no living soul knows this except myself, or realises or understands the extraordinary work I have been doing."

His face lit up, his eyes sparkled and it seemed to Manfred that he grew taller in this moment of exaltation. Pulling open a drawer of a table which stood against the wall he brought out a long porcelain plate and laid it down. From a wire-netted cupboard on the wall he took two tin boxes and with an expression of disgust which he could not disguise, turned the contents upon the slab. It was apparently a box full of common garden mould and then Leon saw to his amazement a wriggling little red shape twisting and twining in its acute discomfort. The little red fellow sought to hide himself and burrowed sinuously into the mould.

"Curse you! Curse you!" The doctor's voice rose until it was a howl. His face was twisted and puckered in his mad rage. "How I hate you!"

If ever a man's eyes held hate and terror, they were the eyes of Dr. Felix Viglow.

Manfred drew a long breath and stepped back a pace the better to observe him. Then the man calmed himself and peered down at Leon.

"When I was a child," he said in a voice that shook, "I hated them and we had a nurse named Martha, a beastly woman, a wicked woman, who dropped one down my neck. Imagine the horror of it!"

Leon said nothing. To him the earthworm was a genus of chaetopod in the section *oligochaeta* and bore the somewhat pretentious name of *lumbricus terrestris*. And in that way, Dr. Viglow, eminent naturalist and scientist, should have regarded this beneficent little fellow.

"I have a theory," said the doctor. He was calmer now and was wiping the sweat from his forehead with a handkerchief, "that in cycles every type of living thing on the earth becomes in turn the dominant creature. In a million years' time man may dwindle to the size of an ant and the earthworm, by its super-intelligence, its cunning and its ferocity, may be pre-eminent in the world! I have always thought that," he went on when neither Leon nor Manfred offered any comment. "It is still my thought by day and my dream by night. I have devoted my life to the destruction of this menace."

Now the earthworm is neither cunning nor intelligent and is moreover notoriously devoid of ambition.

The doctor again went to the cupboard and took out a wide-necked bottle filled with a greyish powder. He brought it back and held it within a few inches of Leon's face.

"This is the work of twelve years," he said simply. "There is no difficulty in finding a substance which will kill these pests, but this does more."

He took a scalpel and tilting the bottle brought out a few grains of the powder on the edge of it. This he dissolved in a twenty-ounce measure which he filled with water. He stirred the colourless fluid with a glass rod, then lifting the rod he allowed three drops to fall upon the mould wherein the little reptile was concealed. A few seconds passed, there was a heaving of the earth where the victim was concealed.

"He is dead," said the doctor triumphantly and scraped away the earth to prove the truth of his words. "And he is not only dead, but that handful of earth is death to any other earthworm that touches it."

He rang a bell and one of his attendants came in.

"Clear away that," he said with a shudder and walked gloomily to his desk.

Leon did not speak all the way back to the house. He sat curled up in the corner of the car, his arms tightly folded, his chin on his breast. That night without a word of explanation he left the house, declining Manfred's suggestion that he should walk with him and volunteering no information as to where he was going.

Gonsalez walked by the cliff road, across Babbacombe Downs and came to the doctor's house at nine o'clock that night. The doctor had a large house and maintained a big staff of servants, but amongst his other eccentricities was the choice of a gardener's cottage away from the house as his sleeping place at night.

It was only lately that the doctor had chosen this lonely lodging. He had been happy enough in the big old house which had been his father's, until he had heard voices whispering to him at night and the creak of boards and had seen shapes vanishing along the dark corridors, and then in his madness he had conceived the idea that his servants were conspiring against him and that he might any night be murdered in his bed. So he had the gardener turned out of his cottage, had refurnished the little house, and there, behind locked doors, he read and thought and slept the nights away. Gonsalez had heard of this peculiarity and approached the cottage with some caution, for a frightened man is more dangerous than a wicked man. He rapped at the door and heard a step across the flagged floor.

"Who is that?" asked a voice.

"It is I," said Gonsalez and gave the name by which he was known.

After hesitation the lock turned and the door opened.

"Come in, come in," said Viglow testily and locked the door behind him. "You have come to congratulate me, I am sure. You must come to my wedding too, my friend. It will be a wonderful wedding, for there I shall make a speech and tell the story of my discovery. Will you have a drink? I have nothing here, but I can get it from the house. I have a telephone in my bedroom."

Leon shook his head.

"I have been rather puzzling out your plan, Doctor," he said, accepting the proffered cigarette, "and I have been trying to connect those postal bags which I saw being loaded at the door of your laboratory with the discovery which you revealed this afternoon."

Dr. Viglow's narrow eyes were gleaming with merriment and he leant back in his chair and crossed his legs, like one preparing for a pleasant recital.

"I will tell you," he said. "For months I have been in correspondence with farming associations, both here and on the Continent. I have something of a European reputation," he said, with that extraordinary immodesty which Leon had noticed before. "In fact, I think that my treatment for phylloxera did more to remove the scourge from the vineyards of Europe than any other preparation."

Leon nodded. He knew this to be the truth.

"So you see, my word is accepted in matters dealing with agriculture. But I found after one or two talks with our own stupid farmers that there is an unusual prejudice against destroying"—he did not mention the dreaded name but shivered—"and that of course I had to get round. Now that I am satisfied that my preparation is exact, I can release the packets in the post office. In fact, I was just about to telephone to the postmaster telling him that they could go off—they are all stamped and addressed—when you knocked at the door."

"To whom are they addressed?" asked Leon steadily.

"To various farmers—some fourteen thousand in all in

various parts of the country and Europe and each packet has printed instructions in English, French, German and Spanish. I had to tell them that it was a new kind of fertiliser or they may not have been as enthusiastic in the furtherance of my experiment as I am."

"And what are they going to do with these packets when they get them?" asked Leon quietly.

"They will dissolve them and spray a certain area of their land—I suggested ploughed land. They need only treat a limited area of earth," he explained. "I think these wretched beasts will carry infection quickly enough. I believe," he leant forward and spoke impressively, "that in six months there will not be one living in Europe or Asia."

"They do not know that the poison is intended to kill—earthworms?" asked Leon.

"No, I've told you," snapped the other. "Wait, I will telephone the postmaster."

He rose quickly to his feet, but Leon was quicker and gripped his arm.

"My dear friend," he said, "you must not do this."

Dr. Viglow tried to withdraw his arm.

"Let me go," he snarled. "Are you one of those devils who are trying to torment me?"

In ordinary circumstances, Leon would have been strong enough to hold the man, but Viglow's strength was extraordinary and Gonsalez found himself thrust back into the chair. Before he could spring up, the man had passed through the door and slammed and locked it behind him.

The cottage was on one floor and was divided into two rooms by a wooden partition which Viglow had had erected. Over the door was a fanlight, and pulling the table forward Leon sprang on to the top and with his elbow smashed the flimsy frame.

"Don't touch that telephone," he said sternly. "Do you hear?"

The doctor looked round with a grin.

"You are a friend of those devils!" he said, and his hand was on the receiver when Leon shot him dead.

Manfred came back the next morning from his walk and found Gonsalez pacing the lawn, smoking an extra long cigar.

"My dear Leon," said Manfred as he slipped his arm in the other's. "You did not tell me."

"I thought it best to wait," said Leon.

"I heard quite by accident," Manfred went on. "The story is that a burglar broke into the cottage and shot the doctor when he was telephoning for assistance. All the silverware in the outer room has been stolen. The doctor's watch and pocket-book have disappeared."

"They are at this moment at the bottom of Babbacombe Bay," said Leon, "I went fishing very early this morning before you were awake."

They paced the lawn in silence for a while and then:

"Was it necessary?" asked Manfred.

"Very necessary," said Leon gravely. "You have to realise first of all that although this man was mad, he had discovered not only a poison but an infection."

"But, my dear fellow," smiled Manfred, "was an earthworm worth it?"

"Worth more than his death," said Leon. "There isn't a scientist in the world who does not agree that if the earthworm was destroyed the world would become sterile and the people of this world would be starving in seven years."

Manfred stopped in his walk and stared down at his companion.

"Do you really mean that?"

Leon nodded.

"He is the one necessary creature in God's world," he said soberly. "It fertilises the land and covers the bare rocks with earth. It is the surest friend of mankind that we know, and now I am going down to the post office with a story which I think will be sufficiently plausible to recover those worm poisoners."

Manfred mused a while then he said:

"I'm glad in many ways—in every way," he corrected. "I rather liked that girl, and I'm sure that impossible person isn't so impossible."

The Courtyard
of the Fly

Vincent Cornier

VINCENT CORNIER WAS THE PEN-NAME OF WILLIAM Vincent Corner (1898–1976), who was born near Redcar and died in Hastings, having spent some years in France and South Africa in between. During his lifetime, his principal champion was the American editor Fred Dannay, better known as one half of the Ellery Queen writing duo. Dannay was founder and editor of *Ellery Queen's Mystery Magazine*, and he rhapsodised about Cornier's "amazing" mysteries. Cornier had a particular gift for the "impossible crime" story, and flourished during the Golden Age, but his baroque style of storytelling fell out of favour, and after the early Fifties, he published few stories. His bibliography remains uncertain, but as far as I know, he never published a novel.

Golden Age enthusiasts such as Stephen Leadbetter and Arthur Vidro helped to keep the memory of his fiction alive, and in 2011, Mike Ashley edited an enjoyable collection of his stories about Barnabas Hildreth (also known as "The

Black Monk"!), *The Duel of Shadows*, which showcased Cornier's ingenuity.

"The Courtyard of the Fly" features neither Hildreth nor Cornier's other series character, Sir Richard Brantygham, but offers a good illustration of his style. The story first appeared in *Cassell's Magazine* in February 1932.

———

SOME THIRTY-SEVEN YEARS AGO, WHEN THE PAGES OF the *Almanac de Gotha* were slim passports to the narrowest society civilisation has yet produced, a cartouche with the word "Labordien" appeared within its yellow backing. Around and about the name were seven royal escutcheons. None of your "by appointment to—"; not even the indiscretion of an address.

Those were unnecessary. Everyone knew that Henri Labordien was a master-artist in the craft of pearl mounting. Henri Labordien and pearls were not to be thought of apart. Nations, through their rulers, trusted him with awesome treasures; and trust continued until that night which was marked by the appearance of the fly and the subsequent loss of a Russian Grand Duchess's rope of superbly matched pearls.

The fly (according to Henri Labordien and Tobias Lockwood, the only other man to see it) was a black and orange monstrosity as large as a mouse. It darted with a rapidity that was swifter than the bolt of a swallow. It hissed.

Oh, yes, it hissed—a tremulous and poignant sound like a horny finger slashed across silk. Henri Labordien heard the noise coming to him; Tobias Lockwood had heard it going away, yet each agreed that this was its nature.

Now here was a fly that was unlike one's ordinary experience of flies, in appearance and faculty. The police, investigating the mystery of the vanished Russian treasure, paid a great deal of attention to it. One of their company, a constable called Hamilton—afterwards destined to become Superintendent Hamilton of the C.I.D.—went so far as to roughen his finger-tips with pumice and to draw them, a hundred times, over silken fabric, until his ears were educated to the sound these other men had heard.

What he could not experiment with was any known species of the insect world capable of clawing up a rope of pearls weighing a quarter of a pound and flying away with it.

According to Henri Labordien and Tobias Lockwood, that was what this fly had done.

Labordien had been sitting at his bench by an open window in his riverside house—the June evening was glowering and sultry with impending storm—when out of the sombre twilight the big fly darted into his workroom. He heard it hiss past him and turned to follow its flight. Before he could take the jewellers' eyeglass from his right eye, the fantastic insect went out again into the open air. Somewhat startled, Labordien got to his feet and picked up a welt of leather in order to crush the thing if it came back. It was loathsome and it looked deadly, as though it carried venom. In his opinion it was a phenomenon hatched from some cargo of sub-tropical fruit—bananas or such—carried by the Thames barges that were always passing this suburb of London. That was, of course, his later and considered opinion. At the moment of reaching out for the piece of leather he had no time for ordered thought.

Even as his hand touched the sheepskin, the big fly came back. This time it alighted on the long string of pearls laid upon his workbench. For a second or so it quivered, then it rose and went out of the window for the last time. The Dmitrioevitsch pearls went with it, and the world-famous Henri Labordien was ruined.

Stuttering with astonishment, shaking his head, he saw the glitter of the gems and the sullen mass of the great fly going into evening space. Among some plane trees, at the end of his courtyard, fringing the narrow road before the river embankment, fly and necklace disappeared.

He could not lean out of the window at once, since the littered expanse of the bench prevented him; but after a moment, when he had swept aside his tools and cabinets and gold and soldering-plant, he clambered up and shrieked for aid. So urgent was his call that half a dozen people were thronging his little courtyard in a matter of two to three minutes. Among them were his next-door neighbour Colonel Brough, the constable Hamilton, and Tobias Lockwood—a shabby and pallid-faced man who clawed at P.C. Hamilton even as that officer came towards the door.

To a heterogeneous crowd, then, Henri Labordien told of his loss. Therein lay his greatest mistake. It might have been possible, had his tale not been given such publicity, for him to carry on with his craft for years to follow. The affair might have been hushed up. Peculiarly enough, Labordien's story was corroborated by this out-of-work clerk, Tobias Lockwood. After P.C. Hamilton had cleared the courtyard of all save Labordien, Colonel Brough, Lockwood and himself, he listened to a second narrative of the hideous fly.

It appeared that Lockwood was sauntering along the embankment, beneath the gently stirring planes, when a rattle on the pavement attracted his attention. To his amazement he looked down to see a lane of shimmering jewels—undoubtedly the lost pearls—almost at his feet. For a time all conscious action ebbed from Lockwood's body. He simply halted, petrified with astonishment, and gaped at the fortune. Before he could find it in himself to pick up the necklace, the fly was in the air again. Straight for his face it came.

———

It stung him. Lockwood showed P.C. Hamilton the bleeding little wound in his ear where the thing had attacked him. The fly had stung and, while its victim had danced with the sudden agony of that sting, the insect alighted on the pearls. A momentary quivering, then again the monstrous creature took itself into the air, carrying the pearls.

Which way had it gone? Towards the river or along the embankment? Tobias Lockwood could not tell. Hadn't he enough to put up with, him with his stung ear, without watching the damned thing?

P.C. Hamilton, Colonel Brough—a frankly suspicious and guffawing sceptic—and the distracted Labordien listened to Lockwood with growing amazement. The colonel bluntly grunted that the proper place to harken to Lockwood's fat-headed tale was in the local police charge-room. Whereat P.C. Hamilton looked up from his notebook and asked the dapper military officer if by any chance he also doubted Mr. Labordien's story. To that question Colonel Brough had no answer.

All was entered up and all was done that could be done, but the pearls were never traced nor the mystery cleared up in its slightest facet.

The twentieth century dawned. The colonel moved from the house next door to Labordien and the stricken little jewel expert was left without any old friend at hand. Since his grotesque story about the fly was never accounted anything but a ridiculous camouflage for his own appropriation of the forty-thousand-guinea necklace (Lockwood's corroboration was conveniently treated as the yarning of a well-paid accomplice) Labordien found every door closed against him. In the place of his former fame he had the friendship of P.C. Hamilton.

The solid young man never rested from his task of attempting to solve the wild mystery. On duty and off duty, he was a constant caller at Labordien's lonely house. Gradually a friendship sprang up between the men— growing as the years grew, throughout the War—until Superintendent Hamilton's retirement.

It was nearly thirty-seven years later—Labordien was now old and bald and very gentle in his ways; Hamilton a sturdy and iron-grey man inclined to excessive fatness— when the fly once again came across the courtyard from the direction of the river.

Labordien's workroom had long been converted to a sort of study—a bookish place with a Whistleresque view of the bending river. As of old, the window facing the courtyard and the plane trees was wide open. And, as of old, the night was in June—sultry and overcast by massing thunder-clouds.

Labordien dropped the book he had been reading. Every vestige of colour went out of his face. He could not mistake that curiously abrupt hissing; no more could he deny his eyes their certitude that they had looked on the grisly insect once more. Trembling and suddenly terrified, he got up out of his chair.

"All right, Henri," a hearty voice boomed up to him from some place not discoverable. "Don't you get alarmed. It's only Hamilton, you know."

"*Hamilton*! Where—where are you? What are you doing? That fly—that beastly thing's been in here!"

"I know that." Still the voice came from the courtyard, but there was no sighting the speaker. "I sent it."

The jocular tone faded and an earnest ring came into Hamilton's voice.

"Be careful, Henri. Stand to one side, well away from the window, and put your spectacles on the table. Turn 'em broadside on, facing the river, and keep back."

Mechanically, Henri Labordien did as he was bidden to do.

The silken hiss sounded quite distinctly. A big orange and black fly rushed through the opening. Lightly it fell— across the spectacles. For a second it hovered and was still, then it darted like a coloured bolt from the room. The spectacles went with it.

Weakly, Labordien sat down and covered his face with his hands. Whatever Hamilton's devilry was, it was too violently akin to the experience of years ago for comfort.

Without his glasses he could not see very clearly, but he could hear a lot of rustling of leaves from the plane trees. Then a rough and guttural coughing, as of a man clearing his throat from dust. After that, steps which he recognised as those of Hamilton came across the courtyard and to the lower door. Without ceremony Hamilton clumped in and rapidly mounted the stairs. There was a rattle on the table and a laugh.

"There are your specks, Henri! Sorry I risked 'em. But now our old friend Brough is nicely settled in chokey with a few years penal staring him in the face, hang him!"

"*Brough*—you mean, Colonel Brough?"

"That's the gentleman! Got him at last. He stole those pearls, you know. I was always dead certain of it, but never could get proof. That's the charge… half a lifetime old, but none the less certain."

"Brough stole—stole those pearls?" Old Labordien was pitifully shaken. He gulped his drink and blinked. "Am I still in command of my senses?"

"You are! Listen, Henri, don't talk." The ex-superintendent rubbed his big hands together jubilantly. "The mystery of that theft is solved at last and I'm only sorry that poor Toby Lockwood isn't alive to be vindicated. Brough stole those pearls, and it was the cunningest job I ever knew."

"Remember how you used to sit by the open window, day in and day out, on your jewel work?" Labordien nodded. "And Brough could not fail to see what treasure you had in your hands every now and then. The open window lured him; the devil suggested means. For more years than I care to recollect I've tried to find out what those means were."

"And have you succeeded?"

"Yes! When I was in Scotland the other day I walked along a river bank and I heard a sound. It was that finger-on-silk sound I've had in my ears for years. Not only that but, with the sound, a big silver blue fly came whizzing past my face. 'Sorry,' a voice called out; 'my fault for not watching the bank—carry on!' The fly had been thrown by a salmon angler just below me. And lo and behold! the mystery of the stolen pearls was solved.

"The fly was, I learned a 'Silver Doctor.' I betook myself

to various authorities, practical and otherwise, until I learned that a good salmon fisher could drop such a fly into a floating coco-nut shell at thirty yards' range, nine times out of ten.

"I went into Colonel Brough's history. He was adept at salmon fishing. Among his possessions we've found a beautiful rod and a cabinet of flies—double-hooked 'uns—one of which clawed those pearls out of your possession.

"He was up one of those plane trees. He cast out his fly, lengthening and ever lengthening his line, until he had just the amount out he required. The first fly you saw was a false cast—the second was dead accurate. The twin hooks got across the necklace and hauled the thing up into the tree.

"Unfortunately for him he excitedly dropped the necklace, or else it fell off the hooks at the last minute, right under Lockwood's eyes. Brough cast again—a short cast now and infinitely more accurate. He tore Lockwood's ear, again crossed the fallen necklace and finally secured the treasure. He probably pocketed it then, leaving his rod hidden among the plane tree branches. No one dreamed of searching up there. He just had time to drop to earth and look as though he'd come out of his front door before the courtyard was filled up.

"The fly he used was a 'Durham Ranger'—black and orange and vermilion. It ranged all right for him, eh? The silken hiss was the noise of the almost invisible gut-cast, to which the artificial fly was fastened. It cuts through the air with that precise sound."

"But surely this is all mere surmise—theory?"

"Not on your life, Henri. You noticed how I, the veriest

tyro in fly-casting, managed to grab your glasses in two shots? After only a month's practice I could do that, out of the tree where he lurked. You may be sure that Brough did the job just like that. Your good name will be restored and my professional pique will be ended and all things are satisfactory."

"If only I could hope," Labordien's old voice quavered to a half-fearful, half-joyful note, "that all you say is true, I'd be a happy man after all these years of loss."

Deliberately ex-Superintendent Hamilton poured drinks into two glasses. He passed one to Labordien.

"Then drink to happiness, Henri, old friend. Brough confessed within an hour of his arrest. Here's to better days!"

The Yellow Slugs

H. C. Bailey

HENRY CHRISTOPHER BAILEY (1878–1961) WAS ONE of the towering figures of Golden Age detective fiction, renowned above all for his short stories featuring the amiable yet occasionally ruthless Reggie Fortune. The Fortune stories fell out of favour after the Second World War, and they were always something of an acquired taste. But Bailey continues to attract devotees, and his best stories are notable for their darkness. Writing in *The Observer* in 1935, the leading critic Torquemada summed up the range of opinions: "Mr. Fortune's position among readers of detective stories is unique. Some cannot read about him at any price; many regard him as merely one of several first-class practitioners; but many more still, the other and my side idolatry, mark time between Mr. Bailey's chronicles."

This chilling story is widely considered to be one of his finest pieces of work. It appeared in *The Windsor Magazine* in March 1935 and in that year it was included in *Mr. Fortune*

Objects, which Ellery Queen regarded as his best volume of short stories.

THE BIG CAR CLOSED UP BEHIND A FLORID FUNERAL procession which held the middle of the road. On either side was a noisy congestion of lorries. Mr. Fortune sighed and closed his eyes.

When he looked out again he was passing the first carriage of another funeral, and saw beneath the driver's seat the white coffin of a baby. For the road served the popular cemetery of Blaney.

Two slow miles of dingy tall houses and cheap shops slid by, with vistas of meaner streets opening on either side. The car gathered speed across Blaney Common, an expanse of yellow turf and bare sand, turbid pond and scrubwood, and stopped at the brown pile of an old poor law hospital.

Entering its carbolic odour, Mr. Fortune was met by Superintendent Bell. "Here I am," he moaned. "Why am I?"

"Well, she's still alive, sir," said Bell. "They both are."

Mr. Fortune was taken to a ward in which, secluded by a screen, a little girl lay asleep.

Her face had a babyish fatness, but in its pallor looked bloated and unhealthy. Though the close July air was oppressive and she was covered with heavy bedclothes, her skin showed no sign of heat and she slept still as death.

Reggie sat down beside her. His hands moved gently within the bed… He listened…he looked…

A nurse followed him to the door. "How old, do you think?" he murmured.

"That was puzzling me, sir. She's big enough for seven or

eight, but all flabby. And when she came to, she was talking almost baby talk. I suppose she may be only about five."

Reggie nodded. "Quite good, yes. All right. Carry on."

From the ward he passed to a small room where a nurse and a doctor stood together watching the one bed.

A boy lay in it, restless and making noises—inarticulate words mixed with moaning and whimpering.

The doctor lifted his eyebrows at Reggie. "Get that?" he whispered. "Still talking about hell. He came absolutely unstuck. I had to risk a shot of morphia. I—" He broke off in apprehension as Reggie's round face hardened to a cold severity. But Reggie nodded and moved to the bed...

The boy tossed into stertorous sleep, one thin arm flung up above a tousled head. His sunken cheeks were flushed, and drops of sweat stood on the upper lip and the brow. Not a bad brow—not an uncomely face but for its look of hungry misery—not the face of a child—a face which had been the prey of emotions and thwarted desires...

Reggie's careful hands worked over him...bits of the frail body were laid bare... Reggie stood up, and still his face was set in ruthless, passionless determination.

Outside the door the doctor spoke nervously. "I hope you don't—"

"Morphia's all right," Reggie interrupted. "What do you make of him?"

"Well, Mr. Fortune, I wish you'd seen him at first." The doctor was uncomfortable beneath the cold insistence of a questioning stare. "He was right out of hand—a sort of hysterical fury. I should say he's quite abnormal. Neurotic lad, badly nourished—you can't tell what they won't do, that type."

"I can't. No. What age do you give him?"

"Now you've got me. To hear him raving, you'd think he

was grown up, such a flow of language. Bible phrases and preaching. I'd say he was a twelve-year-old, but he might only be eight or ten. His development is all out of balance. He's unhealthy right through."

"Yes, that is so," Reggie murmured. "However. You ought to save him."

"Poor little devil," said the doctor.

In a bare, grim waiting-room Reggie sat down with Superintendent Bell, and Bell looked anxiety. "Well, sir?"

"Possible. Probable," Reggie told him. "On the evidence."

"Ah. Cruel, isn't it? I hate these child cases."

"Any more evidence?" Reggie drawled.

Bell stared at his hard calm gloomily. "I have. Plenty."

The story began with a small boy on the bank of one of the ponds on Blaney Common. That was some time ago. That was the first time anybody in authority had been aware of the existence of Eddie Hill. One of the keepers of the common made the discovery. The pond was that one which children used for the sailing of toy boats. Eddie Hill had no boat, but he loitered round all the morning, watching the boats of other children. There was little wind, and one boat lay becalmed in the middle of the pond when the children had to go home to dinner.

An hour later the keeper saw Eddie Hill wade into the pond and run away. When the children came back from dinner there was no boat to be seen. Its small owner made weeping complaint to the keeper, who promised to keep his eyes open, and some days later found Eddie Hill and his little sister Bessie lurking among the gorse of the common with the stolen boat.

It was taken from them and their sin reported to their mother, who promised vengeance.

Their mother kept a little general shop. She had been there a dozen years—ever since she married her first husband. She was well liked and looked up to; a religious woman, regular chapel-goer and all that. Her second husband, Brightman, was the same sort—-hardworking, respectable man; been at the chapel longer than she had.

The day-school teachers had nothing against Eddie or the little girl. Eddie was rather more than usually bright, but dreamy and careless; the girl a bit stodgy. Both of 'em rather less naughty than most.

"Know a lot, don't you?" Reggie murmured. "Got all this today?"

"No, this was all on record," Bell said. "Worked out for another business."

"Oh. Small boy and small girl already old offenders. Go on."

The other business was at the chapel Sunday school. Eddie Hill, as the most regular of its pupils, was allowed the privilege of tidying up at the end of the afternoon. On a Sunday in the spring the superintendent came in unexpectedly upon the process and found Eddie holding the money-box in which had been collected the contributions of the school to the chapel missionary society.

Eddie had no need nor right to handle the money-box. Moreover, on the bench beside him were pennies and a sixpence. Such wealth could not be his own. Only the teachers ever put in silver. Moreover, he confessed that he had extracted the money by rattling the box upside down, and his small sister wept for the sin.

The superintendent took him to the police station and charged him with theft.

"Virtuous man," Reggie murmured.

"It does seem a bit harsh," Bell said. "But they'd had suspicions about the money-box before. They'd been watching for something like this. Well, the boy's mother came and tried to beg him off, but of course the case had to go on. The boy came up in the Juvenile Court—you know the way, Mr. Fortune; no sort of criminal atmosphere, magistrate talking like a father. He let the kid off with a lecture."

"Oh, yes. What did he say? Bringin' down mother's grey hairs in sorrow to the grave—wicked boy—goin' to the bad in this world and the next—anything about hell?"

"I couldn't tell you." Bell was shocked. "I heard he gave the boy a rare old talking to. I don't wonder. Pretty bad, wasn't it, the Sunday-school money-box? What makes you bring hell into it?"

"I didn't. The boy did. He was raving about hell today. Part of the evidence. I was only tracin' the origin."

"Ah. I don't like these children's cases," Bell said gloomily. "They don't seem really human sometimes. You get a twisted kind of child and he'll talk the most frightful stuff—and do it too. We can only go by acts, can we?"

"Yes. That's the way I'm goin'. Get on."

The sharp impatience of the tone made Bell look at him with some reproach. "All right, sir. The next thing is this morning's business. I gave you the outline of that on the phone. I've got the full details now. This is what it comes to. Eddie and his little sister were seen on the common; the keepers have got to keep an eye on him. He wandered about with her—he has a casual, drifting sort of way, like some of these queer kids do have—and they came to the big pond. That's not a children's place at all; it's too deep; only dog bathing and fishing. There was nobody near; it was pretty early. Eddie and Bessie went along the bank, and a labourer who was scything thistles says the little girl was crying, and Eddie seemed to be scolding her, and then he fair chucked her in and went in with her. That's what it looked like to the keeper who was watchin' 'em. Him and the other chap, they nipped down and chucked the life-buoy; got it right near, but Eddie didn't take hold of it; he was clutching the girl and sinking and coming up again. So the keeper went in to 'em and had trouble getting 'em out. The little girl was unconscious, and Eddie sort of fought him." Bell stopped and gave a look of inquiry, but Reggie said nothing, and his face showed neither opinion nor feeling. "Well, you know how it is with these rescues from the water," Bell went on. "People often seem to be fighting to drown themselves and it don't mean any-thing except fright. And about the boy throwing the girl in—that might have been just a bit of a row or play—it's happened often—not meant vicious at all; and then he'd panic, likely enough." Again Bell looked an anxious ques-tion at the cold, passionless face. "I mean to say, I wouldn't have bothered you with it, Mr. Fortune, but for the way the boy carried on when they got him out. There he was with his little sister unconscious, and the keeper doing artificial respiration, and he called out, 'Don't do it. Bessie's dead. She must be dead.' And the keeper asked him, 'Do you want her dead, you little devil?'And he said, 'Yes, I do. I had to.' Then the labourer chap came back with help and they got hold of Eddie; he was raving, flinging himself about and screaming if she lived she'd only get like him and go to hell, so she must be dead. While they brought him along here he was sort of preaching to 'em bits of the Bible, and mad stuff about the wicked being sent to hell and tortures for 'em."

"Curious and interestin'," Reggie drawled. "Any particular torture?"

"I don't know. The whole thing pretty well gave these chaps the horrors. They didn't get all the boy's talk. I don't wonder. There was something about worms not dying, they told me. That almost turned 'em up. Well—there you are, Mr. Fortune. What do you make of it?"

"I should say it happened," Reggie said. "All of it. As stated."

"You feel sure he could have thrown that fat little girl in? He seemed to me such a weed."

"Yes. Quite a sound point. I took that point. Development of both children unhealthy. Girl wrongly nourished. Boy inadequately nourished. Boy's physique frail. However. He could have done it. Lots of nervous energy. Triumph of mind over matter."

Bell drew in his breath. "You take it cool."

"Only way to take it," Reggie murmured, and Bell shifted uncomfortably. He has remarked since that he had seen Mr. Fortune look like that once or twice before—sort of inhuman, heartless, and inquisitive; but there it seemed all wrong, it didn't seem his way at all.

Reggie settled himself in his chair and spoke—so Bell has reported, and this is the only criticism which annoys Mr. Fortune—like a lecturer. "Several possibilities to be considered. The boy may be merely a precocious rascal. Having committed some iniquity which the little girl knew about, he tried to drown her to stop her giving him away. Common type of crime, committed by children as well as their elders."

"I know it is," Bell admitted. "But what could he have done that was worth murdering his sister?"

"I haven't the slightest idea. However. He did steal.

Proved twice by independent evidence. Don't blame if you don't want. 'There, but for the grace of God, go I.' I agree. Quite rational to admit that consideration. We shall certainly want it. But he knew he was a thief; he knew it got him into trouble—that's fundamental."

"All right," said Bell gloomily. "We have to take it like that."

"Yes. No help. Attempt to murder sister may be connected with consciousness of sin. I should say it was. However. Other possibilities. He's a poor little mess of nerves; he's unsound, physically, mentally, spiritually. He may not have meant to murder her at all; may have got in a passion and not known what he was doing."

"Ah. That's more likely." Bell was relieved.

"You think so? Then why did he tell everybody he did mean to murder her?"

"Well, he was off his head, as you were saying. That's the best explanation of the whole thing. It's really the only explanation. Look at your first idea: he wanted to kill her so she couldn't tell about some crime he'd done. You get just the same question, why did he say he meant murder? He must know killing is worse than stealing. However you take the thing, you work back to his being off his head." Reggie's eyelids drooped. "I was brought here to say he's mad. Yes. I gather that. You're a merciful man, Bell. Sorry not to satisfy your gentle nature. I could swear he's mentally abnormal. If that would do any good. I couldn't say he's mad. I don't know. I can find you mental experts who would give evidence either way."

"I know which a jury would believe," Bell grunted.

"Yes. So do I. Merciful people, juries. Like you. Not my job. I'm lookin' for the truth. One more possibility. The boy's motive was just what he said it was—to kill his little sister so she shouldn't get wicked and go to hell. That fits the other facts. He'd got into the way of stealing; it had been rubbed into him that he was doomed to hell. So, if he found her goin' the same way, he might think it best she should die while she was still clean."

"Well, if that isn't mad!" Bell exclaimed.

"Abnormal, yes. Mad—-I wonder," Reggie murmured.

"But it's sheer crazy, sir. If he believed he was so wicked, the thing for him to do was to pull up and go straight, and see that she did too."

"Yes. That's common sense, isn't it?" A small, contemptuous smile lingered a moment on Reggie's stern face. "What's the use of common sense here? If he was like this—sure he was going to hell; sure she was bein' driven there too—kind of virtuous for him to kill her to save her. Kind of rational. Desperately rational. Ever know any children, Bell? Some of 'em do believe what they're taught. Some of 'em take it seriously. Abnormal, as you say. Eddie Hill is abnormal." He turned and looked full at Bell, his blue eyes dark in the failing light. "Aged twelve or so—too bad to live—or too good. Pleasant case."

Bell moved uneasily. "These things do make you feel queer," he grunted. "What it all comes to though—we mean much the same—the boy ought to be in a home. That can be worked."

"A home!" Reggie's voice went up, and he laughed. "Yes. Official home for mentally defective. Yes. We can do that. I dare say we shall." He stood up and walked to the window and looked out at the dusk. "These children had a home of their own. And a mother. What's she doing about 'em?"

"She's been here, half off her head, poor thing," said Bell. "She wouldn't believe the boy meant any harm. She told me he couldn't, he was so fond of his sister. She said it must have been accident."

"Quite natural and motherly. Yes. But not adequate. Because it wasn't accident, whatever it was. We'd better go and see mother."

"If you like," Bell grunted reluctantly.

"I don't like," Reggie mumbled. "I don't like anything. I'm not here to do what I like." And they went.

People were drifting home from the common. The mean streets of Blaney had already grown quiet in the sultry gloom.

Shutters were up at the little shop which was the home of Eddie Hill, and still bore in faded paint his father's name. No light showed in the windows above. Bell rapped on the door, and they waited in vain. He moved to a house door close beside the shop. "Try this. This may be theirs too," he said, and knocked and rang.

After a minute it was opened by a woman who said nothing, but stared at them. From somewhere inside came the sound of a man's voice, talking fervently.

The light of the street lamp showed her of full figure, in neat black, and a face which was still pretty but distressed.

"You remember me, Mrs. Brightman," said Bell. "I'm Superintendent Bell."

"I know." She was breathless. "What's the matter? Are they—is Eddie—what's happened?"

"They're doing all right. I just want a little talk with you."

"Oh, they're all right. Praise God!" She turned; she called out: "Matthew, Matthew dear, they're all right."

The man's voice went on talking with the same fervour, but not in answer.

"I'll come in, please," said Bell.

"Yes, do. Thank you kindly. Mr. Brightman would like to see you. We were just asking mercy."

She led the way along a passage, shining clean, to a room behind the shop. There a man was on his knees praying, and most of the prayer was texts: "And we shall sing of mercy in the morning. Amen. Amen." He made an end.

He stood up before them, tall and gaunt, a bearded man with melancholy eyes. He turned to his wife. "What is it, my dear? What do the gentlemen want?"

"It's about the children, Matthew." His wife came and took his arm. "It's the police superintendent, I told you. He was so kind."

The man sucked in his breath. "Ay, ay. Please sit down. They must sit down, Florrie." There was a fluster of setting chairs. "This is kind, sir. What can you tell us tonight?"

"Doin' well. Both of 'em," Reggie said.

"There's our answer, Florrie," the man said, and smiled, and his sombre eyes glowed. "There's our prayers answered."

"Yes. I think they're going to live," said Reggie. "But that's not the only thing that matters. We have to ask how it was they were nearly drowned."

"It was an accident. It must have been," the woman cried. "I'm sure Eddie wouldn't—he never would, would he, Matthew?"

"I won't believe it," Brightman answered quickly.

"Quite natural you should feel like that," Reggie nodded. "However. We have to deal with the facts."

"You must do what you think right, sir, as it is shown you." Brightman bent his head.

"Yes, I will. Yes. Been rather a naughty boy, hasn't he?"

Brightman looked at his wife's miserable face and turned

to them again. "The police know," he said. "He has been a thief—twice he has been a thief—but little things. There is mercy, surely there is mercy for repentance. If his life is spared, he should not be lost; we must believe that."

"I do," Reggie murmured. "Any special reason why he should have been a thief?"

Brightman shook his head. "He's always had a good home, I'm sure," the woman moaned. She looked round her room, which was ugly and shabby, but all in the cleanest order.

"What can I say?" Brightman shook his head. "We've always done our best for him. There's no telling how temptation comes, sir, and it's strong and the little ones are weak."

"That is so. Yes. How much pocket-money did they have?"

"Eddie has had his twopence a week since he was ten," Brightman answered proudly. "And Bessie has her penny."

"I see. And was there anything happened this morning which upset Bessie or Eddie?"

"Nothing at all, sir. Nothing that I know." Brightman turned to his wife. "They went off quite happy, didn't they?"

"Yes, of course they did," she said eagerly. "They always loved to have a day on the common. They took their lunch, and they went running as happy as happy—and then this," she sobbed.

"My dearie." Brightman patted her.

"Well, well." Reggie stood up. "Oh. By the way. Has Eddie—or Bessie—ever stolen anything at home here— money or what not?"

Brightman started and stared at him. "That's not fair, sir. That's not a right thing to ask. There isn't stealing between little ones and their mother and father."

"No. As you say. No," Reggie murmured. "Good night. You'll hear how they go on. Good night."

"Thank you, sir. We shall be anxious to hear. Good night, sir," said Brightman, and Mrs. Brightman showed them out with tearful gratitude. As the door was opened, Brightman called: "Florrie! Don't bolt it. Mrs. Wiven hasn't come back."

"I know. I know," she answered, and bade them good night and shut the door.

A few paces away, Reggie stopped and looked back at the shuttered shop and the dark windows. "Well, well. What does the professional mind make of all that?"

"Just what you'd expect, wasn't it?" Bell grunted.

"Yes. Absolutely. Poor struggling shopkeepers, earnestly religious, keeping the old house like a new pin. All in accordance with the evidence." He sniffed the night air. "Dank old house."

"General shop smell. All sorts of things mixed up."

"As you say. There were. And there would be. Nothing you couldn't have guessed before we went. Except that Mrs. Wiven is expected—whoever Mrs. Wiven is."

"I don't know. Sounds like a lodger."

"Yes, that is so. Which would make another resident in the home of Eddie and Bessie. However. She's not come back yet. So we can go home. The end of a beastly day. And tomorrow's another one. I'll be out to see the children in the morning. Oh, my Lord! Those children." His hand gripped Bell's arm...

By eight o'clock in the morning he was at the bedside of Bessie Hill—an achievement of stupendous but useless energy, for she did not wake till half past.

Then he took charge. A responsible position, which he

interpreted as administering to her cups of warm milk and bread and butter. She consumed them eagerly; she took his service as matter of course.

"Good girl." Reggie wiped her mouth. "Feelin' better?"

She sighed and snuggled down, and gazed at him with large eyes. "Umm. Who are you?"

"They call me Mr. Fortune. Is it nice here?"

"Umm. Comfy." The big eyes were puzzled and wondering. "Where is it?"

"Blaney Hospital. People brought you here after you were in the pond. Do you remember?"

She shook her head. "Is Eddie here?"

"Oh, yes. Eddie's asleep. He's all right. Were you cross with Eddie?"

Tears came into the brown eyes. "Eddie was cross wiv me," the child whimpered. "I wasn't. I wasn't. Eddie said must go into ve water. I didn't want. But Eddie was so cross. Love Eddie."

"Yes. Little girl." Reggie stroked her hair. "Eddie shouldn't have been cross. Just a little girl. But Eddie isn't often cross, is he?"

"No. Love Eddie. Eddie's dear."

"Why was he cross yesterday?"

The brown eyes opened wider. "I was naughty. It was Mrs. Wiven. Old Mrs. Wiven. I did go up to her room. I didn't fink she was vere. Sometimes is sweeties. But she was vere. She scolded me. She said I was little fief. We was all fiefs. And Eddie took me away and oh, he was so cross; he said I would be wicked and must not be. But I aren't. I aren't. Eddie was all funny and angry, and said not to be like him and go to hell, and then he did take me into pond wiv him. I didn't want. I didn't want!"

"No. Of course not. No. Poor little girl. Eddie didn't understand. But it's all right now."

"Is Eddie still cross wiv me?" she whimpered.

"Oh, no. No. Eddie won't be cross any more. Nobody's cross, little girl." Reggie bent over her. "Everybody's going to be kind now. You only have to be quiet and happy. That's all."

"Oooh." She gazed up at him. "Tell Eddie I'm sorry."

"Yes. I'll tell him." Reggie kissed her hand and turned away.

The nurse met him at the door. "Did she wake in the night?" he whispered.

"Yes, sir, asking for Eddie. She's a darling, isn't she? She makes me cry, talking like that of him."

"That won't do any harm," Reggie said, and his face hardened. "But you mustn't talk about him."

He went to the room where Eddie lay. The doctor was there, and turned from the bedside to confer with him. "Not too bad. We've put in a long sleep. Quite quiet since we walked. Very thirsty. Taken milk with a dash of coffee nicely. But we're rather flat."

Reggie sat down by the bed. The boy lay very still. His thin face was white. Only his eyes moved to look at Reggie, so little open, their pupils so small that they seemed all greenish-grey. He gave no sign of recognition, or feeling, or intelligence. Reggie put a hand under the clothes and found him cold and damp, and felt for his pulse.

"Well, young man, does anything hurt you now?"

"I'm tired. I'm awful tired," the boy said.

"Yes. I know. But that's going away."

"No, it isn't; it's worse. I didn't ought to have waked up." The faint voice was drearily peevish. "I didn't want to. It's no good. I thought I was dead. And it was good being dead."

"Was it?" Reggie said sharply.

The boy gave a quivering cry. "Yes, it was!" His face was distorted with fear and wonder. "I thought it would be so dreadful and it was all quiet and nice, and then I wasn't dead, I was alive and everything's awful again. I've got to go on still."

"What's awful in going on?" said Reggie. "Bessie wants you. Bessie sent you her love. She's gettin' well quick."

"Bessie? Bessie's here in bed like I am?" The unnatural greenish eyes stared.

"Of course she is. Only much happier than you are."

The boy began to sob.

"Why do you cry about that?" Reggie said. "She's got to be happy. Boys and girls have to be happy. That's what they're for. You didn't want Bessie to die."

"I did. You know I did," the boy sobbed.

"I know you jumped in the pond with her. That was silly. But you'd got rather excited, hadn't you? What was it all about?"

"They'll tell you," the boy muttered.

"Who will?"

"The keepers, the p'lice, the m-magistrate, everybody. I'm wicked. I'm a thief. I can't help it. And I didn't want Bessie to be wicked too."

"Of course you didn't. And she isn't. What ever made you think she was?"

"But she was." The boy's voice was shrill. "She went to Mrs. Wiven's room. She was looking for pennies. I know she was. She'd seen me. And Mrs. Wiven said we were all thieves. So I had to."

"Oh, no, you hadn't. And you didn't. You see? Things don't happen like that."

"Yes, they do. There's hell. Where their worms don't die."

The doctor made a muttered exclamation.

Reggie's hand held firm at the boy's as he moved and writhed. "There's God too," he murmured. "God's kind. Bessie's not going to be wicked. You don't have to be wicked. That's what's come of it all. Somebody's holding you up now." His hand pressed. "Feel?" The boy's lips parted; he looked up in awe. "Yes. Like that. You'll see me again and again. Now good-bye. Think about me. I'm thinking about you.".... He stayed a while longer before he said another "Good-bye."

Outside, in the corridor, the doctor spoke: "I say, Mr. Fortune, you got him then. That was the stuff. I thought you were driving hard before. Sorry I spoke."

"I was." Reggie frowned. His round face was again of a ruthless severity. "'Difficult matter to play with souls,'" he mumbled. "We've got to." He looked under drooping eyelids. "Know the name of the keeper who saw the attempted drowning? Fawkes? Thanks."

He left the hospital and walked across the common.

The turf was parched and yellow, worn away on either side, paths loosened by the summer drought. Reggie descried the brown coat of a keeper, made for him, and was directed to where Fawkes would be.

Fawkes was a slow-speaking, slow-thinking old soldier, but he knew his own mind.

There was no doubt in it that Eddie had tried to kill Bessie, no indignation, no surprise. Chewing his words, he gave judgment. He had known Eddie's sort, lots of 'em. 'Igh strung, wanting the earth, kicking up behind and before 'cause they couldn't get it. He didn't mind 'em. Rather 'ave 'em than young 'uns like sheep. But you'ad to dress 'em down proper. They was devils else. Young Eddie would 'ave to be for it.

That business of the boat? Yes, Eddie pinched that all

right. Smart kid; you'd got to 'and him that. And yet not so smart. Silly, lying up with it on the common; just the way to get nabbed. Ought to 'ave took it 'ome and sailed it over at Wymond Park. Never been spotted then. But 'im and 'is sister, they made a reg'lar den up in the gorse. Always knew where to look for 'em. Silly. Why, they was up there yesterday, loafing round, before 'e did 'is drowning act.

"Take you there? I can, if you like."

Reggie did like. They went up the brown slopes of the common to a tangle of gorse and bramble over small sand-hills.

"There you are." The keeper pointed his stick to a patch of loose sand in a hollow. "That's young Eddie's funk-'ole. That's where we spotted 'em with the blinking boat."

Reggie came to the place. The sand had been scooped up by small hands into a low wall round a space which was decked out with pebbles, yellow petals of gorse, and white petals of bramble.

"Ain't that just like 'em!" The keeper was angrily triumphant. "They know they didn't ought to pick the flowers. As well as you and me they do, and they go and do it."

Reggie did not answer. He surveyed the pretence of a garden and looked beyond. "Oh, my Lord!" he muttered. On the ground lay a woman's bag.

"'Allo, 'allo." The keeper snorted. "They've been pinching something else."

Reggie took out his handkerchief, put his hand in it, and thus picked up the bag. He looked about him; he wandered to and fro, going delicately, examining the confusion of small footmarks, further and further away.

"Been all round, ain't they?" the keeper greeted him on his return.

"That is so. Yes." Reggie mumbled and looked at him with searching eyes. "Had any notice of a bag lost or stolen?"

"Not as I've 'eard. Better ask the 'ead keeper. 'E'll be up at the top wood about now."

The wood was a thicket of birch and crab-apple and thorn. As they came near, they saw on its verge the head keeper and two other men who were not in the brown coats of authority. One of these was Superintendent Bell. He came down the slope in a hurry.

"I tried to catch you at the hospital, Mr. Fortune," he said. "But I suppose you've heard about Mrs. Wiven?"

"Oh. The Mrs. Wiven who hadn't come back," Reggie said slowly. "No. I haven't heard anything."

"I thought you must have, by your being out here on the common. Well, she didn't come back at all. This morning Brightman turned up at the station very fussy and rattled to ask if they had any news of his lodger, Mrs. Wiven. She never came in last night, and he thought she must have had an accident or something. She'd been lodging with them for years. Old lady, fixed in her habits. Never went anywhere, that he knew of, except to chapel and for a cup o' tea with some of her chapel friends, and none of them had seen her. These fine summer days she'd take her food out and sit on the common here all day long. She went off yesterday morning with sandwiches and a vacuum flask of tea and her knitting. Often she wouldn't come home till it was getting dark. They didn't think much of her being late; sometimes she went in and had a bit o' supper with a friend. She had her key, and they left the door unbolted, like we heard, and went to bed, being worn out with the worry of the kids. But when Mrs. Brightman took up her cup of tea this morning and found she wasn't in her room,

Brightman came running round to the station. Queer business, eh?"

"Yes. Nasty business. Further you go the nastier."

Bell looked at him curiously and walked him away from the keeper. "You feel it that way? So do I. Could you tell me what you were looking for out here—as you didn't know she was missing?"

"Oh, yes. I came to verify the reports of Eddie's performances."

"Ah! Have you found any error?"

"No. I should say everything happened as stated."

"The boy's going to get well, isn't he?"

"It could be. If he gets the chance."

"Poor little beggar," Bell grunted. "What do you really think about him, Mr. Fortune?"

"Clever child, ambitious child, imaginative child. What children ought to be—twisted askew."

"Kind of perverted, you mean."

"That is so. Yes. However. Question now is, not what I think of the chances of Eddie's soul, but what's been happening. Evidence inadequate, curious, and nasty. I went up to the private lair of Eddie and Bessie. Same where he was caught with the stolen boat. I found this." He showed Bell the woman's bag.

"My oath!" Bell muttered, and took it from him gingerly. "You wrapped it up! Thinkin' there might be fingerprints."

"Yes. Probably are. They might even be useful."

"And you went looking for this—not knowing the woman was missing?"

"Wasn't lookin' for it," Reggie snapped. "I was lookin' for anything there might be. Found a little pretence of a garden they'd played at—and this."

"Ah, but you heard last night about Mrs. Wiven, and this morning you go up where Eddie hides what he's stolen. Don't that mean you made sure there was something fishy? You see when we're blind, Mr. Fortune."

"Oh, no. I don't see. I knew more than you did. Little Bessie told me this morning she was in Mrs. Wiven's room yesterday, privily and by stealth, and Mrs. Wiven caught her and called her a thief, and said they were all thieves. I should think little Bessie may have meant to be a thief. Which would agree with Eddie's effort to drown her so she should die good and honest. But I don't see my way."

"All crazy, isn't it?" Bell grunted.

"Yes. The effort of Eddie is an incalculable factor. However. You'd better look at the bag."

Bell opened it with cautious fingers. A smell of peppermint came out. Within was a paper bag of peppermint lozenges, two unclean handkerchiefs marked E.W., an empty envelope addressed to Mrs. Wiven, a bottle of soda-mint tablets, and some keys.

"Evidence that it is the bag of the missing Mrs. Wiven strong," Reggie murmured. He peered into it. "But no money. Not a penny." He looked up at Bell with that cold, ruthless curiosity which Bell always talks about in discussing the case. "Stealin' is the recurrin' motive. You notice that?"

"I do." Bell started at him. "You take it cool, Mr. Fortune. I've got to own it makes me feel queer."

"No use feelin' feelings," Reggie drawled. "We have to go on. We want the truth, whatever it is."

"Well, all right, I know," Bell said gloomily. "They're searching the common for her. That's why I came out here. They knew her. She did sit about here in summer." He went back to the head keeper and conferred again...

Reggie purveyed himself a deck-chair, and therein sat extended and lit a pipe and closed his eyes…

"Mr. Fortune!" Bell stood over him. His lips emitted a stream of smoke. No other part of him moved. "They've found her. I suppose you expected that."

"Yes. Obvious possibility. Probable possibility." It has been remarked that Mr. Fortune has a singular capacity for becoming erect from a supine position. A professor of animal morphology once delivered a lecture upon him—after a hospital dinner—as the highest type of the invertebrates. He stood up from the deck-chair in one undulating motion. "Well, well. Where is the new fact?" he moaned.

Bell took him into the wood. No grass grew in it. Where the sandy soil was not bare, dead leaves made a carpet. Under the crab-apple trees, between the thorn-brakes, were nooks obviously much used by pairs of lovers. By one of these, not far from the whale-back edge of rising ground which was the wood's end, some men stood together.

On the grey sand there lay a woman's body. She was small; she was dressed in a coat and skirt of dark grey cloth and a black and white blouse. The hat on her grey hair was pulled to one side, giving her a look of absurd frivolity in ghastly contrast to the distortion of her pallid face. Her lips were closely compressed and almost white. The dead eyes stared up at the trees with dilated pupils.

Reggie walked round the body, going delicately, rather like a dog in doubt how to deal with another dog.

Beside the body was a raffia bag which held some knitting, a vacuum flask, and an opened packet of sandwiches.

Reggie's discursive eyes looked at them and looked again at the dead face, but not for long. He was more interested in the woman's skirt. He bent over that, examined it from side to side, and turned away and went on prowling further and further away, and as he went he scraped at the dry sand here and there.

When he came back to the body, his lips were curved in a grim, mirthless smile. He looked at Bell. "Photographer," he mumbled.

"Sent a man to phone, sir," Bell grunted.

Reggie continued to look at him. "Have you? Why have you?"

"Just routine." Bell was startled.

"Oh. Only that. Well, well." Reggie knelt down by the body. His hands went to the woman's mouth… He took something from his pocket and forced the mouth open and looked in… He closed the mouth again, and sat down on his heels and contemplated the dead woman with dreamy curiosity… He opened her blouse. Upon the underclothes was a dark stain. He bent over that and smelt it; he drew the clothes from her chest.

"No wound, is there?" Bell muttered.

"Oh, no. No." Reggie put back the clothes and stood up and went to the flask and the sandwiches. He pulled the bread of an unfinished sandwich apart, looked at it, and put it down. He took the flask and shook it. It was not full. He poured some of the contents into its cup.

"Tea, eh?" said Bell. "Strong tea."

"Yes. It would be," Reggie murmured. He tasted it and spat, and poured what was in the cup back into the flask and corked it again and gave it to Bell.

"There you are. Cause of death, poisoning by oxalic acid or binoxalate of potassium—probably the latter—commonly called salts of lemon. And we shall find some in that awful tea. We shall also find it in the body. Tongue and mouth, white, contracted, eroded. Time of death, probably round about twenty-four hours ago. No certainty."

"My oath! It's too near certainty for my liking," Bell muttered.

"Is it?" Reggie's eyelids drooped. "Wasn't thinkin', about what you'd like. Other interestin' facts converge."

"They do!" Bell glowered at him. "One of the commonest kinds of poisoning, isn't it?"

"Oh, yes. Salts of lemon very popular."

"Anybody can get it."

"As you say. Removes stains, cleans brass and what not. Also quickly fatal, with luck. Unfortunate chemical properties."

"This boy Eddie could have got some easy."

"That is so. Yes. Lethal dose for a penny or two anywhere."

"Well, then—look at it!"

"I have," Reggie murmured. "Weird case. Ghastly case."

"Gives me the horrors," said Bell. "The old lady comes out here to spend the day as usual, and somebody's put a spot of poison in her drop o' tea and she dies; and her bag's stolen, and found without a farthing where the boy Eddie hides his loot. And, about the time the old lady's dying, Eddie tries to drown his sister. What are you going to make of that? What can you make of it? It was a poison any kid could get hold of. One of 'em must have poisoned her to steal her little bit o' money. But the girl's not much more than a baby. It must have been Eddie that did it—and that goes with the rest of his doings. He's got the habit of stealing. But his little sister saw something of it, knew too much, so he put up this drowning to stop her tongue—and then, when she was saved, made up this tale about killing her to keep her honest. Devilish, isn't it? And when you find a child playing the devil—my oath! But it is devilish clever—his tale would put the stealing and all the rest on the baby. And we can't prove anything else. She's too little to be able to get it clear, and he's made himself out driven wild by her goings on. If a child's really wicked, he beats you."

"Yes, that is so," Reggie drawled. "Rather excited, aren't you? Emotions are not useful in investigation. Prejudice the mind into exaggeratin' facts and ignorin' other facts. Both fallacies exhibited in your argument. You mustn't ignore what Bessie did say—that she went into Mrs. Wiven's room yesterday morning and Mrs. Wiven caught her. I shouldn't wonder if you found Bessie's fingerprints on that bag."

"My Lord!" Bell stared at him. "It's the nastiest case I ever had. When it comes to babies in murder—"

"Not nice, no. Discoverin' the possibilities of corruption of the soul. However. We haven't finished yet. Other interestin' facts have been ignored by Superintendent Bell. Hallo!" Several men were approaching briskly. "Is this your photographer and other experts?"

"That's right. Photographer and fingerprint men."

"Very swift and efficient." Reggie went to meet them. "Where did you spring from?"

"By car, sir." The photographer was surprised. "On the road up there. We had the location by phone."

"Splendid. Now then. Give your attention to the lady's skirt. Look." He indicated a shining streak across the dark stuff. "Bring that out."

"Can do, sir," the photographer said, and fell to work.

Reggie turned to Bell. "Then they'll go over the whole of her for fingerprints, what? And the sandwich paper. And the flask. Not forgettin' the bag. That's all. I've finished here. She can be taken to the mortuary for me."

"Very good," Bell said, and turned away to give the orders, but, having given them, stood still to stare at the thin glistening streak on the skirt.

Reggie came quietly to his elbow. "You do notice that? Well, well." Bell looked at him with a puzzled frown and was met for the first time in this case by a small, satisfied smile which further bewildered him. He bent again to pore over the streak. "It's all right." Reggie's voice was soothing. "That's on record now. Come on." Linking arms, he drew Bell away from the photographers and the fingerprint men. "Well? What does the higher intelligence make of the line on the skirt?"

"I don't know. I can't make out why you think so much of it."

"My dear chap! Oh, my dear chap!" Reggie moaned. "Crucial fact. Decisive fact." He led Bell on out of the wood and across the common, and at a respectful distance Bell's two personal satellites followed.

"Decisive, eh?" Bell frowned. "It was just a smear of something to me. You mean salts of lemon would leave a shiny stain?"

"Oh, no. No. Wouldn't shine at all."

"Has she been sick on her skirt?"

"Not there. No. Smear wasn't human material."

"Well, I thought it wasn't. What are you thinking of?"

"I did think of what Eddie said—where their worm dieth not."

"My God!" Bell muttered. "Worms?" He gave a shudder. "I don't get you at all, sir. It sounds mad."

"No. Connection is sort of desperate rational. I told you Eddie was like that. However. Speakin' scientifically, not a worm, but a slug. That streak was a slug's trail."

"Oh. I see." Bell was much relieved. "Now you say so, it did look like that. The sort o' slime a slug leaves behind. It does dry shiny, of course."

"You have noticed that?" Reggie admired him. "Splendid!"

Bell was not pleased. "I have seen slugs before," he grunted. "But what is there to make a fuss about? I grant you, it's nasty to think of a slug crawling over the woman as she lay there dead. That don't mean anything, though. Just what you'd expect, with the body being all night in the wood. Slugs come out when it gets dark."

"My dear chap! Oh, my dear chap!" Reggie moaned. "You mustn't talk like that. Shakes confidence in the police force. Distressin' mixture of inadequate observation and fallacious reasonin'."

"Thank you. I don't know what's wrong with it." Bell was irritated.

"Oh, my Bell! You shock me. Think again. Your general principle's all right. Slugs do come out at night. Slugs like the dark. That's a general truth which has its particular application. But you fail to observe the conditions. The body was in a wood with no herbage on the ground: and the ground was a light dry sand. These are not conditions which attract the slug. I should have been much surprised if I'd found any slugs there, or their tracks. But I looked for 'em—which you didn't, Bell. I'm always careful. And there wasn't a trace. No. I can't let you off. A slug had crawled over her skirt, leavin' his slime from side to side. And yet his slime didn't go beyond her skirt on to the ground anywhere. How do you suppose he managed that? Miracle—by a slug. I don't believe in miracles if I can help it, I object to your simple faith in the miraculous gastropod. It's lazy."

"You go beyond me," said Bell uneasily. "You grasp the whole thing while I'm only getting bits. What do you make of it all?"

"Oh, my Bell!" Reggie reproached him. "Quite clear. When the slug walked over her, she wasn't lying where she was found."

"Is that all?" Bell grunted. "I dare say. She might have had her dose, and felt queer and lay down, and then moved on to die where we found her. Nothing queer in that, is there?"

"Yes. Several things very queer. It could be. Oxalic poisoning might lay her out and still let her drag herself somewhere else to die. Not likely she'd take care to bring her flask and her sandwiches with her. Still less likely she'd lie long enough for a slug to walk over her and then recover enough to move somewhere else—and choose to move into the wood, where she wouldn't be seen. Why should she? She'd try for help if she could try for anything. And, finally, most unlikely she'd find any place here with slugs about. Look at it; it's all arid and sandy and burnt up by the summer. No. Quite unconvincin' explanation. The useful slug got on to her somewhere else. The slug is decisive."

"Then you mean to say she was poisoned some other place, and brought here dead?" Bell frowned. "It's all very well. You make it sound reasonable. But would you like to try this slug argument on a jury? They'd never stand for it, if you ask me. It's all too clever."

"You think so?" Reggie murmured. "Well, well. Then it does give variety to the case. We haven't been very clever so far. However. Study to improve. There is further evidence. She'd been sick. Common symptom of oxalic poisoning. But she'd been sick on her underclothes and not on her outside clothes. That's very difficult. Think about it. Even juries can be made to think sometimes. Even coroners, which is very hard. Even judges. I've done it in my time, simple as I am. I might do it again. Yes, I might. With the aid of the active and intelligent police force. Come on."

"What do you want to do?"

"Oh, my Bell! I want to call on Mr. and Mrs. Brightman. We need their collaboration. We can't get on without it."

"All right. I don't mind trying 'em," Bell agreed gloomily. "We've got to find out all about the old woman somehow. We don't really know anything yet."

"I wouldn't say that. No," Reggie mumbled. "However. One moment."

They had come to the edge of the common by the hospital, where his car waited. He went across to it and spoke to his chauffeur.

"Just calmin' Sam," he apologised on his return. "He gets peevish when forgotten. Come on."

They arrived again at the little general shop. Its unshuttered window now enticed the public with a meagre array of canned goods and cartons which had been there some time. The door was shut but not fastened. Opening it rang a bell. They went in, and found the shop empty, and for a minute or two stood in a mixture of smells through which soap was dominant.

Mrs. Brightman came from the room behind, wiping red arms and hands on her apron. Her plump face, which was tired and sweating, quivered alarm at the sight of them. "Oh, it's you!" she cried. "What is it? Is there anything?"

"Your children are doing well," said Reggie. "Thought I'd better let you know that."

She stared at him, and tears came into her eyes. "Praise God!" she gasped. "Thank you, sir, you're very kind."

"No. You don't have to thank me. I'm just doin' my job."

But again she thanked him, and went on nervously: "Have you heard anything of Mrs. Wiven?"

"I want to have a little talk about her. Is Mr. Brightman in?"

"No, he isn't, not just now. Have you got any news of her, sir?"

"Yes. There is some news. Sorry Mr. Brightman's out. Where's he gone?"

"Down to the yard, sir."

"Out at the back here?"

"No. No. Down at his own yard."

"Oh. He has a business of his own?"

"Yes, sir, a little business. Furniture dealing it is. Second-hand furniture."

"I see. Well, well. We could get one of the neighbours to run down and fetch him, what?" Reggie turned to Bell.

"That's the way," Bell nodded. "What's the address, ma'am?"

She swallowed. "It's just round the corner. Smith's Buildings. Anybody would tell you. But he might be out on a job, you know; I couldn't say."

Bell strode out, and the messenger he sent was one of his satellites.

"Well, while we're waitin', we might come into your nice little room," Reggie suggested. "There's one or two things you can tell me."

"Yes, sir, I'm sure, anything as I can, I'll be glad. Will you come through, please?" She lifted the flap of the counter for him, she opened the curtained glass door of the room behind. It was still in exact order, but she had to apologise for it. "I'm sorry we're all in a mess. I'm behindhand with my cleaning, having this dreadful trouble with the children and being so worried I can't get on. I don't half know what I'm doing, and then poor Mrs. Wiven being lost—" She stopped, breathless. "What is it about Mrs. Wiven, sir? What have you heard?"

"Not good news," Reggie said. "Nobody will see Mrs. Wiven alive again."

The full face grew pale beneath its sweat, the eyes stood out. "She's dead! Oh, the poor soul! But how do you know? How was it?"

"She's been found dead on the common."

Mrs. Brightman stared at him: her mouth came open and shook; she flung her apron over her head and bent and was convulsed with hysterical sobbing.

"Fond of her, were you?" Reggie sympathised.

A muffled voice informed him that she was a dear old lady—and so good to everybody.

"Was she? Yes. But I wanted to ask you about the children. What time did they go out yesterday?" Still sobbing under her apron, Mrs. Brightman seemed not to hear. "Yesterday morning," Reggie insisted. "You must remember. What time was it when Eddie and Bessie went out?"

After a moment the apron was pulled down from a swollen, tearful face. "What time?" she repeated looking at her lap and wiping her eyes. "I don't know exactly, sir. Just after breakfast. Might be somewheres about nine o'clock."

"Yes, it might be," Reggie murmured. "They were pulled out of the pond about ten."

"I suppose so," she whimpered. "What's it got to do with Mrs. Wiven?"

"You don't see any connection?"

She stared at him. "How could there be?"

The shop-door bell rang, and she started up to answer it. She found Bell in the shop. "Oh, have you found Mr. Brightman?" she cried.

"No, not yet. Where's Mr. Fortune?"

Reggie called to him, "Come on, Bell," and she brought him into the back room and stood looking from one to the other. "So Mr. Brightman wasn't in his yard?"

"No, sir. Nobody there. At least, they couldn't make anybody hear."

"Well, well," Reggie murmured.

"But I told you he might have gone off on a job. He often has to go to price some stuff or make an offer or something."

"You did say so. Yes," Reggie murmured. "However. I was asking about the children. Before they went out yesterday—Bessie got into trouble with Mrs. Wiven, didn't she?"

The woman looked down and plucked at her apron.

"You didn't tell us that last night," Reggie said.

"I didn't want to. I didn't see as it mattered. And I didn't want to say anything against Bessie. She's my baby." Her eyes were streaming. "Don't you see?"

"Bessie told me," said Reggie.

"Bessie confessed! Oh, it's all too dreadful. The baby! I don't know why this was to come on us. I brought 'em up to be good, I have. And she was such a darling baby. But it's God's will."

"Yes. What did happen?" said Reggie.

"Mrs. Wiven was always hard on the children. She never had a child herself, poor thing. Bessie got into her room, and Mrs. Wiven caught her and said she was prying and stealing like Eddie. I don't know what Bessie was doing there. Children will do such, whatever you do. And there was Bessie crying and Eddie all wild. He does get so out of himself. I packed 'em off, and I told Mrs. Wiven it wasn't nothing to be so cross about, and she got quite nice again. She was always a dear with me and Brightman. A good woman at heart, sir, she was."

"And when did Mrs. Wiven go out?" said Reggie.

"It must have been soon after. She liked her days on the common in summer, she did."

"Oh, yes. That's clear," Reggie stood up and looked out at the yard, where some washing was hung out to dry. "What was Mrs. Wiven wearing yesterday?"

"Let me see—" Mrs. Brightman was surprised by the turn in the conversation. "I don't rightly remember—she had on her dark coat and skirt. She always liked to be nicely dressed when she went." Under the frown of this mental effort swollen eyes blinked at him. "But you said she'd been found. You know what she had on."

"Yes. When she was on the common. Before she got there—what was she wearing?"

Mrs. Brightman's mouth opened and shut.

"I mean, when she caught Bessie in her room. What was she wearing then?"

"The same—she wouldn't have her coat on—I don't know as I remember—but the same—she knew she was going out—she'd dress for it—she wouldn't ever dress twice in a morning."

"Wouldn't she? She didn't have that overall on?" Reggie pointed to a dark garment hanging on the line in the yard which stretched from house to shed.

"No, she didn't, I'm sure. That was in the dirty clothes."

"But you had to wash it today. Well, well. Now we want to have a look at Mrs. Wiven's room."

"If you like. Of course, nothing's been done. It's all

untidy." She led the way upstairs, lamenting that the house was all anyhow, she'd been so put about.

But Mrs. Wiven's room was primly neat and as clean as the shining passage and stairs. The paint had been worn thin by much washing, the paper was so faded that its rose-bud pattern merged into a uniform pinkish grey. An old fur rug by the bedside, a square of threadbare carpet under the rickety round table in the middle of the room, were the only coverings of the scoured floor. The table had one cane chair beside it, and there was a small basket chair by the empty grate—nothing else in the room but the iron bedstead and a combination of chest of drawers, dressing-table, and wash-stand, with its mirror all brown spots.

Mrs. Brightman passed round the room, pulling this and pushing that. "I haven't even dusted," she lamented.

"Is this her own furniture?" Reggie asked.

"No, sir, she hadn't anything. We had to furnish it for her."

"Quite poor, was she?"

"I don't really know how she managed. And, of course, we didn't ever press her; you couldn't. She had her savings, I suppose. She'd been in good service, by what she used to say."

"No relations?"

"No, sir. She was left quite alone. That was really why she came to us, she was that lonely. She'd say to me she did so want a home, till we took her. When she was feeling down, she used to cry and tell me she didn't know what would become of her. Of course, we wouldn't ever have let her want, poor dear. But it's my belief her bit of money was running out."

Reggie gazed about the room. On the walls were many cards with texts.

"Mr. Brightman put up the good words for her," Mrs. Brightman explained, and gazed at one of the texts and cried.

"'In my Father's house are many mansions.'" Reggie read it out slowly, and again looked round the bare little room.

Mrs. Brightman sobbed. "Ah, she's gone there now. She's happy."

Bell was moving from one to the other of the cupboards beside the grate. Nothing was in them but clothes. He went on to the dressing-table. "She doesn't seem to have any papers. Only this." He lifted a cash-box, and money rattled in it.

"I couldn't say, I'm sure," Mrs. Brightman whimpered.

Reggie stood by the table. "Did she have her meals up here?" he asked.

Mrs. Brightman thought about that. "Mostly she didn't. She liked to sit down with us. She used to say it was more homey."

Reggie fingered the table-cloth, pulled it off, and looked at the cracked veneer beneath. He stooped, felt the strip of old carpet under the table, drew it back. On the boards beneath was a patch of damp.

Mrs. Brightman came nearer. "Well there!" she said. "That comes of my not doing out the room. She must have had a accident with her slops and never told me. She always would do things for herself."

Reggie did not answer. He wandered round the room, stopped by the window a moment, and turned to the door.

"I'm taking this cash-box, ma'am," said Bell.

"If you think right—" Mrs. Brightman drew back. "It's not for me to say—I don't mind, myself." She looked from one to the other. "Will that be all, then?"

"Nothing more here." Reggie opened the door.

As they went downstairs, the shop bell rang again, and she hurried on to answer it. The two men returned to the room behind the shop.

"Poor old woman," Bell grunted. "You can see what sort of a life she was having—that dingy room and her money running out—I wouldn't wonder if she committed suicide."

"Wouldn't it be wonderful. No," Reggie murmured. "Shut up." From the shop came a man's voice, lazy and genial.

"Good afternoon, mum. I want a bit o' salts o' lemon. About two penn'worth would do me. 'Ow do you sell it?"

There was a mutter from Mrs. Brightman. "We don't keep it."

"What? They told me I'd be sure to get it 'ere. Run out of it, 'ave you? Ain't that too bad!"

"We never did keep it," Mrs. Brightman said. "Whoever told you we did?"

"All right, all right. Keep your hair on, missus. Where can I get it?"

"How should I know? I don't rightly know what it is."

"Don't you? Sorry I spoke. Used for cleaning, you know."

Bell glowered at Reggie, for the humorous cockney voice was the voice of his chauffeur. But the cold severity of Reggie's round face gave no sign.

"We don't use it, nor we don't keep it, nor any chemist's stuff," Mrs. Brightman was answering.

"Oh, good day!" The bell rang again as the shop door closed.

Mrs. Brightman came back. "Running in and out of the shop all day with silly people," she panted. She looked from one to the other, questioning, afraid.

"I was wonderin'," Reggie murmured. "Did Mrs. Wiven have her meals with you yesterday—or in her room?"

"Down here." The swollen eyes looked at him and looked away. "She did usual, I told you. She liked to."

"And which was the last meal she ever had?"

Mrs. Brightman suppressed a cry. "You do say things! Breakfast was the last she had here. She took out a bit o' lunch and tea."

"Yes. When was that put ready?"

"I had it done first thing, knowing she meant to get out—and she always liked to start early. It was there on the sideboard waiting at breakfast."

"Then it was ready before the children went out? Before she had her quarrel with Bessie?"

Mrs. Brightman swallowed. "So it was."

"Oh. Thank you. Rather strong, the tea in her flask," Reggie mumbled.

"She always had it fairly strong. Couldn't be too strong for her. I'm just the same myself."

"Convenient," Reggie said. "Now you'll take me down into the cellar, Mrs. Brightman."

"What?" She drew back so hastily that she was brought up by the wall. "The cellar?" Her eyes seemed to stand out more than ever, so they stared at him, the whites of them more widely bloodshot. With an unsteady hand she thrust back the hair from her sweating brow. "The cellar? Why ever do you want to go there? There's nothing in the cellar."

"You think not?" Reggie smiled. "Come down and see."

She gave a moaning cry; she stumbled away to the door at the back, and opened it, and stood holding by the door-post, looking out to the paved yard.

From the shed in it appeared Brightman's bearded face. "Were you looking for me, dearie?" he asked, and brought his lank shape into sight, brushing it as it came.

She made a gesture to him; she went to meet him and muttered: "Matthew! They're asking me to take 'em down to the cellar."

"Well, to be sure!" Brightman gave Reggie and Bell a glance of melancholy, pitying surprise. "I don't see any reason in that." He held her up, he stroked her and gently remonstrated. "But there's no reason they shouldn't go to the cellar if they want to, Florrie. We ain't to stand in the way of anything as the police think right. We ain't got anything to hide, have we? Come along, dearie."

An inarticulate quavering sound came from her.

"That's all right, my dearie, that's all right," Brightman soothed her.

"Is it?" Bell growled. "So you've been here all the time, Mr. Brightman. While she sent us to look for you down at your own place. Why didn't you show up before?"

"I've only just come in, sir," Brightman said quietly. "I came in by the back. I was just putting things to rights in the washhouse. The wife's been so pushed. I didn't know you gentlemen were here. You're searching all the premises, are you? I'm agreeable. I'm sure it's in order, if you say so. But I don't know what you're looking for."

"Mrs. Brightman will show us," said Reggie, and grasped her arm.

"Don't, don't," she wailed.

"You mustn't be foolish, dearie," said Brightman. "You know there's nothing in the cellar. Show the gentlemen if they want. It's all right. I'll go with you."

"Got a torch, Bell?" said Reggie.

"I have." Bell went back into the room. "And here's a lamp, too." He lit it.

Reggie drew the shaking woman through the room

into the passage. "That's the door to your cellar. Open it. Come on."

Bell held the lamp overhead behind them. Reggie led her stumbling down the stairs, and Brightman followed close.

A musty, dank smell came about them. The lamplight showed a large cellar of brick walls and an earth floor. There was in it a small heap of coal, some sacks and packing-cases and barrels, but most of the dim space was empty. The light glistened on damp.

"Clay soil," Reggie murmured, and smiled at Brightman. "Yes. That was indicated."

"I don't understand you, sir," said Brightman.

"No. You don't. Torch, Bell." He took it and flashed its beam about the cellar. "Oh, yes." He turned to Bell. With a finger he indicated the shining tracks of slugs. "You see?"

"I do," Bell muttered.

Mrs. Brightman gave a choked, hysterical laugh.

Reggie moved to and fro. He stooped. He took out his pocketbook and from it a piece of paper, and with that scraped something from a barrel side, something from the clay floor, and sighed satisfaction.

Standing up, he moved the ray of the torch from place to place, held it steady at last to make a circle of light on the ground beneath the steps. "There," he said, and Mrs. Brightman screamed. "Yes. I know. That's where you put her. Look, Bell." His finger pointed to a slug's trail which came into the circle of light, stopped, and went on again at another part of the circle. "It didn't jump. They don't."

He swung round upon Mrs. Brightman. He held out to her the piece of paper cupped in his hand. On it lay two yellow slugs.

She flung herself back, crying loathing and fear.

"Really, gentlemen, really now," Brightman stammered. "This isn't right. This isn't proper. You've no call to frighten a poor woman so. Come away now, Florrie dearie." He pulled at her.

"Where are you going?" Reggie murmured. She did not go. Her eyes were set on the two yellow slugs. "'Where their worm dieth not,'" Reggie said slowly.

She broke out in the screams of hysterical laughter; she tore herself from Brightman, and reeled and fell down writhing and yelling.

"So that is that, Mr. Brightman." Reggie turned to him.

"You're a wicked soul!" Brightman whined. "My poor dearie!" He fell on his knees by her; he began to pray forgiveness for her sins.

"My oath!" Bell muttered, and ran up the steps shouting to his men...

Some time afterwards the detective left the little shop.

On the other side of the street, aloof from the gaping, gossiping crowd, superior and placid, his chauffeur smoked a cigarette. It was thrown away; the chauffeur followed him, fell into step beside him. "Did I manage all right, sir?" The chauffeur invited praise.

"You did. Very neat. Very effective. As you know. Side, Sam, side. We are good at destruction. Efficient incinerators. Humble function. Other justification for existence, doubtful. However. Study to improve. What we want now is a toyshop."

"Sir?" Sam was puzzled.

"I said a toyshop," Reggie complained. "A good toyshop. Quick."...

The last of the sunlight was shining into the little room at the hospital where Eddie Hill lay. Upon his bed stood part of a bridge built of strips of metal bolted together, a bridge of grand design. He and Reggie were working on the central span.

There was a tap at the door, a murmur from Reggie, and the nurse brought in Bell. He stood looking at Reggie with reproachful surprise. "So that's what you're doing," he protested.

"Yes. Something useful at last." Reggie sighed. "Well, well. We'll have to call this a day, young man. You've done enough. Mustn't get yourself tired."

"I'm not tired," the boy protested eagerly. "I'm not, really."

"No. Of course not. Ever so much better. But there's another day tomorrow. And you have a big job. Must keep fit to go on with it."

"All right." The boy lay back, looked at his bridge, looked wistfully at Reggie. "I can keep this here, can I, sir?"

"Rather. On the table by the bed. So it'll be there when you wake. Nice, making things, isn't it? Yes. You're going to make a lot now. Good-bye. Jolly, tomorrow, what? Good-bye." He went out with Bell. "Now what's the matter with you?" he complained.

"Well, I had to have a word with you, sir. This isn't going to be so easy. I thought I'd get you at the mortuary doing the post-mortem."

"Minor matter. Simple matter. Only the dead buryin' their dead. The boy was urgent. Matter of savin' life there."

"I'm not saying you're not right," said Bell wearily. "But it is a tangle of a case. The divisional surgeon reports Mrs. Brightman's mad. Clean off her head."

"Yes. I agree. What about it?"

"Seemed to me you pretty well drove her to it. Those slugs—oh, my Lord."

"Got you, did it? It rather got me. I'd heard Eddie talk

of 'the worm that dieth not.' I should say he's seen that cellar. Dreamed of it. However. I didn't drive the woman mad. She'd been mad some time. Not medically mad. Not legally mad. But morally. That was the work of our Mr. Brightman. I only clarified the situation. He almost sent the boy the same way. That's been stopped. That isn't going to happen now. That's the main issue. And we win on it. Not too bad. But rather a grim day. Virtue has gone out of me. My dear chap!" He took Bell's arm affectionately. "You're tucked up too."

"I don't mind owning I've had enough," said Bell. "This sort of thing tells me I'm not as young as I was. And it's all a tangle yet."

"My dear chap! Oh, my dear chap!" Reggie murmured. "Empty, aren't we? Come on. Come home with me."

While Sam drove them back, he declined to talk. He stretched in the corner of the car and closed his eyes, and bade Bell do the same. While they ate a devilled sole and an entrecôte Elise, he discussed the qualities of Elise, his cook, and of the Romanée which they drank, and argued bitterly (though he shared it) that the cheese offered in deference to Bell's taste, a bland Stilton, was an insult to the raspberries, the dish of which he emptied.

But when they were established in big chairs in his library, with brandy for Bell and seltzer for himself, and both pipes were lit. "Did you say a tangle?" he murmured. "Oh, no. Not now. The rest is only routine for your young men and the lawyers. It'll work out quite easy. You can see it all. When Mrs. Brightman was left a widow with her little shop, the pious Brightman pounced on her and mastered her. The little shop was only a little living. Brightman wanted more. Children were kept very short—they might fade out, they might go to the bad—either way the devout Brightman would be relieved of their keep; and meanwhile it was pleasant making 'em believe they were wicked. Old Mrs. Wiven was brought in as a lodger—not out of charity as the wretched Mrs. Brightman was trained to say; she must have had a bit of money. Your young men will be able to trace that. And they'll find Brightman got it out of her and used it to set up his second-hand furniture business. Heard of that sort of thing before, what?"

"I should say I have," Bell grunted. "My Lord, how often. The widow that falls for a pious brute—the old woman lodger with a bit of money."

"Oh, yes. Dreary old game. And then the abnormal variations began. Pious bullyin' and starvin' didn't turn the boy into a criminal idiot. He has a mind. He has an imagination, poor child. Mrs. Wiven didn't give herself up to Brightman like his miserable wife. She had a temper. So the old game went wrong. Mrs. Wiven took to fussin' about her money. As indicated by Bessie. Mrs. Wiven was going to be very awkward. Your young men will have to look about and get evidence she'd been grumbling. Quite easy. Lots of gossip will be goin'. Some of it true. Most of it useful at the trial. Givin' the atmosphere."

Bell frowned. "Fighting with the gloves off, aren't you?"

"Oh, no. No. Quite fair. We have to fight the case without the children. I'm not going to have Eddie put in the witness-box, to be tortured about his mad mother helpin' murder. That might break him up for ever. And he's been tortured enough. The brute Brightman isn't going to hurt him any more. The children won't be givin' evidence. I'll get half the College of Physicians to certify they're not fit, if they're asked for. But that's not goin' to leave Mr.

Brightman any way out. Now then. Things bein' thus, Brightman had his motive to murder Mrs. Wiven. If he didn't stop her mouth she'd have him in jail. Being a clever fellow, he saw that Eddie's record of stealin' would be very useful. By the way—notice that queer little incident, Bessie bein' caught pilferin' by Mrs. Wiven yesterday morning? Brightman may have fixed that up for another black mark against the children. I wonder. But it didn't go right. He must have had a jolt when Mrs. Wiven called out they were all thieves. Kind of compellin' immediate action. His plan would have been all ready, of course—salts of lemon in her favourite strong tea; a man don't think of an efficient way of poisonin' all of sudden. And then the incalculable Eddie intervened. Reaction of Mrs. Wiven's explosion on him, a sort of divine command to save his sister from hell by seeing she died innocent. When Brightman had the news of that effort at drowning, he took it as a god-send. Hear him thanking heaven? Boy who was wicked enough to kill a little sister was wicked enough for anything. Mr. Brightman read his title clear to mansions in the skies. And Mrs. Wiven was promptly given her cup o' tea. She was sick in her room, sick on her overall and on her underclothes. Evidence for all that conclusive. Remember the damp floor. I should say Mrs. Brightman had another swab at that today. She has a craze about cleaning. We saw that. Feels she never can get clean, poor wretch. Well. Mrs. Wiven died. Oxalic poisoning generally kills quick. I hope it did. They hid the body in the cellar. Plan was clever. Take the body out in the quiet of the night and dump it on the common with a flask of poisoned tea—put her bag in Eddie's den. All clear for the intelligent police. Devil of a boy poisoned the old lady to steal her money, and was drownin' his little sister so she shouldn't tell on him. That's what you thought, wasn't it? Yes. Well-made plan. It stood up against us last night."

"You did think there was something queer," Bell said.

"I did," Reggie sighed. "Physical smell. Damp musty smell. Probably the cellar. And the Brightmans didn't smell nice spiritually. However. Lack of confidence in myself. And I have no imagination. I ought to have waited and watched. My error. My grave error. Well. It was a clever plan. But Brightman was rather bustled. That may account for his errors. Fatal errors. Omission to remove the soiled underclothes when the messed-up overall was taken off. Failure to allow for the habits of *limax flavus*."

"What's that?" said Bell.

"Official name of yellow slug—cellar slug. The final, damning evidence. I never found any reason for the existence of slugs before. However. To round it off—when you look into Mr. Brightman's furniture business, you'll find that he has a van, or the use of one. You must prove it was used last night. That's all. Quite simple now. But a wearin' case." He gazed at Bell with large, solemn eyes. "His wife! He'd schooled her thorough. Ever hear anything more miserably appealing than her on her dear babies and poor old Mrs. Wiven? Not often? No. Took a lot of breakin' down."

"Ah. You were fierce," Bell muttered.

"Oh, no. No." Reggie sighed. "I was bein' merciful. She couldn't be saved. My job was to save the children. And she—if that brute hadn't twisted her, she'd have done anything to save 'em too. She'd been a decent soul once. No. She won't be giving evidence against me."

"Why, how should she?" Bell gaped.

"I was thinkin' of the day of judgment," Reggie murmured.

"Well, well. Post-mortem in the morning. Simple straight job. Then I'll be at the hospital if you want me. Have to finish Eddie's bridge. And then we're going to build a ship. He's keen on ships."

Pit of Screams

Garnett Radcliffe

HENRY GARNETT RADCLIFFE (1898–1971) WAS BORN IN County Meath and educated at Campbell College, Belfast, and at Sandhurst. He served in India on the North-West Frontier and with the RAF in South Arabia and Socotra. Later, he became a civil servant. In some respects he seems like an Irish counterpart to the American "pulp writers," with a penchant for "weird tales" reflected in short story titles such as "The Mirror of Dancing Death," "The Octopus Man," "The Rat's Accomplice," and "The Abominable Snowman of Katayadu." He also wrote under the name Stephen Travers. Among his occasional novels, *The Great Orme Terror* (1934), set in the vicinity of Llandudno, is unquestionably one of the most preposterous mysteries that I have read.

Yet he didn't lack the ability to entertain, and that stern judge Dorothy L. Sayers included one of his less lurid mysteries in one of her prestigious anthologies.

For the chance to read "Pit of Screams," I'm indebted to

Jamie Sturgeon, who supplied me with a copy of the story as it appeared in *Suspense* in November 1958. I agree with him that it seems almost certain to be a retitled version of a story that, during the pandemic, we were unable to locate, "Pit of Punishment," which appeared in *Argosy* in the U.S. in December 1938.

HAVE SNAKES HYPNOTIC POWERS? WHY ASK ME? IT IS THE British soldier who has served in India, and the tourist, who tell snake stories. I'm a retired businessman whose acquaintance with India has been confined mainly to Calcutta and Bombay, where you would be as likely to meet a snake as in Piccadilly.

All the same, your question has stirred a memory. When I was a young man I was once in a place called Togarapore in the Central Provinces, a small, independent native state with its own customs. The British administration didn't concern itself much about Togarapore. You see, everyone knew the Rajah was an enlightened, humane young man who'd been educated at Eton and Oxford.

In London and Deauville and Cannes the best people called him "Bobby." He dressed English-fashion and rode with the Pytchley when he was in England.

In Togarapore he dressed like a Rajput or a Bengali dancing-girl or in nothing at all, as the whim took him.

People called him the Lord of Blood, but when they did so they spoke in a whisper, after making sure there were no strangers present.

Yes, he was a Jekyll and Hyde. More British than the British, and more Rajput than a Rajput. Togarapore had a Civil Service, a secret police, a library, a theatre and one of the best hospitals in India.

Also, it had the Pit of Screams.

My story concerns both the Civil Service and the Pit of Screams.

I knew the Civil Service—at least I knew the Ministry of Finance. My business interests had made it necessary for me to contact them. There were only three—a Persian called Ali Dad Makmud and his two Dogra clerks. The clerks were both younger men. Their names were Chirandah Dass and Hirnam Singh.

Chirandah Dass was short, plump and smiling; Hirnam Singh was tall and pock-marked; and apart from their being Dogras they had only one thing in common—they were both excellent clerks.

Their books (kept in English) were miracles of neatness; their writing could be read as easily as print. Had it not been so, Ali Dad Makmud would never have employed them, at thirty rupees a month, which in those days was good pay for a clerk.

Their work was very confidential. They had to prepare the annual budget after Ali Dad Makmud and the Rajah had decided whom and what to tax. And the taxes in Togarapore were always paid.

The Rajah liked money almost as much as he liked brandy, horses and dancing-girls, and those who didn't pay on the first demand got no second chance. They were taken to the Pit of Screams, and after the snakes had dealt with them the Rajah inherited their estates.

Yes, I am coming to the Pit of Screams. But at the moment my story concerns itself with the Finance Ministry. You see, while I was there the Rajah suddenly decided to make a cut in his Civil Service, and it was on the Ministry of Finance that the axe fell.

Why? Because there had been a leakage of budget

secrets. A rumour about a certain new tax had reached the merchants before it should have done and that meant a big loss in revenue to the Rajah. And he knew he must have been betrayed by one of those three, Ali Dad Makmud, Chirandah Dass or Hirnam Singh.

So the axe fell.

Rather I should say that Ali Dad Makmud, who as Minister of Finance was the most responsible, fell. He fell quite literally from the pole in the centre of the Pit of Screams into the bed of expectant snakes below.

In the centre of the Pit where the ground was level and sandy there was a pole about fifteen feet high. It was made of rough, knotted wood and not difficult to climb, at least not difficult for a man spurred by terror. All criminals who were placed in the Pit swarmed up it like monkeys pursued by a leopard. And when they could climb no higher they clung there for as long as their strength endured.

Although he was stout and not young, Ali Dad clung to the pole for a very long time before he fell; and all the time he was screaming, as people who were executed in that Pit always did scream. The snakes knew the sound. When they heard it they would come from their holes in the rocky sides of the Pit, a crawling rivulet of death.

When they reared themselves around the foot of the pole to stare at their victim they looked pretty, like flowers swaying in a breeze. They were Togara vipers, long and thin with mottled bodies and green and red hoods. From the top of the pole they must have looked like tulips.

Yes, Ali Dad Makmud screamed for a long time before he fell. I think even the Rajputs, crowded together to watch on the sloping ground above the Pit, were glad when his numbed hands lost their grip.

The tulips rose to greet him as fox-hounds greet a fox thrown to them by the huntsmen, and then Togarapore had no Minister of Finance.

The purge was not yet complete. The two Dogra clerks still remained. Either or both of them might have been guilty of betraying the budget secret, and the Rajah's appetite for blood had only been whetted by what had happened to Ali Dad Makmud.

All that restrained him from sending them both to the Pit of Screams was that to do so would leave himself without an efficient clerk who understood the finance system.

Which of the two should he purge, which should he keep? Was plump little Chirandah Dass or tall, thin Hirnam Singh to be made redundant? Both protested their innocence with equal vehemence; both were excellent clerks.

Now in some ways the Rajah was a very practical man. Since he hated Chirandah Dass and Hirnam Singh equally, but had to keep one of them to do the accounts, he decided to retain the most efficient. A logical, simple solution. And to determine which *was* the most efficient, he devised an examination that was equally simple and equally logical.

Another advantage of the plan was that the carrying out of the test would be a spectacle unusual even for Togarapore, a place that had seen some very strange spectacles indeed.

As a distinguished visitor out of whom the Rajah hoped to make money, I was invited to the theatre where the test was to be made. I sat in the stalls among the minor nobility and laid bets on Chirandah Dass while we waited for the curtain to go up.

Why did I want Chirandah Dass to win? Well, he was younger than Hirnam Singh, a clean, laughing boy with an honest face. And he'd a little wife who wore flowers in her hair and flowers round her neck. They had a baby like a squirrel. I'd often seen the three of them laughing and play-ing in the State gardens where the Rajah's blue peacocks strutted among the flower beds.

We sat in the theatre waiting for the show to begin, and everybody made wagers. A Rajput would bet on the fall of a leaf, or the hour of his mother's death. The odds were heavily on Hirnam Singh. He was a different type from Chirandah Dass. An older, harder man with bold eyes and a tight mouth. He had strong nerves, and this contest the Rajah had devised was a war of nerves in very truth.

When the curtain rose we saw that the stage had been arranged like an office. There were two tables and chairs, a great pile of files, blotting-paper, ink, pens, pencils, rulers— all the weapons a clerk uses in his fight to earn his daily bread. Each table was equipped exactly the same, and the chairs had been placed so that the writers would face one another. Behind, at a little distance from the tables, were other chairs. They were for senior clerks who were to judge the contest like the umpires at a boxing-match.

A battle of clerks! The laughter of the Rajput nobles rose like a great storm when they saw what the Rajah had planned. There would be pens and ink instead of swords and blood in this strange duel, but for the loser death waited in the Pit of Screams.

Chirandah Dass and Hirnam Singh were brought on to

the stage. They came separately and we cheered them as if they had been boxers stepping into the ring. By far the loudest shout was for Hirnam Singh.

He looked like a winner. Calm and confident, as if the fight were already won. He bowed in acknowledgement of the applause and spoke so that all could hear.

"By the names of the gods and the grass on the graves of my ancestors, I swear I am innocent of the charge," he cried. "And now by my skill as a clerk I will prove the truth. Chirandah Dass betrayed the secret for a bribe, and Chirandah Dass will pay the penalty."

You should have been there to hear the shout that went up. When it died Chirandah Dass was led on the stage.

Fear was stamped on his face. He tried to hide it, but it was there for all to see. The test called for nerves of iron, and even though I believed him to be innocent, I felt my heart sink.

His lips quivered, his hands shook. We could hardly hear his voice. "I am innocent…" he said.

First they drew for tables. Everything had to be very fair. The Lord of Blood had learned English sportsmanship at Eton and Oxford.

He was present himself to see that everything was done according to the Queensberry rules. His eyes were bloodshot and he was a little drunk. He might have been a Riviera playboy, in his flannels and spotted silk scarf. Yet, when I looked at him, slim and dark, with his gleaming teeth, I seemed to see one of the Togara vipers.

For the benefit of the spectators it was explained what the clerks would have to do. Their task was to enter in brand-new ledgers particulars from the files that held the records of the principal tax-paying landowners of Togarapore. Names, addresses, date of birth, number of children and so forth. Then the income and allowances and amount of tax payable had to be entered in the appropriate columns. At the end of each page these columns of figures had to be added up and the totals carried forward. It was not difficult work, but it called for concentration and accuracy. And remember that the Dogras would be writing in English, a language not their own.

Also, remember the conditions in which they were working. The audience, the dreaded presence of the Lord of Blood, the hubbub of voices applauding and jeering by turn. Above all, the knowledge that the slightest slip or blot or failure to complete the page in an allotted time meant death—and a horrible death.

Concentration, accuracy and speed were what this contest called for. Hirnam Singh looked from the start as if he possessed these qualities. When he lifted his pen to examine the nib it was as if he had drawn his sword to try the blade. His smile was cool and confident.

But Chirandah Dass! Although he tried, he could not disguise his fear. We could see the sweat and the shaking hands. His arm seemed wooden when he tried to take his pen. Hirnam Singh, who was ruling columns as calmly as if he were in his own office, laughed in mockery.

I saw Chirandah Dass raise his head to stare at him across the tables. A new light, the hard light of anger came into his eyes. He was a clerk, but he came of Dogra fighting stock. His anger and his confidence were growing. And we who had backed him shouted our applause. Our horse had made a bad start but he was in the race. As he warmed to the task we saw that his hands moved as quickly and accurately as those of Hirnam Singh.

He had lost a lot of precious time. We held our breath, expecting to see him gonged before he had totted up the totals on the first page. But he counted them, it seemed, with one sweep of the eye. His pen moved like lightning, the page swished over, and we could breathe again.

Hirnam Singh's eyes flickered and we saw him crouch low over the table. He must have heard the scratching of Chirandah Dass's nib like the hoofs of a pursuer. His hand was like a brown spider darting across the page. The files passed from the "IN" tray on his left to the "OUT" tray on his right as quickly and precisely as if they were being carried on a conveyor belt through a machine.

Line by line, file by file, page by page he forged ahead. Chirandah Dass was working at tremendous speed, but had not yet settled into a proper rhythm. Little things kept worrying him: the shadow of his hand on the paper, the perspiration trickling into his eyes, the flies hovering round him as if he were a sick animal. It was very hot and there was no punkah.

But he was a born clerk. As his nib warmed to its work he seemed to forget the annoyances in an utter concentration of brain and hand. He had so much to live for.

Time went on. Now the first thrill had passed it became wearisome to the spectators. We left the theatre, fed, drank, slept and returned at intervals to see how the race proceeded.

They were both working like machines. All through the long, hot day they wrote without a pause. Chirandah Dass had found his rhythm. Letter by letter, word by word he was creeping up on his rival.

When night fell and the lights were turned on, both showed signs of exhaustion. Hirnam Singh now looked the more worried of the two. His eyes were wild and his skin glistened. He kept glancing across the tables at Chirandah's nib following him as relentlessly as death.

Again the theatre filled. The Rajah reappeared. We saw him in a box making merry with a party of friends. He was all Rajput now, magnificently robed in purple, with diamonds in his turban.

As the marathon proceeded the excitement mounted. Hirnam Singh was swaying in his chair. He began to chant figures and words aloud as he wrote. That seemed to break Chirandah Dass's concentration. He screamed at Hirnam Singh to be quiet but the other only raised his voice.

Then Chirandah Dass also began to chant. They tried to drown each other's voices, yelling like challenging cocks across the tables. And still those red-eyed, sweat-soaked clerks drove their pens without blot or falter. Still the files shot like shuttlecocks across the tables.

No thrill in clerking? I who am now old and have travelled the world and lived through wars will never forget that night. My heart, soul and mind were with Chirandah Dass. I knew he was fighting for his wife and baby. The little wife who loved flowers, and the baby like a bright-eyed squirrel.

More time passed. The clerks were too exhausted to shout now. They leaned sideways on the tables and the nimble pens now crawled along the lines like horses dragging a heavy load.

Suddenly a great shout went up. Chirandah Dass had drawn level with his rival. The sound must have been to him like wine. He straightened himself with a last access of strength and again his nib began to fly. But Hirnam Singh didn't move. He was lying across the table and his pen had dropped from his hand.

Victory for Chirandah Dass! But then—while we were still roaring our plaudits—he too stopped writing. His face was ghastly as he stared at a completed column of figures. And I guessed what had happened.

He'd missed an entry, the running total was wrong and the entire page would have to be altered.

The judges crowded round to examine the ledger. We saw them whispering and gesticulating. And then the subedar sounded the gong that meant the disqualification of Chirandah Dass.

He'd been beaten in the very moment of victory, and Hirnam Singh's supporters were shouting, waving and flinging flowers. At last silence fell. The Rajah had left his box and come on to the stage.

"The Gods have declared their judgment," the Rajah said. "Chirandah Dass is the guilty one and I sentence him to die in the Pit of Screams."

At midday the sun was very hot. There was a great crowd round the Pit of Screams. The Rajah had declared a holiday.

Because I was a visitor whom he wished to honour, the Rajah invited me to stand beside him. With the crowd pressing behind us we leaned over a low wall and watched the vipers creeping towards the pole in the centre.

Chirandah Dass had climbed almost to the top. As long

as he could cling there he was safe. He was brave although he was little more than a boy, and even when he saw the snakes he did not scream.

"They will mesmerise the Dogra dog until he falls," the Rajah laughed in my ear. "Have a drink, old boy. You won't see anything as amusing as this in Calcutta."

A waiter gave us glasses of brandy mixed with champagne. We leaned far over the wall with our glasses in our hands. The Rajah threw some of the contents of his glass to see if he could splash a viper.

"A libation to the snakes," he cried. "Soon the man will begin to scream and then it will be more funny."

Chirandah Dass didn't scream. He was smiling towards a place a little to our right. I looked to where he was smiling and I saw his wife. Yes, by the Rajah's order she had to watch her husband die.

She sat very still, like a child absorbed by a play. There was no fear or horror in her face. I saw the way they smiled at one another, and I could read her thoughts as if she had spoken them aloud.

"She means to go with him," I thought. "She has poison she will take when the end comes."

We waited. The khitmagar refilled our glasses. I felt a little giddy, as if the snakes were calling me into the Pit of Screams. Chirandah Dass was growing weak. We saw his hands slip; the vipers stiffened in expectation and the crowd surged forward.

He recovered, and again there was silence. We knew the end was near. The Dogra was shivering as a tree shivers just before it falls. Time seemed to stand still. Someone cried, "He's falling!" and a rustle passed over the crowd like wind. His right hand, too numb to hold on any longer, had dropped to his side. His head sank, his body sagged against the pole.

Silence while we held our breath. Then the end came—sudden and sharp as an explosion. A scream such as even the Pit of Screams had never heard; the shadow of a falling body on the sand…

No, it was not Chirandah Dass who had fallen. It was the Rajah, the Lord of Blood himself. In his drunken excitement he had leaned too far over the low wall and had over-balanced.

No one could help him. He alighted unhurt upon the sand, picked himself up and ran screaming like the sadist and coward he was. But the sides of the pit were high and the mottled ones were faster than he. They caught him before he could climb out of the pit and struck him again and again as he lay writhing on the rocks.

They were too busy to pay attention to Chirandah Dass. While they were still clustered round the screaming thing that had been the Lord of Blood, he dropped from the pole and made a dash for safety. He climbed the side of the pit farthest from where the Rajah lay, climbed as far as he could up the wall, and cheering men lifted him to safety and the kisses of his little wife.

In Togarapore to this day they will tell you that the snakes hypnotised the Rajah so that he fell. But what do *you* think?

He was giddy from drink and the sun? Yes, that's another possible explanation. It is bad to drink brandy and champagne at midday. But neither is correct. What really killed the Rajah was a tear running down the cheek of that girl wife.

I was a young man in those days, very strong and with hot blood. When I saw that tear I bent, unnoticed, and jerked his ankles so that he somersaulted like the rat he was into the Pit of Screams.

Hanging by a Hair

Clifford Witting

CLIFFORD WITTING (1907–1968) IS AN AUTHOR whose reputation is currently enjoying a deserved revival after half a century of obscurity. He was working in a bank at the time he wrote an enjoyable first novel, *Murder in Blue* (1937), which demonstrated a facility for light, humorous prose. His agreeable storytelling is especially in evidence in *Midsummer Murder*, his second novel, published in the same year as his debut, which deals with a series of sniper killings in a small English town. *Measure for Murder* (1941), which has a theatrical background, is an example of the way he liked to do something a little different with the conventional detective story. His last book appeared in the year of his death, and he also dabbled in screenwriting; he was responsible for two scripts in the BBC anthology series *Detective*, one based on a Father Brown story and the other on his own novel, *Subject: Murder.*

John Cooper has discussed Witting's books interestingly

in four articles for *CADS*, an irregularly published magazine about detective fiction, which is a mine of information about neglected authors; I am indebted to him for drawing my attention to "Hanging by a Hair." This story features Witting's series detectives Charlton and Bradfield and as far as is known is his only published short detective story. It was originally published on April 19, 1950 in the *Evening Standard*.

BINDWEED... IN HIS BACK GARDEN IN THE LITTLE Downshire town of Paulsfield, Arthur Marstead, B.A., tore more stems away. Bindweed—fragrant and lovely, but twining itself round other plants and choking them to death. Or so he supposed.

He was an historian, not a gardener, and would rather have spent this Saturday afternoon on his new book about Prince Rupert of Bavaria than toiling out there in his shirt-sleeves. But his wife had so decreed—his wife who now sat watching him through the open french windows, with Rufus on her lap.

Funny how the two women in his life both adored cats, yet were in every other way so different; his wife thin-lipped and critical, old before her time; Violet meek and timid, with the insipid prettiness of the girls on the covers of her beloved novelettes.

It was this that had drawn him to Violet Florimer. Had she been less pliable, less of a soft refuge from the eternal nagging of his wife, he might have put an end to the affair before it went too far. But Violet had attached herself to him and clung like—bindweed.

Pausing in his work, he felt for the cigarettes in his trouser pocket, but before he could pull out the packet his wife called to him. Just like her.

He walked towards the house, a tall man in the middle thirties, with a premature stoop, untidy hair, eyes peering through horn-rimmed spectacles, and a general air of absent-minded anxiety. He stepped into the room, to find that his wife had summoned him to close the windows because Rufus had sneezed in his sleep.

On Rufus were lavished the love and care that he himself should have enjoyed. He disliked Rufus—disliked him above all other cats except one, which was Tiggles, Violet's blue Persian. With Rufus the antagonism was mutual and Rufus held aloof, but Tiggles—like Violet—maddened him with cloying attentions.

He closed the french windows as quietly as possible. Yet it brought a reproof. With a vague apology, he went along the passage and back into the garden.

How he hated them—his wife and Rufus, Violet and Tiggles.

He went into the shed at the bottom of the garden to get out the lawn-mower, then remembered that it needed attention. The spanner was on the shelf.

While he was fumbling with the heavy spanner, there came to him a solution to all his difficulties.

Unknowingly, his wife furthered his plans by announcing after tea that she was going to see *Murder in the Cathedral* at Paulsfield's only theatre, the Royal.

She did not invite him to escort her; they had not been out together for over a year.

When she had left the house, he went up to her bedroom.

Her other handbag was on the dressing-table and he took from it all the cash it contained—a pound note and two half-crowns. Not nearly enough, but he might be luckier at Heathview Cottage.

He went along to his own bedroom to pack. He took his suitcase, heavy with books of reference and the Prince Rupert manuscript, down into the hall, where he put on his raincoat before going out to the shed.

On his way back to the house he was spoken to over the fence by Miss Blanch. A nuisance, she was a nosey old woman.

The bus took him from Paulsfield to Lulverton. On the outskirts of Lulverton, standing by itself, was Heathview Cottage, where Violet lived alone.

He left the suitcase at Lulverton station and, with his raincoat now over his arm, walked out to the cottage. He was reasonably certain that nobody saw him go in—and that his departure was also unnoticed.

Back at the station, he was just in time to catch a train to London, where he boarded a north-bound express.

It was Mrs. Webb, the cleaner, who found Violet Florimer's body on the settee in the front room of Heathview Cottage, her skull fractured by heavy blows, delivered, said the police surgeon, from behind.

When Detective-inspector Charlton examined the room with young Detective-sergeant Bradfield, they found some interesting things.

On the carpet was a spanner, its condition leaving no doubt that it had been used for the crime. From the wound, the surgeon extracted some fragments of green paint. On the table was a cash-box, forced open and empty.

On the seat and arms of an easy chair by the window were woollen fibres, some red, the others light brown. In various parts of the room were hairs from a blue Persian cat. The chair by the window bore hairs from a cat of another colour.

"Ginger," said Peter Bradfield. "That's curious."

Charlton looked down at Tiggles. "Yes, very curious."

They might not have got so swiftly on the track of Arthur Marstead had not Mrs. Webb confided in Mrs. Parsons, whom she obliged twice a week. Mrs. Parsons telephoned her sister, Miss Blanch, who went to the police.

Charlton and Bradfield drove from Lulverton to interview her at Paulsfield police station.

"This is very painful for me," said Miss Blanch, enjoying every moment of it, "but yesterday evening, while his wife was at the theatre, Mr. Marstead left home with a heavy suitcase and hasn't come back.

"Poor Violet Florimer! A dear girl, but too easily led."

"Why connect the two things, Miss Blanch?" said Charlton.

"Well, I don't like saying it, but Mr. Marstead has been seeing more of Violet than his wife would approve of if she knew. Yesterday afternoon he was mending his mower with a big spanner, and in the evening, just before he left, he went down to the shed and came back putting something into his pocket."

"Did you see what it was?"

"No, but what else could it have been but the one the charwoman saw on the floor?"

The two detectives called on Mrs. Marstead.

"We understand," said Charlton, "that you're concerned about your husband's absence."

She hesitated, then said:

"It is worrying. Yesterday evening I went to the Royal. My husband doesn't like mystery thrillers, so he didn't come. When I got home afterwards, he wasn't in, but I thought he'd gone for a walk, so went to bed. This morning he was still missing—and so was his suitcase."

"He didn't leave a note?"

She shook her head.

"Would you say he had much money on him?"

"No, because he took some of mine—out of my other bag. A pound note and some silver."

"It might not have been your husband who took the money. Do you mind if I have the bag tested for fingerprints? I shan't need the other things."

Next morning the Leicester police called at a boarding-house in that city, and within the hour Arthur Marstead was on his way back to Lulverton.

"Mr. Marstead," Charlton began, "you're not obliged to say anything, but if you do, it may be given in evidence."

"I don't know what it's all about, but fire away."

"I believe I'm right in saying that on Saturday evening you called on Miss Violet Florimer. Was that so?"

"It certainly wasn't."

"You were good enough to let us examine your suit. On the right trouser-leg there were hairs from a blue Persian cat."

"What of it?"

"Miss Florimer's cat is a blue Persian."

Charlton went off on another tack.

"We've seen your wife, sir. She says you—er—borrowed money before you left."

"Quite so. I was hard up."

"When you booked your room in Leicester, you paid in advance with new ten-shilling notes. Where did you get them?"

"I told you—from my wife."

"But I gather from her that there was only a pound note and some silver involved."

"What are you getting at?"

"Did you take the money from Miss Florimer?"

"No, definitely not."

"I've been in touch with Miss Florimer's bank here. On Saturday morning she drew a considerable sum in new ten-shilling notes. On one of these the cashier had written a number in red. The same number, also in red, appears on one of the notes with which you paid for your room.

"I don't know whether you realise your position, Mr. Marstead. Murder is—"

"*Murder?* For God's sake, who?"

"Miss Florimer."

"You're mad! She's not dead! She can't be!"

"She was found yesterday morning with a fractured skull."

Marstead jumped to his feet.

"Are you suggesting I did it?"

"I'm suggesting nothing, sir. I'm trying to find out how it happened. Please sit down."

Marstead obeyed.

"Sorry for the outburst," he smiled wryly. "I'd better tell you the whole truth. For some time past Violet Florimer and I have been lovers. On Saturday evening I decided to leave my wife for good, so I packed my things and came to Lulverton to tell Miss Florimer what I proposed to do.

"My idea was that she should follow me to Leicester in a week or two, which would give my wife grounds for divorce."

"How did Miss Florimer receive your suggestion?"

"She wasn't there."

"So what did you do?"

"The back door was unlocked. I went in and sat down to wait."

"Where did you sit?"

"In the chair on the window side of the fireplace."

"Please go on."

"I wanted to be well away before my wife came home, so after about 20 minutes I decided to drop Miss Florimer a line from Leicester.

"This is where I come to the awkward part. You see, I needed money badly and I couldn't wait for Miss Florimer, so I—well, I broke open her cash-box. I was going to pay it back, of course."

Charlton looked at him.

"Mr. Marstead, your story about waiting for Miss Florimer is untrue. You did *not* sit in the chair you mention. The seat was covered with hairs from a blue Persian cat, and the only traces on your clothes were on the trouser-leg."

Marstead tried to speak.

"And *your* finger-prints were found on the spanner used for the crime."

"Spanner?"

"Yes, the one from your shed."

The man seemed stunned.

"No," he muttered half to himself. "No, not that."

Alone in the office with his chief, Bradfield said:

"Looks a clear case, sir."

"Yes, Peter," Charlton agreed, rising to his feet, "there's not much doubt. Let's have another word with the wife."

Mrs. Marstead's tone was sharp when she greeted them.

"Why didn't you tell me about the murder?" she demanded.

"I didn't want to distress you. I'm sorry to disturb you again, but have you a cat?"

"What a ridiculous question! Yes, we have."

She raised her voice to call:

"Rufus!"

In leisurely response, a marmalade cat sauntered out.

"See for yourselves," she said. "Why did you want to know?"

"Miss Florimer's murderer brought hairs from a cat of that colour into Heathview Cottage."

"My husband?"

"No, madam. I've reason to think it was you."

Sergeant Bradfield had to wait till next day for an explanation.

"Peter," smiled Charlton, "have you ever seen *Murder in the Cathedral*?"

"T. S. Eliot, isn't it?"

"Yes—all about Thomas Becket. Would you call it a mystery thriller?"

"Scarcely."

"Mrs. Marstead did, which proves she hadn't seen it. No, she spied on her husband instead. After he'd left for the cottage, she went home and got the spanner from the shed. Whether she intended then to murder Miss Florimer, we don't know, but she took it to the cottage in her large handbag."

"Can we prove that?"

"You know the green paint we found in the wound and on the spanner? It came off Marstead's lawn-mower, and there were some tiny traces of it in the handbag. That's why I took it away, for testing at the labs.

"Marstead wanted freedom from both women. He went to the cottage for the sole purpose of getting money.

"If Miss Florimer had been there, he would have tried to borrow it; as she wasn't, he saw his chance and pinched it."

"And Mrs. Marstead?"

"Miss Florimer was home again by the time she called. I'd say the two women talked for a while, Miss Florimer on the settee, and Mrs. Marstead in the chair by the window.

"At some point in the conversation Mrs. Marstead must have gone behind Miss Florimer, then killed her, with the spanner held in her gloved hand. She gambled on her husband being blamed."

"Pleasant type. How did you arrive at all this, sir?"

"From the chair by the window, we removed hairs from two cats—ginger and blue Persian. There were no ginger hairs on Marstead's clothes, but there were plenty on his wife's—ginger *and* blue Persian.

"Also, the woollen fibres we found on the chair were identical with Mrs. Marstead's tweed coat.

The Man Who
Shot Birds

Mary Fitt

MARY FITT WAS THE PRINCIPAL PEN-NAME OF A DIS-
tinguished classical scholar, Kathleen Freeman (1897–
1959), who lectured in Greek for many years. She was born
in Birmingham, but the family moved to Cardiff in 1911,
and she remained in Wales. Her first published work, in
1926, was *The Work and Life of Solon, with a translation of
his poems*, while her post-war publications included *The
Pre-Socratic Philosophers; a companion to Diels* and *The
Philoctetes of Sophocles, a modern version*. In her spare time,
she wrote poetry, children's fiction, mainstream novels, and
a study of Jane Austen, but it is as a detective novelist that
she is best remembered, her first mystery, *Murder Mars the
Tour*, appearing in 1936.

Her principal series character, a police officer called
Mallett, is mentioned in this story. Although he is rather
colourless, Fitt's writing has a distinctive quality, with
plenty of unorthodox touches, sometimes verging on the

eccentric. As a result, her work is interesting but inconsistent. Even when the setting—as in the country house milieu of *Death at Heron's Mere* (1941)—is conventional, she liked to try to do something a little different, and her ambition as a writer was recognised by her election to membership of the Detection Club in 1950. This is the title story from a collection first published in 1954.

—————

1

"Curiously enough," said Dr. Manners, "I know a story in which the detection of a murder turned on the behaviour of a bird: in this instance a jackdaw."

"Really?" said Mr. Pitt with interest. "Do tell me: I can believe anything of jackdaws. If I hadn't got Georgina I think I might have liked a jackdaw as a pet—and they are among the few birds that seem to enjoy domesticity."

"So I've heard," said Dr. Manners. "But I have no personal experience. This story was told me by Fitzbrown—in fact it happened to him, and I came in at the very end. You know Fitzbrown? He practises in the country outside Chode."

"Yes, I've met him," said Mr. Pitt. "He works a good deal with Mallett, doesn't he?"

Manners nodded:

"A very decent chap: abnormally clever in some ways. We were students together at Broxeter. This little adventure happened during our student days. But I say: why don't we get him to tell the story himself? How would it be if I fixed up a meeting—a dinner at my house, or his?"

"I should enjoy it," said Mr. Pitt.

It was soon arranged that Dr. Manners should drive Mr. Pitt over to Chode one evening to dine with Dr. Fitzbrown. Superintendent Mallett was also to be one of the party, and Fitzbrown insisted that if he told his story of the jackdaw the others should each contribute a story too, however short, derived from their own experience.

2

YES (SAID DR. FITZBROWN OVER THE BRANDY AND cigars), this story is perfectly true. It was my first direct contact with crime, though I did not know this till later.

I was a fourth-year medical student at Broxeter, working very hard and not inclined to pay much attention to anything that was going on around me unless it was physically abnormal. I couldn't even play games because of a bad heart due to rheumatic fever, and I was therefore rather a morose individual at the time. My nature is sociable, and I resented the cut in my activities. So for that winter and spring, rather than see the other fellows having a good time, I moved out of Broxeter to Bugle Head. I thought I'd like to be near the sea, and as it's only four miles out I could easily travel to and fro by train.

I found a furnished flat at the top of a tall old house at the far end of the town, quite near the railway halt and also near the sea; in fact I could see the sea through a gap in the houses opposite. From the back windows of my flat I could see across the railway line to the fields and a hill, on the slope of which was a church with a cemetery, and at the very top a cluster of pines forming a rookery.

Here I spent the loneliest winter of my life, refusing all invitations and thereby earning a reputation for having gone a little queer—but as I couldn't manage both work and play I had no choice, and of course I wanted to get fit again as quickly as possible. So I kept to the sober grind, catching the morning train at the halt, coming back in the evening, and for exercise I took walks along the cliff or across the fields to the cemetery. You may not believe it, but I was rather cemetery-minded in those days.

During the winter months I usually walked along the cliff. But as spring came on and trippers began to appear I found myself wanting to turn inland across the railway line to the fields. One could not be quite sure of avoiding trippers even here, because in the cemetery on the hill there happened to be the sort of thing they love—namely a grandiose, newly-made tomb. And when I tell you that this monument, a huge affair in polished grey granite, had been erected by his wife to a man who twelve months before had been murdered, you can well understand what an attraction it was to the day-visitors and how it always had its little cluster of admirers.

You remember the case, Mallett, though it was before you came here: the chap was a millionaire, one of those bogus shipowners who bought and sold ships on paper during the '14–18 war. He got rich suddenly and died before his money melted away—as you may remember, he was hit on the head by a burglar in his own house; and at the time I'm speaking of, the thug who killed him was still uncaught.

There was no mystery about the actual killing: it was simply the consequence of an interrupted burglary. This millionaire-chap—what was his name? Oh yes, I remember: Reuben-Smith, John Reuben-Smith: the hyphen came after he won his millions—this Reuben-Smith inhabited an enormous house on the cliff overlooking the sea, with his wife and such servants as they could get from time to time by outbidding their neighbours. His wife was a handsome purse-proud blonde, whose one idea was that Reuben-Smith should cover her with jewels; and since she was a walking advertisement designed to tempt burglars, they were burgled. Reuben-Smith had his head smashed in, and many of the jewels were removed, including a diamond star consisting of forty-nine stones—seven clusters of seven—each worth at least a hundred pounds.

I was not interested in the tomb; and when on a May evening I saw the usual small group gathered round it with children swinging on the aluminium-painted chains, I made a detour towards the pine plantation, from which one got a fine view of the Channel and the coastline. As I climbed the gentle slope towards the knoll I heard a shot: this was followed by a puff of smoke coming from the farther side. Down from one of the pine-trees there fell at my feet a dead rook, and a moment later a man with a shot-gun appeared.

He did not look like a farmer. He wore a mackintosh, though the weather was warm, and a trilby hat pulled down, and the usual cigarette drooped from his lips. I was irritated with him for disturbing the peace of the evening by remind-ing me of what I lived with—death—and surely there is nothing so pathetic as a dead bird?

He came towards me. When he reached me I said:

"Were you bound to do that?"

He answered in the most debased form of our language, a sort of Cockney-American which this type seems to con-sider a proof of smartness:

"So what? I don't have to ask *you*, I reckon."

"I suppose not," I said, "if you have a gun licence. But

can't you do your potting somewhere else, or at some other target? Don't you realise the birds are nesting now?"

He scowled at me. He was a thick-set fellow, shorter than myself and about ten years older, and I wondered if I should knock him down and get it over before *he* hit *me*. But he merely said:

"I guess I can shoot a bloody jackdaw if I want to." And he bent down to pick up the bloodstained bird.

"That's not a jackdaw," I said contemptuously. "That's a rook."

He dropped the bird, which he had been swinging by the legs, and stared with what looked like real concern:

"Rook, is it? What's the difference?"

"Quite a lot," I said, "but I can't stop to teach you ornithology." And I left him.

When I reached the top of the knoll and turned I saw him already at the bottom, making across the fields towards the railway line.

3

A COUPLE OF WEEKS PASSED BEFORE I CLIMBED THE hill again, but meanwhile I had seen the man who shot birds several times. He lived—had rooms, I discovered later—in one of the small houses in the row facing the railway line; their backs abutted on the backs of the houses in the more pompous road where I lived, and from the back windows of my flat I looked down on their tiny back gardens. One day I saw this chap walk down the path, which was about twelve yards long, and throw something into the dustbin: it was the body of a blackbird. As he replaced the lid he looked up and saw me. He gave me what no doubt he would have called a dirty look. I also saw him a couple of times catching the train at the halt nearby. He cast me a furtive glance, but I avoided him. I could not have borne to sit in the same carriage with him, much less run the risk of having him beside me. I had conceived an intense loathing for him.

Then on a June evening a strange thing happened.

I was sitting at a table in the front room of my flat when—just like Edgar Allan Poe—I heard a tapping: but it was on one of the window-panes, not on my door. I looked up, startled. Then I laughed. My visitor was a jackdaw.

I opened the window and let him in, delighted to be so honoured. He hopped in, first on to my shoulder, then on to the table, where he strutted about importantly, examining everything with attentive eye and occasionally with sharp beak. I brought him some food, which he accepted. Then he set out to explore the rest of the room, and in fact the rest of the flat, while I returned to my books.

I forgot about him.

When I went to bed at two a.m. I never gave him a thought. It was therefore a surprise to wake up and find him roosting on the end of my bed—and there were signs of his presence which I did not think would amuse the woman who came in to get my breakfast and clean. So I ventured to show him politely to the open window, at first with feeble cries of "Shoo!"—feeble because I didn't want to offend him permanently—and then with gesticulation, and finally, when this merely caused him to ruffle his feathers without stirring, I tried to take hold of him.

He pecked me severely. It was only after I had put on a leather gauntlet-glove that I was able to carry him to the window, and when I had put him out he flew in again. I had to catch him, put him out again—ignoring his indignant "Tchak!"—and firmly close the window. Even then he stalked up and down on the window-sill, angrily trying the window frame and the glass with his beak. At last, defeated, he flew off, and I saw him disappear head first down the highest chimney of the large house next to mine, which happened at that time to be only partly occupied.

Next day he came again, in the evening. This time he got into the kitchen through the open window, and had eaten most of my supper, set out for me on a tray by the maid, before I heard him. When I appeared in the kitchen doorway he greeted me with a joyous "Tchak!", flew on to my shoulder, and began nibbling the lobe of my ear. It was clear that he was not easily offended.

When the nibbling became painful and I was forced to get my gauntlet-glove and remove him, he flew on to the sitting-room mantelpiece beside the black marble clock and stood coolly looking at me from the top of the pediment: the clockcase was shaped like the maker's idea of the Parthenon.

I decided to go on with my work until bedtime. Then I'd put him out. I was too busy to bother just now, and, anyway, I was getting fond of him.

There was peace for about five minutes. Then a tearing sound roused me from a consideration of the central nervous system. The jackdaw was busily removing the beads off the mantelpiece cover.

Now he was welcome to the beads so far as I was concerned, but the furnished flat I rented belonged to an old lady who lived on the ground floor, and she had a great regard for her possessions. I knew she regularly made tours of inspection when I was out, and I didn't want to have to buy her a new mantelpiece cover, so it seemed to me that the time had again come to persuade my guest to leave.

He watched me warily as I approached. He knew what was coming. When I was within arm's length he gave a malicious "Tchak!", flew past me, snatched up a red pencil from the table, flew out at the door and through one of the back windows—and I saw him disappear down his chimney-pot, carrying my red pencil no doubt to an admiring wife and family.

I was still standing there laughing when I looked down and saw the man who had shot the rook and the blackbird. He had seen the whole incident. He was staring up at the chimney with his gun in his hands—he had been sitting on a chair in his back garden cleaning the gun—and although it was still pointing to the ground, I could tell from his attitude that he had the greatest difficulty in refraining from risking a shot. When he caught sight of me looking down at him from my window he gave me a malevolent look, sat down again slowly, and began polishing his gun again.

4

What was I to do?

Below me lived this man who for some reason wanted to shoot jackdaws—for I was convinced that he had mistaken the blackbird, too, for a jackdaw, as he had mistaken the rook: his dismay about the rook showed *that*. I had taken a dislike to him over the rook; I loathed him because of the blackbird; but now I was really concerned. I did not want him to kill "my" jackdaw, as I called my rather difficult guest. Yet what could I do? If I said anything to the man with the gun, he'd probably shoot Jack out of spite. But how could I

warn Jack? This business of the impossibility of communi-
cation between man and the animals can be very frustrating.

I could only hope that the gunman wouldn't risk a shot
so close to houses, and that he'd remain satisfied with the
rookery. Yet now, when I walked to the top of the hill,
the gunman was never there—and he *was* watching that
chimney-pot. Evening after evening I saw him sitting there
cleaning his gun and watching. Somebody must have told
him that the bird who lived there really was a jackdaw—and
he had some complex about jackdaws.

5

Meanwhile, Jack continued to visit me.

Unaware of danger, he came every evening. He walked
round, ate some supper, pulled a few beads, spangles or tas-
sels off my landlady's furniture, sat on my shoulder, nibbled
my ear-lobes and generally made himself at home. I had
resigned myself to cleaning up after him.

Then he began "collecting" again: I won't say "stealing,"
for how could his bird's brain recognise the human distinc-
tion of "mine" and "thine"?

I had hidden everything bright that could attract his eye.
Having stripped all the beads off the mantelpiece cover, he
had to search quite hard, and I thought I had thwarted him
until one evening when I had carelessly left a shilling on a
side-table for the gas-meter. It was a bright new shilling.
We made a simultaneous dive for it—I saw his intention—
but I was a second too late. He actually wrenched it from
my fingers, and away he went with this new bauble to his
chimney-pot. I watched anxiously, my chief concern being
that he should get away with it.

He did.

Then the matter became serious.

Within a week he had "collected" two thermometers, one cuff-link, several collar-studs, a paper-weight—all without any great value, though it was inconvenient to lose them. His nest, I thought, must look like a junk-shop. But I hadn't the heart to keep the windows shut in case that swine of a gunman should get him. Besides, the weather was very warm.

But things didn't come to a head until he took my gold watch.

This watch had belonged to my mother. It was set in diamonds, and I always carried it in a special pocket which I had had made for it in all my jackets. I valued it greatly, not so much because it was valuable in itself, but because it had been my mother's, and she had died only a year before.

6

I DIDN'T KNOW WHAT TO DO.

I had to get that watch back somehow. Yet I didn't want to call in outside help. If I did, it would mean that Jack and his family would be smoked out or pushed out with a sweep's brush, their nest destroyed and possibly themselves also. And there was always the malignant gunman waiting for his opportunity. Nobody would stop him now if he shot down the marauding bird: in fact he'd be regarded as a public benefactor.

I decided to go about things in my own way.

I did nothing that evening. Next morning on some pretext I went downstairs and had a talk with my landlady, old Mrs. Coakley.

"Oh, by the way," I said, when I had paid my rent and admired her budgerigar, "that house on the corner—the house next to this on the southward side—does anyone live in it?"

She told me that it had been made into flats like her own, but not all of them were taken, because the rents were too high. She assured me I wouldn't care for those flats at all, and she gave me many reasons.

I assured her in my turn that I had no intention of moving. I had merely wondered if the house was unoccupied, as I had never seen anyone coming in and out. I added very tentatively that one never even saw smoke coming out of the chimneys, and in some of these the birds seemed to be nesting.

She caught my drift at once.

"You're thinking of the jackdaws," she said. "Yes: I ought to have warned you. They're getting to be a great nuisance—at least, one of them is. People round here are complaining. He *takes* things. I hope you don't let him in at all. He is very destructive." She gave me a sharp look with her beady eyes. Beads! Good lord! I was reminded of the mantelpiece cover, and my courage failed me.

"Oh no," I said hastily, "of course not. I just wondered."

"He is a *tame* jackdaw, you see," said Mrs. Coakley. "He used to belong to an old couple who lived in that house before it was turned into flats. So every year he comes back to that same chimney. But something will have to be done about it if there's any further trouble."

"Oh, no trouble at all as far as I'm concerned," I said. "I merely mentioned the matter at random." But I could see she didn't believe me. I had done what I least had wanted to do: I had put ideas into her head. The next thing would be she'd be telling the other flat-owner to call in the sweep...

I went away, hoping she'd forget.

7

IT WAS THEREFORE CLEARER THAN EVER THAT NO ONE must be told about the loss of my gold watch. I must try to recover it myself without attracting any attention.

I studied the layout carefully and came to the conclusion that the best plan would be to climb over the roofs to that chimney after dark and try to take a look inside. Perhaps by using a fishing-rod and a strong hook, as I'd read that professional thieves do, I might be able to retrieve the watch if only I could see it—and I might be able to see it with the help of a torch.

I could not make the attempt until after dark, and as it was June I had a long time to wait. I spent the evening making my preparations: deciding on the right clothes, a dark suit, cycling clips, rubber-soled shoes, dark gloves, a piece of burnt cork to rub over my face; choosing a suitable fish-hook and line. Among the books on my shelves there was one on criminal investigation: this suggested that the professional used a fish-hook on a thread, so I decided to do the same. The writer added that such a possession found on the person of a suspect was always damning... Well, I had to take that risk. Few men can have been called upon to steal back their own property from a jackdaw.

After midnight I started out. The night was not perfectly dark—there was a luminosity in the sky which I didn't care for—but still, if no one were watching, I doubted if I would be seen. I climbed out through the skylight in my bathroom and began the journey.

I was not used to roof-climbing, and it took me some while to reach the chimney. It was a high one, but luckily I was able to look down it by standing precariously on an ornamental stone coping that surrounded the roof. I was excited. Drawing out my torch and my string with the fish-hook, I stood on tiptoe on the coping and peered down into the chimney...

There was a rustling and a faint "Tchak!" as my light shone down... But I could make out nothing distinctly.

What to do next? I did not know. I called out "Jack! Jack!" idiotically, hoping he'd leave the nest and give me a chance to try my fishing-line... But nothing happened. I must have made a fine target now, against the far-from-velvet-black sky...

As I stood poised there, wondering if I could drop something in to rouse the occupants, the problem was solved for me. I heard a shot. I felt a sharp pain in my leg. I lost my grip on the chimney—my other foot gave way—and I fell...

8

WHEN I WOKE UP THERE WAS A DETECTIVE-SERGEANT beside my bed. No bones were broken: I had fallen on to a compost heap. The only trouble was the shot in my leg, which had been removed. And now explanations were demanded.

I gave them. There was no help for it. I assure you I felt like the basest of traitors as I told my story, because I knew I was buying my exculpation at the expense of poor Jack—Jack who had honoured me with his rather formidable friendship. Of course I was not believed. The police could not believe that a man with his face blackened and carrying a fishing-line with hook, creeping across roofs in the middle of the night, was merely birds'-nesting. The most charitable explanation was the rumour going round the medical school that I was mad, and it was pointed out that I had become very queer and morose since my illness... Bob Jones, who was house-surgeon at the time, will tell you my temperature went up on every occasion I was questioned and that I talked in my sleep. But what I said he never would tell me.

Well, of course, the police went to the house where Jack lived and got the nest down with a sweep's brush, as I had expected. They didn't find any young birds, but they did find a huge treasure: not only my gold watch but lots of other things belonging to the neighbours—and at the bottom of the pile of sticks lay the diamond star that had been stolen from Mrs. Reuben-Smith when her husband had been murdered by the burglar.

Meanwhile they had got hold of the man who had potted at me and questioned him. His story was straightforward enough. His name was Gallon, he said: he worked at a greyhound racing track in Broxeter. He had lived in various big towns doing odd jobs of this sort and had come to Broxeter about three years ago. After a year or so he had moved out to Bugle Head, staying in various rooms, and finally in Railway Terrace: liked a bit of country life, fishing and shooting. Had been brought up on a farm...

Asked why he shot at me, he said he happened to look out of his window and saw a man creeping across the roofs: assumed he was a cat-burglar about to break into the house on the corner. The whole neighbourhood was on the alert for burglars since Mr. Reuben-Smith had been murdered: thought he'd better make sure *this* guy didn't get away.

When they told me this story I said:

"The man's a liar."

They asked me why.

"Pooh!" I said, happy to be able to scoff at *them* for a change. "Brought up on a farm, was he?—and he didn't know a rook from a jackdaw!" I went on to tell them of my first encounter with Gallon.

9

BY NOW THEY HAD THOROUGHLY COMBED THE CHIM-ney, had got down every stick of poor Jack's nest, and made a list of the stolen property. It wasn't all there. Jack was not there either, and one of the policemen who saw him hovering round the next day said he went off finally in the direction of the cemetery. I was relieved: I knew that in the breeding-season jackdaws often join up with rooks, so I assumed that he'd got his real nest up there and was simply using the chimney-pot nest as a store-room. But I didn't pass on this bit of knowledge.

The star with the forty-nine diamonds was identified by Mrs. Reuben-Smith: it was discoloured with soot and was entangled in some thread which had originally been gilt, the experts decided, of the kind sometimes used in embroidery. There were lots of other things, beads and spangles and so on, which had been pulled off coverlets and cushions, but naturally there was not much point in trying to find the owners of all these bits and pieces, or so they thought. However, the police did put out a request that anyone living in the neighbourhood who had missed anything from their homes should communicate with them and claim the missing articles: and when one day a landlady from the sea-front came along and said she'd missed some small glass ornaments from her mantelpiece, they didn't think anything of it until she happened to remark:

"And that dratted bird pulled every scrap of gold thread off the mantelpiece cover—would you believe it? And he stole things from the lodgers as well."

They showed her the thread tangled round Mrs. Reuben-Smith's jewel and asked if that could be it. She said yes, it could. They had cleaned it up so that the gilt showed in places, and when she brought along the mantelpiece cover and they examined it they found enough of the thread still clinging to the underside to prove that the thread stolen by Jack was the same.

The question then arose, how did the jewel and the thread get together?

At first it seemed easiest to suppose that Jack had stolen the jewel and the thread at different times and that they'd got mixed up in his rather untidy nest. Then it struck one of the detectives—pardon me, Mallett: this was, as we all know, before you arrived—that the jewel could have been stolen by the burglar before Jack got it, so that Jack had "collected" it not from the Reuben-Smiths but from the burglar.

So they questioned this landlady about her lodgers for the past two years, and when they'd correlated their information they found that the man staying there when the burglary at the Reuben-Smiths occurred was Gallon—Gallon the gunman—the man who shot birds.

10

THIS WASN'T ENOUGH TO HANG GALLON ON, OF course. But I had now come to life again, and this time they had to listen to me. I reminded them of how I had encountered Gallon taking pot shots at the rookery, and I gave it as my opinion that he was the burglar and doubtless the murderer of Reuben-Smith: that he had taken the digs on the sea-front for the express purpose of studying the Reuben-Smiths' house and the movements of the inhabitants, planning the burglary long in advance as professionals do; that he had got away with it and had brought the jewels home, only to have the most valuable of them stolen from him by my friend Jack. How Jack got the opportunity was a matter of conjecture. I should guess that he was already in the room when Gallon returned—roosting after his arduous labours pulling the gilt thread off the mantelpiece cover—and that Gallon didn't see him. Then, when Gallon was taking a last look at his swag, Jack swooped, picked out the most conspicuous object and was gone before Gallon could stop him. Jack was quite capable, as I knew from experience, of wrenching something he coveted out of one's very hand.

After a discreet interval Gallon changed his digs to Railway Terrace, so that he could walk across the fields and do a bit of shooting. He knew that his best piece of loot, worth at least five thousand pounds, had been pinched by a sort of black bird. He also knew from the landlady, who missed her glass ornaments and the gilt thread, that the marauder was a jackdaw. Now he didn't know a jackdaw when he saw one, and he was too stupid to get a book and find out what they were like; but he had been told that there were jackdaws on the hill-top, nesting up there with the rooks on the pine-trees. So he used to go up there and pop at the nests, in the hope of bringing the right one down and getting back the diamond star while no one was looking.

Then when I came he got suspicious.

He saw me looking down from my window and he thought he was being watched. He was convinced of it after our meeting on the hill when I spoke to him about killing rooks: he thought I had been detailed to follow him. So *he* began watching *me*.

And it was through watching me that he sighted Jack and his chimney-pot. So he stopped haunting the rookery and kept his eye on the chimney instead. But he was afraid to climb up there in case I or anyone else spotted him, and he couldn't risk a shot among the houses: he didn't dare draw attention to himself, especially with me there.

However, when one night he looked out and saw a cat-burglar—me—creeping over the roofs towards that chimney, he thought the cache was discovered. I could be a detective—but also I could be a fellow-burglar trying to forestall him. Anyway, he couldn't bear it any longer. He shot.

11

EVEN SO, I DOUBT WHETHER THEY COULD HAVE PINNED it on to him without further evidence. A jury would never have accepted such a story, especially on the testimony of a crazy medical student: a clever lawyer could easily have poured ridicule on the idea that there was any connection other than coincidence between these different facts.

But there was one more trifle—or rather there were two—which cooked Gallon's goose. These trifles were discovered by the Broxeter Forensic Laboratory. The diamond star belonging to Mrs. Reuben-Smith was in the form of a brooch, the sort that women pin into the lapels of their coats: costume-jewellery, I believe it's called. Well, when the chemists had cleaned all the soot off the diamonds and their setting, they found a thread of cloth still clinging to the hinge and with it a greyhound's hair. When they searched Gallon's wardrobe they found the corresponding jacket, greyhound's hairs and all. He must have pinned the brooch in his own jacket for a moment at some time during his proceedings, and that gave him away.

12

I don't know what happened to Jack and his family. The odd thing was, when this adventure was over I found myself completely cured—I suppose because of the long rest—and I was able to leave Bugle Head for good. Neither I nor anyone else, so far as I know, saw Jack in the neighbourhood again after the destruction of his treasure-nest. But one evening at the end of June, shortly before I left, I took a last walk up to the rookery, and on the ground under one of the tallest pines I found a broken thermometer.

Death in a Cage

Josephine Bell

JOSEPHINE BELL WAS THE CRIME-WRITING ALIAS OF Doris Bell Collier (1897–1987), a Cambridge graduate who became a qualified doctor before (like Arthur Conan Doyle) turning to crime. She published her first novel, *Murder in Hospital,* in 1937, and produced books steadily for the next forty-five years. *The Port of London Murders* (1938) has been published as a British Library Crime Classic. Her principal series character was Dr. David Wintringham, and her stories (including this one) frequently make effective use of her medical expertise.

Zoos have provided several crime writers with an exotic setting for murderous deeds. Freeman Wills Crofts' *Antidote to Venom,* originally published in 1938 and reprinted by the British Library in the Crime Classics series, is a notable example, as are John Dickson Carr's *He Wouldn't Kill Patience* (1941) and Ethel Lina White's *The Man Who Loved Lions,* aka *The Man Who Was Not There*

(1943). This story featured in *Choice of Weapons*, a Crime Writers' Association anthology edited by Michael Gilbert and published in 1958. Wintringham appears, but he was reaching the end of his career as an amateur sleuth. *The Seeing Eye*, published in the same year, marked his swan song in novel-length mysteries.

THE FOG THAT NOVEMBER NIGHT WAS THICKEST IN Central and North London. Cars in the Mall, edging blindly about the wide roadway near Buckingham Palace, came to a standstill where the kerbs gave them no help. Queues of traffic formed behind drivers who, mistaking a gap in the pavement for Birdcage Walk, had jammed themselves against the railings. A slow procession moved round Hyde Park. In Knightsbridge the buses went head to tail, scarcely moving.

Further north the fog lay thick upon Regent's Park. The canal was invisible even from the bridges over it. No cars came into the circles of this Park, because the street lamps there are set too far apart to be much use in fog. The unaccustomed absence of traffic joined with the blanket of fog to still all noise. Under the trees the gentle fall of drops from the branches above was startlingly loud.

The constable on duty near the main entrance to the Zoo felt his way along the railings to the turnstiles, moved slowly across the recess where they stand, and found his way to the railings on the other side. He wondered what the animals thought of the fog, especially those poor blighters accustomed to tropical sunlight and dry hot desert lands. They must be taking a poor view of this damp, choking, blinding world, that was capable of seeping through closed doors and windows, as he knew very well, having only recently come on duty from a Station where you could barely see across the width of the charge room.

As if in answer to his thoughts, he had no sooner left the Zoo entrance behind him than a commotion broke out within its enclosure. The night was suddenly filled with shrill noise, splitting the fog, beating in his ears, startling him with its unexpected hysteria.

"Damned senseless brutes!" he thought, furiously, realising at once that the sounds came from the Monkey House, not far away inside the gate.

All his sympathy for suffering dumb animals, oppressed by alien fog, evaporated. He was frightened, and he resented it bitterly. Coming at him, as it had, in his isolated blindness, the fear was unreasonably strong. Suppose something was loose in there? A tiger, a bear, something of that sort. It would be likely to upset the monkeys; it might be after them. It might be anywhere. It might soon be after him!

He stood still, pulling himself together, telling himself not to be a darned fool. He expected the clamour to die away as quickly as it had begun. But it did not do so; if anything it increased in volume and variety.

Screams and cries and chatterings, some half human, some frankly animal, still rent the fog. The constable felt his way back to the turnstiles, and finding them all securely locked, and the gates closed, shouted aloud, to discover if there was anyone about the place.

An answering call came from within the Gardens. Evidently a night watchman was on his way. He shouted that he was going into the Monkey House to see what was the matter.

The constable waited, hearing the noises rise and fall

several times before they died away to an occasional excited scream. Presently the night watchman came over to the barrier.

"Nothing doing," he said, cheerfully.

"Got the jitters, have they, like me? I don't blame them. There's something about the fog at night…"

"They're upset, all right," went on the night watchman. "Jumping round their cages, and that. It's not the fog. The fog doesn't get in there; not to speak of. You see, half of the big ones are behind glass to keep them from catching colds off the public. But they're upset, proper. No one about. None of them injured. No signs of them fighting, which they do, sometimes. I've known them set on one, in the big cages, and nearly worry the life out of the poor little beggar. But no signs of that. Just banging round their cages, the lot of them. I dunno."

"Well, they seem to have got over it, now," said the constable, "judging by the noise."

The night watchman listened.

"More or less," he agreed.

They parted on that, each disappearing from the other's sight when he had taken only three steps on his way. The night watchman went round the outside of the Monkey House several times during the rest of his spell of duty, but there was no further disturbance.

Early the next morning, in a damp mist following the fog of the night before, a keeper taking meat to the birds of prey met a sight that haunted his disturbed nights for many weeks.

Most of his charges, as he passed behind their cage,

looked round at him from their perches, ready to fly down when the food was delivered.

But in the vultures' cage a different order obtained. The three birds were all on the ground, gathered about an object at which they plucked and tore. It looked at first sight like a bundle of old sacking, but the keeper was not long deceived. There was blood on the rags, and it did not take him more than a few seconds to realise, in a moment of horror, that the vultures' meal was, or rather had been, a man.

Assistance came, the birds were driven off and moved to another cage, the police took down the meagre facts and began their enquiries.

The evening papers gave this unique sensation priority over the growing list of fog-caused road accidents. An early headline, "Man loses death fight with giant birds," was hastily discarded when someone remembered that the vulture never attacks the living, but waits for its prey to die before it comes down to feed. Therefore the unknown man must have died in the cage, or been brought into it a corpse.

And there, for a few days, the matter rested. For information was very scarce, and the police had nothing to give away. They had made no progress whatever.

In the first place, they had not identified the dead man. The vultures, being well-cared-for birds, had not actually consumed a great deal of him, but they had made recognition difficult. However, with their usual thoroughness, the police did manage, before the inquest, to decide who he had been. A tramp, recognised vaguely by his clothes, and general build, who had given trouble, in the Park, sleeping out, the summer before, and had been noticed from time to time since, by various constables in the district.

At the inquest other facts of his physical condition came

out. He had been a man of between thirty and forty, under-nourished, emaciated, his lungs full of the cavities and scars of advanced, untreated, tuberculosis.

The coroner, accepting the orthodox account of the habits of vultures, found for natural causes. There was no suggestion of foul play, no wounds, other than the post-mortem mutilations made by the birds, and enough physical disease to have brought about death from inanition and exposure on such a night. Perhaps terror at the discovery of his whereabouts; the sight, through the fog, of those hard eyes and predatory beaks, and obscene necks, had brought on the haemoptysis that appeared to have been the imme-diate cause of death. He must have died there, in the cage, under the watching eyes of his dreadful companions, too weak even to cry out for help.

It was recalled that the night had been unusually foggy. Perhaps the wretched man had been seeking shelter in the Zoo, had stumbled into this cage by mistake. The question of unlocked doors was brought up, argued over, and left unsolved. No keys had been missed, the place had been found locked in the morning, with the exception of the vul-tures' outer cage itself.

And with this anti-climax of a verdict, the sensation itself died a rapid and natural death. Only a few visitors to the Zoo, from that time on, noticed that a baby gorilla, whose birth had been much publicised a couple of months before, was no longer to be seen with its mother, in the cage they had occupied together. The keeper, when asked, was ret-icent. Most animals were shy, he said, and did not always care to show themselves.

But behind the scenes there had been great agitation. For the mother gorilla and her child were not, in fact, hiding themselves from the public gaze. The adult animal, for seven days, had been savage, and utterly unmanageable. The baby had disappeared. Bloodstains had been noticed on the floor of the cage, and a strip of black fur, looking as if it had been torn from the baby gorilla's back, had been recovered near the door of the cage at feeding time. But no detailed search had been possible. The mother animal was too enraged even to be moved to other quarters.

As the days passed, and there was still no sign of the young gorilla, there seemed to be little hope of its survival. The mother now sat for most of the day near the bars of her cage, gazing out through the glass with dull tragic eyes. She moved slowly, and left most of her food untouched. While she was left to herself she seemed entirely listless; only when anyone approached the cage did she exert herself. And then, as the head keeper did not stop telling his colleagues, the look in her eye was enough to give you the willies; plain murder, staring you in the face.

Six weeks later, on a Sunday morning, Dr. David Wintringham, with his two younger children, Beth and Peter, visited the Zoo in company with a Fellow of the Society. It was a privileged visit, as such Sunday morning occasions always are.

The special houses for breeding animals were their chief objective, and here the children spent some time in front of the glass-enclosed cage of a young female chimpanzee, who was sitting with her three-week-old infant beside her.

"It doesn't look right lying on the floor," said Beth. "It ought to have a cot."

"It looks cold without any clothes on," said Peter.

The keeper laughed, saying, "The cage is specially warmed, and air-conditioned. It has ultra-violet light, too."

"It ought to be all right, then," said David.

But Beth was taken with melancholy and clung to it.

"Will the poor mother gorilla have another baby now?" she asked. "The one whose baby disappeared, I mean."

"She killed it herself, didn't she?" said Peter. "And ate it, too."

The keeper and the Fellow exchanged glances.

"She's very ill just now," the latter said, and led the children to another cage. Later he explained to David.

"Miliary tubercle," he told him. "She can't last much longer. She began to ail a week or two after she lost the little one. Perhaps we ought not to have let her have it in the Monkey House, but they both seemed very strong and well, and after all it was four months old when we moved them back. We think she killed it in a fit of temper, perhaps excited by the other animals. She has been moping ever since, and very savage all the time. We haven't moved her for fear of spreading the infection; just screened her cage from the public, and isolated the feeding and cleaning."

"The cage is glass-lined, like this one, isn't it?"

"Yes. All the great apes are very susceptible to T.B. They all used to go that way, in the days before glass covering and ultra-violet light."

"What was the date of the baby's death?" asked David.

"Presumed death," corrected the Fellow.

"Not much doubt now, sir," said the breeding-house keeper. "It would be November 17th she was noticed missing."

He spoke with an air of bereavement that might have

been comical if it had not been so obviously genuine. David saw that he felt as a doctor might who had safely delivered a child only to see it fade away under the mismanagement of the mother. He frowned, but before he had time to ask his next question Beth and Peter had pulled him forward to see another young monkey, and he was not able to return to the subject.

But he did not forget his sudden interest in the baby gorilla's strange disappearance. During the next two days he assembled all the newspapers he could find dated November 16th and 17th, and the week following, and made a collection of newspaper cuttings.

Next, with the help of his friend in the Zoological Society, he arranged to meet, first, the head keeper of the Monkey House, next, the keeper who had been in charge of the big apes, and lastly, the night watchman who had been on duty near the main entrance, not far from the Monkey House, on the night of November 16th.

From the latter he learned of the sudden excitement among the monkeys. The night watchman described how he had gone into their house, seen nothing wrong and left, locking the door again behind him. He told of his conversation with the policeman on the beat outside the gates. He was convinced that he had not seen anyone in or near the Monkey House while he made his inspection.

"But the monkeys were definitely excited?" David asked.

"Yes, sir. Springing all round their cages."

"You saw them. Did you put on the lights, or use a torch?"

"I had me torch."

"What about the gorillas?"

"Mad as the others."

"And the baby gorilla?"

"I didn't see him, but I wasn't on the lookout for him, particular. No reason to be, as far as I knew at the time."

"Quite."

The keepers had even less to say. The junior one had come on duty the next morning, and begun his usual work. He had at once noticed the absence of the young gorilla, which was friendly, and always made a point of coming to him to be made a fuss of. He wondered vaguely if it was ill, but did not report the matter at once.

Later that day he noticed streaks of blood on the floor of the cage. The mother gorilla was too savage that day, and for several days after, to allow him even to clean her cage. She was very hysterical and kept retiring into her sleeping den under her platform, throwing the straw about, and then dashing round and round her cage. He then went to tell the head keeper about it.

The two men had gone back to the cage together. And it was during one of the gorilla's later frenzies that they saw her drop a piece of fur-covered skin near the inner door of the cage. The head keeper, showing considerable courage, had retrieved this.

"You thought it came off the baby gorilla?" David asked.

The keeper nodded. His colleague looked away, seeming to suggest that he found the subject too painful for discussion.

The next day David went to see his friend Stephen Mitchell, a detective superintendent at Scotland Yard. The latter greeted him warily.

"Got some trouble to unload on us?" he asked.

"Possibly. Tell me, Steve, did you have to do any work on that case at the Zoo a couple of months ago?"

"In November? Do you mean the tramp in the vulture's cage?"

"Yes. What do you know about him?"

"No home address. Never gave the same name twice. Used to frequent Regent's Park all last summer, and through the autumn. Two constables were able to identify him in the end as the loafer they had often spoken to. He had no papers on him, and only a shilling or two of money. We really know nothing about him except his partiality to sleeping out in Regent's Park whenever he could. He spoke with a foreign accent, it seems. French or Italian, our more travelled officers have said. Not very tall, nor very old. He must have been practically dying that night when he got into the Zoo. His lungs were in the last stages. No treatment of any kind. None of the London hospitals could claim him as a patient."

"It wouldn't have been exactly to their credit to do so."

"Are you suggesting..."

"God forbid," said David, piously. "No. I saw the account of the inquest. How did he manage to get into the vultures' department?"

"That was the question they wanted us to solve. Local men completely foxed. It's my belief one of the night watchmen let him into the shelter of the passage behind the cages, and one of the cage doors was unlocked, and in the fog he went in unawares, saw the vultures, and died of fright."

"But the outer door of that passage was locked the next morning, wasn't it?"

"I expect the night watchman discovered what had happened, when he went to rouse him out in the morning, before going off duty. So then he would leave ill alone, lock up the door he was responsible for, and keep his mouth shut."

"A bit too slick," said David. "I suppose the night watch-man denied any such action on his part?"

"Emphatically. But I'm not satisfied. The tramp was known to have made his way into the Zoo before. He had been turned out of the Reptile House once, after an exceptionally cold night. Swore first he had hidden in there at closing time. When it was pointed out there was nowhere to hide, he said the night watchman had let him in."

David nodded.

"He would need to be out of the cold or fog with those lungs, poor devil. What about the Monkey House?" he asked, suddenly.

Mitchell was startled.

"What about it?"

"They keep it well heated, too, don't they?"

"Yes. But what…?"

David was not listening, however. He had risen, and was standing beside the superintendent's table.

"Did you say the man was a Mediterranean?" he asked.

"Yes. Italian or Southern French. Not more than forty. Small boned. Good teeth, considering his circumstances."

"Thanks a lot," said David. "I'm off now. The airports first, then the Zoo again. Give me a chit for the airports to open up."

"What's the big idea?"

"The big idea is murder," said David, gravely. "Or at any rate, accessory before and after the fact."

"Who? The tramp?"

"Yes. It was ingenious to put his body in the vultures' cage, to have the identity rubbed out. But the murderer made one fatal mistake."

"So are you making one fatal mistake. There was no

suggestion of foul play. The man died of haemoptysis, possibly brought on by fright."

"Possibly. But he was deliberately exposed to it with the
idea of killing him."

"With what motive? That old night watchman has been
there for years. They wouldn't turn him off, even if he had
given the tramp somewhere to sleep. Besides, he was talking
to one of our chaps at the time there was that commotion in
the Monkey House."

"Glad to hear it. That helps my case."

"Why can't you say what you mean?"

"I will when I've had a go at the airports. You shall come
up to the Zoo with me. You know, if you hadn't been put off
by the coroner, and had braved the gorilla in its cage, and
turned your apparatus on what there was there, you might
have won medals over this."

"If you had minded your own business, a lot of time
wouldn't have been wasted."

"Come across with those chits, Steve."

They met again six hours later in the curator's office at
the Zoo.

"I think we ought to clear this up quickly, now," said
David. "Before anything else happens. So I'll tell you what I
did at the airports. I found what I wanted at…"

He named a line that operated to South America.
Passenger lists had been produced for him, as at the other
ports; employees at the Customs sheds answered questions.
An airplane leaving early on November 17th had had a passenger who carried a cage containing a parrot. He had had
all the correct papers for it, including a certificate that it did
not suffer from psittacosis. It was in a glass-lined cage, ventilated through a special filter.

"The one I was looking for," explained David. "The parrot got through the Customs and the cover was put back on the cage. But the crew of the aircraft never saw the parrot. What they saw, some time after the take-off, was a monkey. And by then the owner had all the right papers for a monkey, including a clean bill of health. Or so they say."

"It was in the cage?"

"The glass-lined, specially ventilated cage. The passenger had been wearing a heavy overcoat, quite a bulky affair. The parrot probably flew down all right, when he got rid of her off the plane, though possibly much surprised to find the natives speaking a foreign tongue. The ape would be pleased to get out of stuffy darkness into the comparative comfort of a warm glass-lined box."

"Ape?"

"Oh, yes. They said monkey because of the size. But it was an ape, travelling in the necessary security for such delicate creatures. A baby gorilla, to be exact."

There was a silence; then the curator said, "Where is it now?"

"At a zoo in the Argentine," answered David. "Bought in all good faith. You'll find it very hard to get it back."

"Then what...?" asked the curator, looking at a specimen on his table.

"I'll show you," said David. "I've brought some ether meth with me."

Using a piece of cotton wool soaked in methylated ether he cleaned the strip of fur that had come from the gorilla's cage. The black skin beneath the silky black hairs lightened until it became greyish-white.

"Unwashed skin doesn't clean up all at once," said David, "as I remember from my far-off student days. Good enough, for now. Black straight hair of the Mediterranean type," he went on. "I think when you've cut sections and done blood tests on that smear under the skin, you'll be able to prove this is human, and belonged to the tramp. You might be able to scrape an old bloodstain in the cage, too, and prove he was in there that night. Ask the junior keeper how much they paid him to kidnap the young gorilla, and exactly at what moment in the proceedings the tramp found his way into the warm Monkey House through the door the keeper had left unlocked in his excitement. Ask him if it was really fright that killed the poor wretch when he found himself pushed into the bereaved animal's cage, perhaps to take her attention off what he was doing to her child. Or if the poor animal caught him by the neck the vultures later so obligingly tore to ribbons. Ask him which of the trolleys or wheelbarrows he used to trundle the body down to the aviaries in the fog. The night watchman was lucky not to come on the scene too soon, or he might have gone the same way. But he didn't get there until after the monkeys began to voice their general dislike of the proceedings, and he only flashed his torch into their house, and left again. The keeper, with the baby gorilla and the corpse of the tramp, were behind the scenes by that time, waiting for the coast to clear. The night watchman has the constable's story as his excellent alibi."

"A terrible story," said the curator, sadly, "if it's true, as I'm afraid it may be. One of our best men; quick-witted, brave, resourceful. All qualities you need in dealing with wild animals."

"And with interfering people when you happen to be committing a crime," said David. "He was very quick and efficient, indeed, because the uproar in the Monkey House when the death fight was on lasted only a few minutes. He was brave, too, to get the tramp's body away from the maddened gorilla. But he was foolish to call the head keeper before this little scrap of skin turned up, or perhaps just unlucky. He should have made sure there was nothing left. But he may not have been feeling too good by then. If he didn't actually see the vultures come down to the body after he left it in their cage, he would surely hear their joyful surprise following him through the fog. And they haven't got very nice ways of expressing themselves."

The case took a conventional course. The keeper, well advised, pleaded guilty to theft, but boldly claimed the tramp as an accomplice. There was no evidence to refute this possibility; only the police knew what an unlikely accomplice the man had been. The keeper was acquitted of murder, and given eighteen months on the lesser charge. Mitchell saw David Wintringham after the trial.

"One thing I'd like to ask you," he said. "What made you start on this?"

"Visit to the Zoo with Beth and Peter. I heard that the female gorilla was dying of miliary T.B. What they used to call galloping consumption. I knew that apes are very susceptible to this disease, and live in glass-lined cages for that reason. I wondered how she had picked up a mass infection sufficient to start her off with such a bang. Then I remembered the tramp in the Park had had advanced T.B. I wondered if the two facts could be related. They turned out to be so. Quite simple."

"Nothing easier," answered the superintendent, bitterly.

The Man Who
Loved Animals

Penelope Wallace

PENELOPE WALLACE (1923–1997) WAS THE DAUGHTER
of Edgar Wallace, the only child of his second marriage
to Violet King. Her father's sudden death was followed
fourteen months later by that of her mother at the age of
thirty-seven. At that point, the Wallace estate was mired
in debt, but the continuing popularity of his work meant
that it was possible to restore financial equilibrium with
such success as to enable Penelope to be educated at
Roedean. Penelope and her husband, George Halcrow,
later managed the family estate, and for the rest of her life,
she worked to preserve the legacy of her father's writing.
In 1969 she founded the Edgar Wallace Society, of which
she remained president until her death. She was also president of the Society of Women Journalists and held various
offices in the Press Club.

She wrote a handful of crime novels, and served for a year
as chair of the Crime Writers' Association. As an author, her

strength lay in the short story; she made a number of contributions to the CWA's annual anthologies of short mystery fiction and "Tell David" was made into an episode of the television series *Night Gallery*. This story first appeared in *Edgar Wallace Mystery Magazine* (where else?) in February 1965.

———————

"Yes, miss, I've always loved animals," he told me.

He took a long drink from his pint, set it carefully on the table and wiped his straggling moustache with a dirty blue handkerchief; then he took off his rimless glasses and tucked them in his top pocket.

"Blind as a bat without them," he confessed, "but it somehow makes it easier, talking. Not that I don't like talking, anyway. Yes," he repeated, "I've always loved animals and I could always get them to do anything for me."

"Please tell me about it," I asked—although I admit that I already knew, because John and Henry had told me about the man and that was why I was buying him a drink in a dingy pub off Commercial Road.

He told me of his reputation as "Sam The Animal Man," of how he had worked the halls and of how he had tried the Circus, but the animals he tamed and trained by kindness were useless for anyone else.

"Did you never hit the animals?" I asked.

"'Course not! Any more than I'd beat my wife—if I had one."

He'd tried working in a zoo but the safety regulations irked him. It seemed incredible that there was no work for such a gifted man.

"I've tried most things, miss," he said. "Even been on

the telly—from Willmouth Zoo and, would you believe it, everyone said it was faked!"

His faded blue eyes blinked over the past.

"Once I worked for a vet. I enjoyed that—helping with the animals…" He stopped abruptly. He had the most readable face I'd ever seen, and now there was a look of shame in his eyes.

"Did you ever fail?" I asked, bluntly.

He was silent for a while, then:

"I might as well tell you the whole story, though it's not often I do." He fortified himself with another drink of beer and went on:

"Yes I did have a failure, miss," he spoke slowly, "when I was with the vet. Often there was animals—old you know, or ill—that had to be put down. I knew it was the best for them; but one day a man brought in a dog—Alsatian it was—said it was vicious. Just not treated right, I reckon, and it was a beauty, young and full of life. All of a sudden I thought I shouldn't be doing this, it's wrong." He paused and I waited. "Well, I suppose I got sort of a fear, and the dog got it too—'orrible bite I got and I couldn't stand any more. I packed the job in—not because of the bite but feeling I'd done wrong."

I could see by his face that it was something that still troubled him; that he'd let down an animal. He was fighting the sadness of the memory and he went on:

"That's about all about me, I reckon. What about you, miss? If you'll forgive me for asking, don't often see a pretty young face like yours in here."

The flattery was charming!

"I'm afraid my life story isn't nearly as interesting," I told him. "I work in an export firm, I had to come down to our warehouse to check some figures, and afterwards it was so hot that I felt I must have a cold drink. The cafés were full so I came here—and met you. You are here often?"

"Most evenings," he agreed. "The landlord lets 'em bring in their dogs—'course it's good for business too; see one bloke'll tell another wot a fierce dog he's got, won't let nobody else speak to him even and the other bloke'll say 'Bet you a pint Sam'll have it eating out of 'is 'and in five minutes' and they bring it in 'ere." Sam chuckled. "Many's the time it's so pally it'd carry a burglar's tools anyway. Sometimes they bring 'em in to ask wot's wrong with 'em. Cats too, and budgies—mostly women that is."

It took me a moment to work out who brought what. He seemed surer on the past than the present. I was getting fond of Sam and hated to deceive him, but I wanted proof that he actually had this ability with animals, and when Henry walked into the bar I made no sign of recognition.

Henry had with him the meanest looking Alsatian I had ever seen. Above a thick leather muzzle, its eyes glowed yellow with hatred. The ears were laid back and as it passed my chair it bared two rows of sharp and hopeful teeth and made a very unpleasant noise in its throat.

I was terrified; I wondered where Henry had found it and whether he had made sure that the muzzle was as strong as it looked. I hoped that Sam wouldn't think it too much of a coincidence… Already Sam had forgotten me. He had taken out his glasses and was wiping them. I noticed that they were firmly in place before he said "Good evening, sir," to Henry. "Nice dog you've got. Mind if I talk to 'im?"

Already the brute was straining at his leash towards the old man.

"Well," said Henry dubiously, "he's not mine. I told a pal I'd look after him for the evening and I'm blowed if I'd have done it if I'd known what I was letting myself in for."

"Just you let me talk to 'im," the old man wheedled and the dog pulled Henry towards him.

"There, there, old boy..." Sam's voice was low, gentle, coaxing. Talking softly, he stroked the dog's head, its ears. The dog put a tentative paw on Sam's knee, and Sam took off the muzzle. The ears were upright now; the yellow look of hate had changed to one of adoration.

The dog swallowed, yawned and lay down at Sam's feet. The old man began to talk to Henry; still softly. He said that Henry should tell his friend that the dog needed affection, not a muzzle...

The barman leant over the bar. "Better than the telly, isn't it?"

Henry nodded, with a nice blend of admiration and surprise.

"It certainly is," I said, and I meant it.

Soon afterwards I left, Sam and Henry bidding me goodnight.

The next morning I went to the house where Sam lived. Henry was very efficient, but I did ask twice in the neighbourhood where I might find Sam, the man who loved animals. I had a rather dejected little kitten in a basket to add point to the query.

When Sam opened the door to me he looked embarrassed—prepared for flight. There was a miaow from the basket and I ceased to exist. He took the basket from me and led the way into a frowsty kitchen. Three sleek cats rubbed his legs—better fed that he was—as he put the basket on the table and examined the kitten.

"It seems tottery," I explained.

"Looks 'alf starved to me," there was accusation and disappointment in his voice. I hastened to explain that it was a stray that had come in that morning and didn't seem able to drink.

"It needs looking after," he said. "Can you do that, miss, being out to work and all, or do you want me…?"

"Yes, please, would you?"

"'Course I would, and pleased to."

I could see that his reference to my work had started a train of thought and I went on, "I've got three days off. I wanted to see you." I hesitated. "I need your help," I told him, the words tumbling out. "It's not just about the kitten. It's something else and it's desperately important. Please, Sam, please help me. I know you can. Please say you will."

My voice was shaking and he pulled out a chair for me.

"I'll put on the kettle and we'll 'ave a nice cuppa."

His voice was gentle—for a while at least he had identified me with the little lost kitten which sat in his hand.

"Now you tell me what I can do to 'elp you," he said.

I told him.

The next day I drove him into the country. We had to take the kitten with us so that Sam could feed it every four hours from a thermos of warm milk.

It was over a week before I saw Sam again.

He was in a side room of a gaunt ward of St. John's Hospital. Thick bandages swathed both arms and covered his neck, and long strips of plaster were on his face and head.

The blue eyes, without glasses, had a faraway look.

The man in Police uniform moved away from the bed as I sat down. I said, "Hullo, Sam."

He peered at me closely. "Who is it?" he asked.

"The girl with the kitten."

"I thought it was, but you sound different, somehow, and you look different, too—older somehow. I suppose it's not 'aving my specs." His voice was faint and painful.

"What happened, Sam?" I asked gently.

"Well, you could say it started to go wrong when I broke my glasses. That was in the pub yesterday morning, some silly—silly fool bumped into me and they broke in my pocket. When I got 'ome I 'unted 'igh and low for my spare set. Don't know where they got to. Always keep 'em on the kitchen mantelpiece. 'Course, I couldn't tell you to put things off as you didn't give me no address; so I went off to this 'Adley 'All you showed me. The big gates was open like you said they'd be"—he stopped and looked at me. I felt as though his unfocused eyes could read my thoughts. "Tell me again, miss. Tell me what you told me the other day."

"I told you, Sam, that I had once foolishly had a lover who was very wealthy and quite unscrupulous, that he had proof that, equally foolishly, I'd once belonged to the Communist Party. I told you that I was marrying a wonderful boy, who would lose his job if it came to light that his wife had been a Communist. I told you that my fiancé knew where these documents were kept in the man's office and that he could get in all right but he couldn't deal with the dogs. So I asked you to go in and quieten them for him."

"Yes," he nodded slowly. "That's what you said. But it wasn't true, was it?"

"Part of it was," I told him. "Please, Sam, I can't stay long. Tell me what happened."

"Would you pass me the water, miss." I passed him the glass and held it while he drank.

"Beer 'ud be better," he said. "You want to know what happened? Well, I found the right door. Funny thing, it had a great notice on it. I couldn't read it but it looked big for Tradesman's Entrance, or anything like that. The door was open and I went in and there was these two great growling dogs. Of course we made friends quickly enough and I waited for your fiancé to show up. I thought 'e'd be watching for me to get in and then pop in the minute 'e 'eard the dogs quiet down. So I got curious and opened one of the doors. Big office it was, far as I could see. Then I opened another door and that was the same, and I started to think it was funny, even a wealthy bloke 'aving two offices the same like that, and I couldn't see why your boy friend didn't turn up. I'd 'ave been in quick enough if it'd been my girl I was trying to 'elp. I couldn't think what was keeping 'im."

I silently cursed John and his tardiness.

"Then I started to think about the notice on the door and the funny way one pair of specs was broken and the other lost. I began to wonder if I was mixed up in something crooked and a little fear seemed to creep into me and I looked out at them dogs. I couldn't see 'em properly but I could feel it and I could feel their fear and not trusting me any more and I could hear as they began to snarl." Fear crossed his face as he relived those minutes. "Then they went for me," he finished simply.

"They say I'm lucky to be alive." He gave me a strange look. "They let me send a message to Mrs. Brown, next door, to look after the cats—and the kitten." He peered over my shoulder. "Is the policeman still there?"

"No. He went long ago." It was true, for the man in uniform who had given me his chair was John.

Sam spoke urgently. "I was right to be worried, wasn't I, miss? The police said it wasn't 'Adley 'All—the place they found me. It was 'Adley Research Establishment. That notice said to keep out. It's one of them secret places. You lied to me, didn't you, miss?"

"Yes, Sam, I did. I had to."

"And your job. Doesn't 'ave anything to do with exports, does it?"

"In a way it does." I had to explain something of what I felt. I owed it to him. "Believe me, Sam, I do what I do because it has to be done. Because I think it's right."

He seemed to accept this.

"I 'aven't told the police about you," he assured me.

I knew that was true because if he had they'd have found me by now—Henry and John had got safely away when they heard the dogs attacking—and I knew they wouldn't trace me from my present visit. If Sam had had his glasses, he still wouldn't have recognised me in the aged "wife" who sat by his bed.

We had been unsuccessful but we were safe—if Sam kept quiet.

"I didn't tell the police about you," Sam said yet again, "and I never will." His face was unafraid. "Will I, miss?"

"No, Sam, you never will."

And I shot him.

The Hornet's Nest

Christianna Brand

CHRISTIANNA BRAND WAS THE WRITING NAME OF Mary Christianna Milne Lewis (1907–88). She arrived on the scene as the Golden Age of detective fiction drew to a close, publishing *Death in High Heels* in 1941, but over the course of almost forty years she produced novels and short stories in the finest traditions of Golden Age mystery. Towards the end of her career she devised a seventh solution to *The Poisoned Chocolates Case* by Anthony Berkeley, which has been published as a British Library Crime Classic. Her principal detective was Inspector Cockrill, who appeared in the splendid wartime whodunit *Green for Danger* (1944)— which was filmed with Alastair Sim cast as Cockrill—and six other novels, one of them as yet unpublished. Cockrill's short cases were gathered by Tony Medawar in a posthumous collection, *The Spotted Cat* (2002), which includes interesting remarks about Brand's literary career.

This story, originally published in *Ellery Queen's Mystery*

Magazine in May 1967 under the title "Twist for Twist," is a rare example of a short story which also offers an elaborate whodunit puzzle falling squarely within the classic tradition. Most writers need the length afforded by a novel to concoct a truly ingenious "fair play" whodunit mystery, but "The Hornet's Nest" illustrates her virtuosity. Brand makes pleasing use of hornets in the story, mainly as a metaphor.

"We've got hornets nesting in that old elm," said Mr. Harold Caxton, gulping down his last oyster and wiping his thick fingers on the table napkin. "Interesting things, hornets." He interrupted himself, producing a large white handkerchief and violently blowing his nose. "Damn these colds of mine!"

"I saw you were treating them," said Inspector Cockrill, referring to the hornets. "There's a tin of that wasp stuff on your hall table."

Harold Caxton ignored him. "Interesting things, I was saying. I've been reading up about them." Baleful and truculent, he looked round at the guests assembled for his wedding feast. "At certain times of the year," he quoted, "there are numerous males called the drones, which have very large eyes and whose only activity is to eat—" he glared round at them again, with special reference to the gentlemen present—"and to participate in the mass flight after the virgin queen."

He cast a speculative eye on his bride. "You are well named, Elizabeth, my dear," he said. "Elizabeth, the virgin queen." And added with ugly significance, "I hope."

"But only one of the hornets succeeds in the mating," said Inspector Cockrill into the ensuing outraged silence.

"And he dies in the process." He sat back and looked Harold Caxton in the face, deliberately, and twiddled his thumbs.

Harold Caxton was really a horrid old man. He had been horrid to his first wife and now was evidently going to be horrid to his second—she had been the late Mrs. Caxton's nurse, quite young still and very pretty in a blue-eyed, broken-hearted sort of way. And he was horrid to his own stout son, Theo, who was only too thankful to live away from papa, playing in an amateurish way with stocks and bonds, up in London; and horrid to his stepson, Bill, who, brought into the family by the now departed wife, had been pushed off to relatives in the United States to be out of Mr. Caxton's way.

And he was horrid to poor young Dr. Ross who, having devotedly attended the first wife in her last illness, now as devotedly attended Mr. Caxton's own soaring blood pressure and resultant apoplectic attacks; and horrid to his few friends and many poor relations, all of whom he kept on tenterhooks with promises of remembrances in his will when one of the choking attacks should have taken him off.

He would no doubt have been horrid to Inspector Cockrill too; but—Mr. Caxton being incapable of keeping peaceably to a law designed for other people as well as for himself—Cockie got in first, and was horrid to *him*. It must have been Elizabeth, the Inspector reflected, who had promoted his invitation to the wedding.

The pretty little nurse had stayed on to help with things after the first wife died, had gradually drifted into indispensability and so into accepting the pudgy hand of the widower. Not without some heart-searching, however; Inspector Cockrill himself had lent a shoulder in an off-duty moment—in those days of Mr. Caxton's uninhibited courtship; and she had had a little weep on his shoulder and told him of the one great love, lost to her, and how she no longer looked for that kind of happiness in marriage, and how she was sick of work, sick of loneliness, sick of insecurity.

"But a trained nurse like you can get wonderful jobs," Inspector Cockrill had protested. "Travel all over the place, see the world." She *had* seen the world, she said, and it was too big, it scared her; she wanted to stay put, she wanted a home; and a home meant a man.

"There are other men?" he had suggested; and she had burst out that there were indeed other men, too many men, all of them—oh, it was dreadful, it was frightening to be the sort of woman that, for some unknown reason, all men looked at, all men gooped at, all men wanted.

"With him at least I'll be safe; no one will dare to drool over me like that—not when he's around."

Inspector Cockrill had somewhat hurriedly disengaged his shoulder. He was a younger man, in those days of Mr. Caxton's second marriage and subsequent departure from this life, and he was taking no chances.

And so the courtship had gone forward. The engagement and imminent wedding had been announced and in the same breath the household staff—faithful apparently in death as in life to the late Mrs. Caxton—had made their own announcement: they had Seen it Coming and were now sweeping out in a body, preferring, thank you very much, not to continue in service under That Nurse.

The prospective bride, unchaperoned, had perforce modestly retired to a London hotel and thereafter left most of the wedding arrangements to Son Theo and Stepson Bill—Theo running up and down from London, Bill temporarily accommodated for the occasion beneath the family roof.

Despite the difficulties of its achievement, Mr. Caxton was far from satisfied with the wedding breakfast. "I never did like oysters, Elizabeth, as you very well know. Why couldn't we have had smoked salmon? And I don't like cold meat—I don't like it in any form. Not in *any* form," he insisted, looking once again at his virgin queen with an ugly leer. Inspector Cockrill surprised a look of malevolence on the faces of all the males present, drones and workers alike, which really quite shocked him.

She protested, trembling. "But Harold, it's been so difficult with no servants. We got what was easiest."

"Very well then. Having got it, let us have it." He gestured to the empty oyster shells. "With all these women around, am I to sit in front of a dirty plate forever?"

The female relations quickly acted on this broad hint, rising from their places like a flock of sitting pheasants and beginning to scurry to and fro, clearing used crockery, passing plates of chicken and ham. "Don't overdo it, my dears," said Mr. Caxton, sardonically watching their endeavours. "You're all out of the will now, you know."

It brought them up short—the crudeness, the utter brutality of it. They stood there staring back at him, the plates in their shaking hands. Half of them, probably, cared not two pins for five, or five-and-twenty pounds in Harold Caxton's will; nevertheless they turned questioning—reproachful?—eyes on the new heiress.

"Oh, but Harold, that's not true," she cried, and above his jeering protests insisted, "Harold has destroyed his old will, yes; but he's made a new one and—well, I mean, no one has been forgotten, I'm sure, who was mentioned before."

The lunch progressed. Intent, perhaps, to show their disinterestedness, the dispossessed scuttled back and forth with the cold meats, potato salad, and sliced cucumber—poured delicious barley water (for Mr. Caxton was a rabid teetotaller) into cut-glass tumblers that were worthy of better things. The bridegroom munched his way through even the despised cold viands in a manner that boded ill, thought Inspector Cockrill, for the wretched Elizabeth, suddenly coming alive to the horror of what she had taken upon herself. She sat silent and shrinking and made hardly any move to assist with the serving.

Son Theo carved and sliced, Stepson Bill handed out plates, even young Dr. Ross wandered round with the green-salad bowl; but the bride sat still and silent, and those three, thought Cockie, could hardly drag their eyes from the small white face and the dawning terror there.

The meat plates were removed, the peaches lifted one by one from their tall bottles and placed, well soused with syrup, on their flowery plates. Stepson Bill dispensed the silver dessert spoons and forks, fanned out ready on the sideboard. The guests sat civilly, spoons poised, ready to begin.

Harold Caxton waited for no one. He gave a last loud trumpeting of his nose, stuffed away his handkerchief, picked up the spoon beside him and somewhat ostentatiously looked to see if it was clean, plunged spoon and fork into the peach, spinning in its syrup, and scooping off a large chunk he slithered it into his mouth, stiffened—stared about him with a wild surmise—gave one gurgling roar of mingled rage and pain, turned first white, then purple, then an even more terrifying dingy dark red, and pitched forward across the table with his face in his plate.

Elizabeth cried out, "He's swallowed the peachstone!"

Dr. Ross was across the room in three strides, grasped the man by the hair and chin, and pushed him back in his chair. The face looked none the more lovely for being covered with syrup, so he wiped it clean with one swipe of a table napkin; and stood for what seemed a long moment, hands on the arms of the chair, gazing down, intent and abstracted, at the spluttering mouth and rolling eyes. Like a terrier, Elizabeth was to say later to Inspector Cockrill, alert and suspicious, sniffing the scent.

Then with another of his swift movements the doctor was hauling Mr. Caxton out of his chair and lowering him to the floor, calling out, "Elizabeth—my bag! On a chair in the hall." But she seemed struck motionless by the sudden horror of it all and only stammered out an imploring, "Theo?"

Stout Theo, nearest to the door, bestirred himself to dash out into the hall, appearing a few moments later with the bag. Stepson Bill, kneeling with the doctor beside the heaving body, took the bag and opened it. Elizabeth, shuddering, said again, "He must have swallowed the stone."

The doctor ignored her. He had caught up the fallen table napkin and was using it to grasp, with his left hand, the man's half-swallowed tongue and pull it forward to free the air passages; at the same time his right hand was groping blindly toward the medical bag. "A fingerstall—rubber finger covering—it's on top, somewhere."

Bill found it immediately and handed it to him; the doctor shuffled it on and thrust the middle finger of his right hand down the gagging throat. "Nothing there," he said, straightening up, absently wiping his fingers on the table napkin, rolling off the rubber finger covering—all again with that odd effect of sniffing the air; then he galvanised into action once more and fell to his knees beside the body. With the heel of his left hand he began a quick, sharp pumping at the sternum, and with his right gestured again toward the medical bag.

"The hypodermic. Adrenalin ampoules in the left-hand pocket."

Bill fumbled, unaccustomed, and the doctor lifted his head for a moment and said sharply, "For heaven's sake—Elizabeth!"

She jumped, startled. "Yes? Yes?" she said, staccato, and seemed to come suddenly to her senses. "Yes, of course. I'll do it." She dropped to her knees beside the bag, found the ampoules, and filled the syringe.

"Keep it ready," he said. "Somebody cut away the sleeve." The doctor used both hands to massage the heart. "While I do this will someone give him the kiss of life? Quickly!"

It was a long time since anyone, his affianced included, had willingly given Mr. Caxton a kiss of any kind and it could not now be said that volunteers came forward eagerly. The doctor said again, "Elizabeth?"—but this time on a note of doubt. She looked down, faltering, at the gaping mouth, dribbling dreadfully. "Must I?"

"You're a nurse," said Dr. Ross. "And he's dying. Quickly, *please!*"

"Yes. Yes, of course I must." She brought out a small handkerchief, scrubbed at her own mouth as though somehow, irrationally, to clean it before so horrible a task, then moved to crouch where she would not interfere with the massage of the heart. "Now?"

Mercifully, Harold Caxton himself provided the answer—suddenly and unmistakably he gave up the ghost. He heaved up into a last great, lunging spasm, screamed briefly, and rolled up his eyes. She sat back on her heels, the handkerchief balled against her mouth, gaping.

Dr. Ross abandoned the heart massage, thrust her aside, himself began a mouth-to-mouth breathing. But he soon admitted defeat. "It's no use," he said, straightening up, his hands to his aching back. "He's dead."

Dead. And there was not one, perhaps, in all that big, ugly, ornate room who did not feel a sort of lightening of relief, a sort of small lifting of the heart—because with the going of Harold Caxton so much of ugliness, crudity, and cruelty had also gone. Not one, at any rate, even pretended to grieve. Only the widowed bride, still kneeling by the heavy body, lifted her head and looked across with a terrible question into the doctor's eyes, then leaped to her feet and darted out into the hall. She came back and stood in the doorway. "The tin of cyanide," she said. "It's gone."

Dr. Ross picked up the dropped table napkin and quietly, unobtrusively, yet very deliberately, laid it over the half-eaten peach.

Inspector Cockrill's underlings dealt with the friends and relations, despatching them to their deep chagrin about their respective businesses, relieved of any further glorious chance of notoriety. The tin had been discovered without much difficulty, hidden in a vase of pampas grass which stood in the centre of the hall table; its lid was off and a small quantity of the poisonous paste was missing, scooped out, apparently with something so smooth as to show no peculiarities of marking—at any rate, to the naked eye. It had been on the hall table since the day before the wedding; Cockie himself had seen it still there, just before lunch.

He thought it all over, deeply and quietly—for it had been a plot, deeply and quietly laid. "I'll see those four myself," he said to his sergeant. "Mrs. Caxton, the son, the stepson, and the doctor."

Establishing himself in what had been Harold Caxton's study, he sent first for Elizabeth. "Well, Mrs. Caxton?"

Her white teeth dug into a trembling lower lip to bite back hysteria. "Oh, Inspector, at least don't call me by that horrible name!"

"It is your name, now; and we're engaged on a murder investigation. There's no time for nonsense, Elizabeth."

"You don't really believe—?"

"You know it," said Cockie. "You're a nurse—you were the first to know it."

"Dr. Ross was the first," she said. "You saw him yourself, Inspector, leaning over Harold when he was lying in that chair, sort of—sort of sniffing, like a terrier on the scent. He could smell the cyanide on his breath, I'm sure he could—like bitter almonds they say it is."

"Who bought the food for the wedding luncheon, Mrs. Caxton?"

"Well, we all—we talked it over, Theo and Bill and I. It was so difficult, you see, with no servants, and me being in London. I ordered most of the stuff to be sent down from Harrod's and Theo brought down—well, one or two things from Fortnum's." Her voice trailed away rather unhappily.

"Which one or two things? The peaches?"

"Well, yes, the peaches. Theo brought them down himself, yesterday. He was up and down from London all the time, helping Bill." But, she cried, imploring, why should Theo possibly have done this terrible thing? "His own father! For that matter, why should anyone?"

"Ah, as to that!" said Cockie. Had not Harold Caxton spoken his own epitaph? *At certain times there are numerous males called the drones, which have very large eyes and whose only activity is to eat and to participate in the mass flight after the virgin queen.* He had seen them himself, stuffing down Mr. Caxton's oysters and cold chicken and ham, their eyes, dilated, fixed with an astonishing unanimity on Mr. Caxton's bride. *Only one of them succeeds in the mating,* he repeated to himself, *and he dies in the process.* That also had been seen to be true.

"Elizabeth," he said, forgetting for a moment that this was a murder investigation and there was to be no nonsense, "from the hornet's-eye view I'm afraid you are indeed a virgin queen."

Then Theo, the young drone Theo, stout and lethargic, playing with his stocks and bonds in his cosy London flat… Inspector Cockrill had known him from his boyhood. "You needn't think, Cockie, that I wanted any of my father's money. I got my share of my mother's when she died."

"Oh, did you?" said Cockrill. "And her other son, Bill?"

"She left that to my father to decide."

"Wasn't that a bit unfair?"

"You can fly across nowadays easily enough, but he never came over from America to see them. My mother had sort of written him off, I suppose. Though I believe they did write to each other, secretly, when she knew she was dying. The servants told me. Father would never have allowed it, of course."

"Of course!" said Cockie. He dismissed the matter of money. "How well, Theo, did you know your father's new wife?"

"Not at all well. I saw her when I came to visit my mother,

and again at the funeral, after she died. But, of course—"

But of course, his tone admitted, a man didn't have to know Elizabeth well to—There was that certain something—an irresistible something—

"You never contemplated marrying her yourself?"

But Theo, lazy and self-indulgent, was not for the married state. "All the same, Inspector, it did make me pretty sick to think of it. I mean, my own father—"

Would Theo, dog in the manger, almost physically revolted by the thought of his beloved in the gross arms of his own father—would Theo kill for that? "Those bottled peaches, Theo. You served them, I know; but who actually opened them? I mean, had they been unsealed in advance?"

"No, because they'd have lost the bouquet of the Kirsch. They were kept sealed right up to the last minute."

"Can you prove that?"

"Elizabeth can bear me out. We nipped in here on the way to the wedding—I drove her down from London—for me to go to the john. And she took a quick dekko just to see that everything looked all right. She'll tell you that the bottles were still sealed up then; you can ask her."

"How quick a dekko? Tell me about this visit."

"Oh, good heavens, Inspector, the whole thing took about three minutes—we were late and you know what the old man was. We rushed in, I dashed into the powder room, and when I came out she was standing at the dining-room door looking in and she said, 'It all looks wonderful,' and what a good job Bill and I had done. Then she went into the powder room and we both got back into the car and went off."

"Was the tin of cyanide on the hall table then?"

"Yes, because she said thank goodness Bill seemed to have got it for her and saved her more trouble with Father."

"No one else was in the house at this time?"

"No, Bill had gone on to the church with my father."

"Okay. Well, send Bill in to me, will you, Theo? And tell him to bring his passport with him."

Bill was ten years older than his stepbrother—well into his thirties; blond-headed, incisive, tough, an ugly customer probably on a dirty night; but rather an engaging sort of chap, for all that. Cockie turned over the pages of the passport. "You haven't been to this country since you were a boy?"

"No, they shipped me out as a kid—the old man didn't want me and my mother doesn't seem to have put up too much of a fight for me. So I wasn't all that crazy to come rushing home on visits."

"Not even when she died?"

"At that time I was—prevented," he said briefly.

"By what, may I ask?"

"By four stone walls," said Stepson Bill ruefully. "Which in my case, Inspector, *did* a prison make. In other words, I was doing time, sir. I got into a fight with a guy and did six months for it. I only got out a few weeks ago."

"A fight about what?"

"About my wife if you have to know," he said sullenly. "I was bumming around, I admit it, and I guess he got her on the rebound. Well, bum or not, I chucked her out and that was the end of her. And I pulled him in, and that was the end of *him*. In the role of seducer, anyway."

"You divorced your wife?"

"Yeah, divorced her." He stared at Inspector Cockrill and the hard bright eyes suddenly had a look, almost of despair. "I think now I made some pretty big mistakes," he said.

"At any rate, having got out, you learned that your

stepfather was marrying the nurse, that your mother's money was in jeopardy, perhaps? So you came across, hot-foot, to look the lady over?"

And having looked her over... Another drone, drawn willy-nilly—the more so having been for long months starved of the company of women; having been deprived of his wife, whom he still loved—drawn into the mass flight after the virgin queen. "It was you, I believe, who brought the poison into the house?"

"Yes, I did. The old man was furious with Elizabeth because she hadn't ordered it. How could she, poor girl, when she wasn't here half the time? So I went and got it at the village drug store, just to save her from more trouble, and put it on the table so he'd think she'd got it."

"But she was in London. How could he expect her to get it?"

"Oh, hell, he didn't care; if it wasn't there, she was responsible."

"And after all this alleged fuss and urgency, it never got used? For hornets, I mean."

"Didn't I tell you?—it was only to make more aggravation for Elizabeth."

"I see. Well, we agree it was you who introduced the cyanide. Didn't you also hand a plate of cold meat to your stepfather?"

"Me? For heavens' sakes, Inspector! Those old girls were running around like a lot of decapitated chickens, snatching plates out of our hands, dumping them down in front of anyone who'd accept them."

"You just might have said specifically to one of them, 'This plate is specially for Mr. Caxton.'"

"I might at that," said Bill cheerfully. "Why don't you just ask around and find out?" He shrugged. "Anyway, what does it matter? The poison wasn't on the meat, was it? It had been put on the peach."

"If it had," said Cockie, "it had been put there by someone very clever." He dwelt on it. "How could it have been put there so that the whole dose—to all intents and purposes—was on the one mouthful he happened to take? And, the first mouthful at that."

And he sent Stepson Bill away and summoned Dr. Ross. "Well, Doctor, so we have it? *Only one mates, and he dies in the process.*"

"You're referring to the thing about hornets?" said Dr. Ross, rather stiffly.

"That's right—to the thing about hornets. But nobody could call *you* a drone, Doctor. So busy with that little bag of yours that you had it with you out in the hall, all ready to hand."

"At intervals of about once a week," said Dr. Ross, "policemen like yourself exhort us not to leave our medical bags in unattended cars." He fixed Inspector Cockrill with a dark and angry eye. "Are you suggesting it was I who murdered my own patient?"

"Will you declare yourself outside the mass flight after the queen, Dr. Ross? You must have seen a good deal of our little queen in the sickroom of the late Mrs. Caxton?"

"I happen to have a little queen of my own, Inspector. Not to mention several little drones, not yet ready for flighting."

"I know," said Cockie. "It must have been hell for you." He said it very kindly, then added, "I accuse you of nothing."

Disarmed, the doctor capitulated immediately,

wretchedly. "I've never so much as touched her hand, Inspector. But it's true—there's something about her... and to think of that filthy old brute—"

"Well, he's gone," said Cockie. "Murdered under your nose and mine. And talking of noses—?"

"I smelled it on his breath. Only the faintest whiff—but it was there. I thought it must be just the Kirsch—the Kirsch on the peaches."

"Such a curious meal!" said Inspector Cockrill, brooding over it. "He was the bridegroom, so you'd think everybody would be falling over themselves to please him. But, no; he didn't like oysters, but he has oysters; he hated cold meat but cold meat is all there is; he was violently teetotal but he's given peaches soaked in liqueur."

Cockrill sat with his chin in his hand, his bright birdlike eyes gazing away into nothingness. "There has been a plan here, Doctor. No simple matter of a lick of poison scraped out of a fortuitous tin, smeared onto a fortuitous peach-in-liqueur. No, a very elaborate, deep-laid, long-thought-out, absolutely sure-fire plan. But who planned it? Who carried it out and with what ultimate motive?" He broke off, then said slowly, "Of course whatever's in the will, as the law is now, she will still be a rich widow—more agreeable to her, presumably, than being a rich wife."

"You don't honestly think that Elizabeth—?"

"Elizabeth had nothing to do with the preparation of the food; she hasn't been in the house for the past three days, except for that brief period when she and Theo dropped in on the way to the church. Each was then alone for only a minute or two—not nearly enough time to have chanced prying open the tin, scooping out the stuff, and poisoning the peaches, which anyway were still in sealed bottles, or the cold meat or the oysters or anything else. Anyway, you'd taste it on cold meat or oysters. On the other hand, Elizabeth is a trained nurse." He mused over it. "He had a bad cold. Could she have persuaded him to take some drug or other? On the way back from the church, for example."

"He was a man who would never touch medicines. He got these periodic colds, and the place was full of pills and potions I'd prescribed for him, but he'd never even try them. Besides," he insisted, as Bill had before him, "wasn't the stuff on the peach?" And it was that fat slob Theo who had been responsible for the peach. Not that he wanted to suggest, he added rather hurriedly, that Theo would have murdered his own father. But—"You needn't think I haven't seen him, gooping at her."

"You needn't think I haven't seen you all gooping at her."

"I've made up my mind," said the doctor, quietly and humbly. "If I can get out of this business with my family still safe and sound, never so long as I can help it will I see Elizabeth again."

"You are a worker," said Cockie, "not a true drone. It will be easier for you. Bill is a drone; he admits it—only *he* calls it a bum."

And so was fat Theo a drone. Bill, Theo, the doctor…

But the doctor had a family of his own whom he had had no intention, ever, of deserting for Elizabeth the virgin queen. And so for that matter had Bill a wife of his own whom, even now, even knowing Elizabeth, he cared for. And Theo was sufficient unto himself and would go no further than a little yearning, a little mooning, an occasional sentimental somersaulting of the fatty heart.

Only one of them mates… Of the four, mass flighting

after the queen, only one in fact had been a mate—and sure enough he had died.

Of the three remaining—which one might be capable of murder simply to prevent that mating?

———————

Investigation, interrogation—the messages to Harrod's, to Fortnum's, to the pharmacist's shop in the village; the telephone calls to Mr. Caxton's lawyers, to Stepson Bill's few contacts in America, to the departed domestic staff…

The afternoon passed and the light summer evening came; and Cockrill stood with the four of them out on the terrace of the big, ugly, anything-but-desirable residence, which must now be all Elizabeth's.

"Elizabeth—Mrs. Caxton—and you three gentlemen. In this business there is only one conceivable motive. Money doesn't come into it. The new will had been signed, so Mr. Caxton's death now or later made no difference to its contents. None of you appears to be in any urgent financial need. So there's only one motive, and therefore only one question: who would commit murder to prevent Harold Caxton from ever going to bed with Elizabeth?"

Theo, Bill, Dr. Ross. Out of these three… Softly, softly, catchee monkey, said Inspector Cockrill to himself. Aloud he said, "This murder was a planned murder—nothing was left to chance. So why, I go on asking myself, should his very first mouthful of peach have been the fatal one? And I answer myself, 'Think about that spoon!'"

"You mean the spoon Theo was using to dish out the peaches?" said Elizabeth quickly. "But no, because Theo didn't hand the plate to his father. He couldn't know which peach he'd get."

"Unless he directed a special plate to his father?" suggested Bill, casting a quizzical eye on Inspector Cockrill. He reassured a suddenly quacking Theo. "Okay, okay, pal, take it easy! We've already worked through that one."

"In any event, it still wouldn't account for the first mouthful being the poisoned one. And Elizabeth," said Inspector Cockrill severely, "please don't go trying to put me off! That was a red herring—to draw my attention away from the *other* spoon—the spoon handed directly to your husband by Bill, here."

She began to cry, drearily, helplessly, biting on the little white screwed-up ball of her handkerchief. "Inspector, Harold is dead—all this won't bring him back. Couldn't you—? Couldn't we—?" And she burst out that if it was all because of her, it was so dreadful for people to be in all this trouble.

"But your husband has been murdered. What do you expect me to do, let it go at that, just because his murderer had a sentimental crush on you?" He came back to the other spoon. "If that spoon had been smeared with poison—"

She stopped crying and raised her head triumphantly. "It couldn't have been. Harold looked at it to see if it was clean—he always did after the servants left. He said that I—" The lower lip began to wobble again. "I know he's dead, but he wasn't very kind," she said.

Not Theo, then, who could not have known that the poisoned peach would reach his father. Not Bill, who could not have poisoned the peach at all.

"And so," said Dr. Ross, "you come to me?"

It was very still out there on the terrace; the sun had gone down and soon the stars would be out, almost invisible in the pale evening sky. They stood, still and quiet, and for a little while all were silent. Then Elizabeth said at last, slowly, "Inspector, Dr. Ross has a wife of his own. He has children."

"He still might not care for the vision of you in the arms of 'that filthy old brute,' as he called him."

"That went for the three of us," said the doctor.

"But it was you that went for Mr. Caxton, Doctor, wasn't it? Or went *to* him, if you prefer. Went to him and put down his throat a finger protected by a rubber fingerstall."

A rubber finger covering—thrust down the throat of a man having an everyday choking attack. A fingerstall dabbed in advance in a tin of poison.

"You don't really believe this?" said Dr. Ross, aghast. "You *can't* believe it! Murder my own patient!" Elizabeth caught at his arm, crying out, "Of course he doesn't mean it!" But the doctor ignored her. "And murder him in such a way! How could I have known he'd have an attack of choking at exactly the right moment?"

"He was always having attacks of choking," said Cockie.

"But Dr. Ross couldn't have *got* the poison," said Elizabeth. "It wasn't he who fetched the bag from the hall." She broke off. "Oh, Theo, I didn't intend—"

"I got the bag," said Theo. "But that doesn't mean anything."

"It could mean it was you who dabbed the fingerstall with poison."

Theo's round face lost colour. "Me, Inspector? How could I have? How could I know anything about it? *I* don't know what they use fingerstalls for and what they don't."

"Anyway, he wouldn't have had time," said Elizabeth. "Not to think it all out, open the poison tin, find the fingerstall in the bag. Fingerstalls are kept in a side pocket, not floating about at the top of a medical bag."

But in fact that was just where it had been—floating about at the top of the medical bag. Bill, crouching beside the doctor over the heaving body, had located it immediately and handed it to him. "I had used it on a patient just before I came to the church," said Dr. Ross. "You can check, if you like. I dipped it in an antiseptic, dried it, and chucked it back into my bag. I was in a hurry to come to the wedding."

In a hurry to come to Elizabeth's wedding. "So the fingerstall was in the front of your mind then, Doctor? When you brought in your medical bag and put it down on the chair in the hall your eye fell on that tin of poison. Everyone was milling about, just back from the ceremony, not thinking of anyone except the bride and bridegroom. You take out a little scoop of the poison, using the fingerstall—just in case an occasion arises. And an occasion does arise. What a bit of luck!"

"Inspector Cockrill," said Elizabeth steadily, "this is all nonsense! Dr. Ross smelled the stuff on Harold's breath long before he needed the fingerstall. You saw him yourself, as I said, sort of sniffing—"

"Sort of sniffing at nothing," said Cockie. "There was nothing to sniff at, was there, Doctor?—not yet. But it placed the poison, you see, in advance of the *true* poisoning with the fingerstall. The man chokes, the doctor leans over him, pretends to be suspicious. *Then* the poisoned fingerstall down the throat—and this time there *is* something to sniff at. And when the fingerstall is examined later, the fact of its having been down the throat of a man already poisoned would account for any traces of cyanide on it. Now all that remains is to pinpoint the earlier source of the poison. Well, that's easy. The doctor wipes off the fingerstall on the napkin, and then—so innocently!—places the napkin over the peach, thus putting poison on the peach." His bright eyes, birdlike, looked triumphantly at them.

They all stood, rigid, staring at the doctor—horrified, questioning. Elizabeth cried out, "Oh—it isn't true!" But a note of doubt had crept into her voice.

"I don't think so—no," said Cockie. "This isn't a crime in which anything was left to chance."

She went over to the doctor, put her two little hands on his arm, laid her forehead for a moment against his shoulder, in a gesture entirely devoid of coquetry. "Oh, thank God! He frightened me."

"He didn't frighten me," said Dr. Ross stoutly; but he looked, all the same, exceedingly pale. To Cockrill he said, "He got these attacks of choking, yes, but only once or twice a year. You couldn't risk all that on the chance of his having one today."

"So that brings us back to you, Theo," said Inspector Cockrill blandly. "You gave him peaches in Kirsch and you *made* him have one."

Theo looked as likely to have a choking attack as his father had. "I *made* him have one?"

"My dear Theo! The man was a rabid teetotaller. You provide him with a peach in a thick syrup of Kirsch, having observed that he has a heavy cold and won't smell the liqueur. He takes a great gulp of it and realises he's been tricked into taking alcohol. You knew your father—he would go off into one of his spluttering rages and if he didn't choke on the peach he'd choke on his own spluttering. And it's true, isn't it, that you know all about choking attacks, and how the air passages can be freed with a finger covered with a fingerstall? You must have seen your father having an attack at least once or twice—he'd been having them for years."

Theo began to splutter, himself. "I couldn't have done it—gone out into the hall, you mean, to get the bag and put stuff on the fingerstall? Elizabeth showed that, earlier—I wouldn't have had time."

"We were all preoccupied, getting your father out of his chair and lowered onto the floor. The seconds pass quickly."

But she couldn't bear it for Theo, either. "Don't listen to him, Theo, don't be frightened. This is no more true than his other theories. He's—he's sort of needling us, trying to make us say something incriminating. If Theo did it, Inspector, what about Dr. Ross? Why should he have sniffed at Harold's breath, when he was lying back in the chair? There would have been nothing to sniff at, not yet. You might say he was pretending; but if it was Theo who put the poison on the fingerstall, why should the doctor have pretended? Unless—"

She broke off, clapped her hand across her mouth, took it away immediately, and began to fiddle with her handkerchief. Inspector Cockrill said, "Yes, Elizabeth? Unless—?"

"Nothing," said Elizabeth. "I just mean the doctor wouldn't have put on an act if it had been Theo who had done it."

"Unless—" He thought about it and his eyes were as brilliant as stars. "Unless, Elizabeth, you were going to say, unless they were in it together."

And the Inspector looked round at the three of them and smiled with the smile of a tiger. "Unless they were all three in it together."

Three men united—united in loving the same woman, united in not wishing actually to possess her, but united in their determination not to let a fourth man have her.

The first casual exchange of thought, of feeling, of their

common disgust and dread; the first casual discussion of some sort of action, some sort of rescue; the vague threats, hardening into determination, into hard fact, into realistic plotting. But—murder! Even backed up by the others, which one of them would positively commit murder? And, none accepting, divide the deed, then, among them—as in an execution where a dozen men fire the bullets and no one man kills.

Bill's task was to acquire the poison and see that it remained available in the hall.

Theo's task was to insure as far as possible that a chance arose to use a poisoned fingerstall.

The doctor's that, of course, was to actually employ it.

But lest that seem too heavy a share of the guilt for one partner to carry, Theo could be the one to go out into the hall and poison the fingerstall, Bill to take the bag from him and hand the poisoned thing to the doctor.

Executioners: does he who administers the poison kill more than he who procures it? Does he who presents the victim to the murder kill the less because he does not do the actual slaying? All for one, and one for all! And all for the purity of Elizabeth, the virgin queen.

Elizabeth stood with him, weeping, in the hall, while a sergeant herded the three men into the huge, hideous drawing room and kept them there till the police car arrived. "I don't believe it—I utterly don't believe it, Inspector. Those three? Together?"

He had said it long ago, from the very beginning: "A very elaborate, deep-laid, long-thought-out, absolutely sure-fire plan."

"Between the doctor and Theo, then, if you must. But Bill—why drag Bill into it?"

"Ah, Bill," the Inspector said. "But without Bill...? You have been very loyal, but I think we must now come out into the open about Bill."

And he was back with her, so many weeks ago now, when Harold Caxton's proposed new marriage had first become an open secret. "But a trained nurse like you can get wonderful jobs," he had said to her. "Travel all over the place, see the world." "I *have* seen the world," she had answered.

"All right," she admitted now, in a small voice. "Yes. I did go to America, I did get married there. Harold knew I'd been married, and divorced. I didn't tell other people because he didn't like anyone else knowing."

Married, and divorced. Married to one who "bumming around" had heard through the old, devoted family servants that his mother's illness would be her last, that the rich old stepfather would soon be a widower. "Inspector, we were desperate. He wouldn't work, he gambled like a maniac, I couldn't keep the two of us. And yet I couldn't leave him. I told you that he was my 'lost love'; well, that was true, in its own way. He was my love, still is, and always will be. I suppose that's the way some women are."

"And some men," admitted Cockie, thinking of the suddenly desolate look when Bill had said, "I think now I made some pretty big mistakes."

"I have been so ashamed, Inspector," she said, weeping again. "Not only of what we were doing, but of all the lies, all the acting."

"Yet you went through with it?"

"You don't know Bill," she said. "But—yes, it's true. He wrote to his mother, secretly, through the servants. He said he knew of a girl, a wonderful nurse, who would soon be coming over to England. He told his mother to say nothing to the old man about it, but to try to get this girl engaged to look after her; of course the girl was me, Inspector. Then he set about getting a divorce. He actually beat up a man he pretended was having an affair with me. He overdid things a bit and got himself a term in prison, but that helped in speeding up the divorce."

"Without a divorce, of course, you couldn't have inherited; the marriage with the old man had to be watertight."

"Inspector," she said in anguish, "don't believe for one moment that this was a murder plot. His stepfather was old, in bad health, he was going to die soon anyway. I think, in fact, Bill imagined him much older and sicker than he was. He hadn't been home for a long time—to a boy his elders seem far more ancient than they really are."

"He was prepared to wait?"

"He saw the thing in terms of a year or two, no longer. Meanwhile, he would remain in England, we could see one another—after all, he was a member of the family. And I could provide him with money, I suppose; and he could keep on gambling."

"But before this happy condition of things you were to come over here, nurse the poor sick mother, then succeed in her place with the widower?"

She turned away her head. "You think it sounds terrible, Inspector; put that way, it seems terrible to me too—and it always has. But—once again, you don't know Bill. What Bill says, you have to do. And I did nurse her; she was dying, I couldn't make any difference to that, but I did nurse her and care for her—almost her last words were of gratitude to me. When she died, I could hardly bear it. I rang up Bill in

America and told him I couldn't go through with it. But—well, he just said—"

"He said you *must* go through with it—and came over here himself to make sure you did?"

"To make sure of that—and of something else," she said faintly.

"Yes," he said, thinking it over. "Of something else too. Because he's still in love with you, Elizabeth, in his own way. And he might drive you to the altar with a horrible old man, but he would never let you get as far as the old man's bed."

And in that determination he had found allies. "I suppose, Inspector, he may have meant to do it himself—God knows he never breathed even a word of such a thing to me. I think back in the States he was visualising more of a—well, an old-man-and-nurse relationship. But anyway he's a gambler—here was this chance and nothing must stand in the way of it. Then he came over here and saw me again; and saw me with his stepfather... And then perhaps, finding how the other two felt about it, I suppose he roped them in. Another gambler's chance, and so typical of Bill. Only this one will come off for a change, because the law can't do anything to them."

"How do you mean—can't do anything to them?"

"Well, but—who has committed any crime? Bill bought a tin of stuff for killing wasps—there's nothing wrong in that. Theo bought a bottle of peaches—there's nothing wrong in that either. The doctor—well, I suppose he did put the fingerstall down Harold's throat. But *he* didn't poison it. None of them has actually done one wrong action. They can't even be put in prison!"

"Only for a very short time," acknowledged Cockie.

"For a short time?"

"Till they're taken out and hanged," said Inspector Cockrill.

"You don't truly mean that? All three of them could be—executed?"

"All three," said Cockie. "For being accessories to a murder—that's the law. The flight of the queen, Elizabeth—*at certain times of the year the drones sit around eating*—well, we saw them do that—*and gazing with huge eyes upon the virgin queen*—well, we saw them do that too. And then, *the mass flight after the queen*—and that, also we've seen. But here something goes wrong with the comparison—because only one succeeds in the mating, and therefore—only one dies."

"You mean that all three—?"

"I mean that all three are not going to die. It would be too inartistic an ending to the metaphor."

"What can save them?" said Elizabeth, beginning to tremble.

"Words can save them—and will save them."

"Words?"

A dozen words—exactly a dozen, carelessly spoken, hardly listened to at all. But with reflection, how clear it had all become! Curious, thought Cockrill, how two brief sentences, barely heard, could so twist themselves about and about until they wound themselves into a rope—into a noose.

Twelve little words, hardly listened to… "Except by me, when I remembered them later. Your husband saying, 'Why couldn't we have had smoked salmon?' and you replying, 'We got what was easiest.'"

A plain-clothes man who all this time had sat quietly on a chair by the front door, got up, as quietly, and came forward; and Inspector Cockrill shot out a hand and circled her little wrist with fingers of steel. "Why should oysters have been easier than smoked salmon, Elizabeth?" he demanded.

A very elaborate, deep-laid, long-thought-out, absolutely sure-fire plan… The ugly collusion between husband and wife to implant in the household of the dying mother a new bride for the rich widower, soon to be. On the husband's part, probably nothing more, nothing worse intended, than an impatient waiting for the end of a life whose expectations had been somewhat underestimated. On her part—ah! *she* had been on the spot to recognise in advance the long years she might yet have to serve with a man who at the least sign of rebellion would pare down her inheritance to the minimum the law allowed. Had she really confessed to Harold Caxton an earlier marriage? Not likely! Of all of them, the one who had had most cause to dread Mr. Caxton's marriage bed had been Elizabeth herself—"the virgin queen."

The plot, then, deeply laid—but in one mind alone. Use the ex-husband, expendable now, as red herring Number One; ensnare with enchantments, long proved irresistible, such other poor fools as might serve to confuse the issue. With gentle insistence, no injury pinpointable, alienate servants too long faithful and now in the way. And, the scene set, sit, sweet and smiling, little hands fluttering, soft eyes mistily blue—and in the back of one's scheming mind, think and think and plan and plan…

"You can't know," she said, spitting it out at him as they drove away from the house, the three men left sick, bewildered, utterly confounded, watching her go; sitting between the Inspector and the sergeant in the smooth black police car, ceaselessly, restlessly struggling against their grip on her wrists. "You can't *know*. It's all a trick, trying to lead me up the garden path."

"No," said Cockrill. "Not any more. We've been up enough garden paths—with *you* leading *me*." His arm gave, slackly, against the tug and pull of her hand but his fingers never gave up their firm hold. "How well you did it!— poking the clues under my nose, snatching each of them back when you saw it wasn't going to work—and all with such a touching air of protecting your poor dear admirers, fallen into this terrible trap for love of you. But I matched you," he said with quiet satisfaction. "Trick for trick."

"You *can't* know," she repeated.

"I knew," he said, "from the moment I remembered his asking why he couldn't have smoked salmon. *You* ordered the meal; so why give him oysters which would only make him angry? If one thought about it—taking all the other factors into consideration—the answer had to be there."

"But the tin of poison! You saw it yourself on the hall table when we came into the dining room. I never left the dining room—so how could I have hidden it in the vase on the hall table?"

"You hid it when you went out to 'look'—it wouldn't take a second and you had your little hankie in your hand, didn't you, all ready to avoid leaving fingerprints." And with his own free hand he struck his knee. "By gum!—you'd thought this thing out, hadn't you?—right down to the last little shred of a handkerchief."

She struggled, sitting there between them, to ease their grip on her wrists. "Let me go, you brutes! You're hurting me."

"Harold Caxton didn't have too comfortable a time a-dying."

"That old hog!" she said viciously. "Who cares how such an animal dies?"

"As long as he dies."

"You'll never prove that I killed him, Inspector. How, for example," she said triumphantly, "could I have taken the poison from the tin?"

"You could have taken it while you were in the house with Theo, on the way to the church. Theo went off to the powder room—"

"For half a minute—how long does a man take, nipping into the loo? To get the stuff out of the tin and do all the rest of it—"

"Ah, but I don't say you did 'do all the rest of it'—not then. 'All the rest of it' had been prepared in advance. We'll find—if we look long enough, and we will—some pharmacist in London where you bought a *second* tin of the cyanide for wasps. The tin in the hall was a blind; there was time enough even during Theo's half minute in the powder room to take a quick scoop out of it—no doubt you'd arranged to have it left on the hall table. That scoop was probably disposed of in the powder room when *you* went there, after Theo."

"You know it all, don't you?" she said sarcastically; but she was growing weary, helpless; she was sitting limply between them now, slumped against the seat.

A very elaborate, deep-laid, long-thought-out, absolutely sure-fire plot, and all of it conceived in the mind of one little woman—a woman consumed, destroyed, by the dangerous knowledge of her own invincibility in the hearts of men. But the cleverness, thought Cockie, the infinite patience! The long preparation, the building-up piece by piece of the "book" itself, of the props, the scenery—the way a producer will work months ahead on a projected stage production.

Then—the stage set at last, the puppet actors

chosen—and curtain up! The "exposition"—"Bill, for goodness sake get the stuff from the pharmacist for me—the old
man will slay me if I don't get his wretched old wasp stuff.
Just leave it on the hall table, let him think I got it for him
and I put it there"; and "Theo, I've ordered the stuff from
Harrod's, but I never thought about a dessert. You could
hop across to Fortnum's and get some of those peaches-
in-Kirsch; I've seen them there and they look delicious.
Teetotal?—oh, lord, so he is! But still, why should everyone
else suffer?—perhaps this will make up to them for having
no champagne. And he's got his usual fearful cold, so he
probably won't even notice."

In the excitement and confusion who would remember
accurately, who would carry in their heads, all the com-
mands and countercommands, all the myriad unimportant
small decisions, and who had made them? Who, for that
matter, of her three cavaliers, would shelter behind her
skirts to cry out, "It was Elizabeth who told me to." So Bill
introduces the poison into the house, and Theo the peach
which is to be found guilty of conveying the poison; and if
the doctor does not bring in his medical bag, then busy little
Elizabeth, ex-nurse, will be there to remind him of police
exhortations not to leave the bag in his car.

The stage is set, the cast assembled, the puppet
actors—Inspector Cockrill himself included, to do the
observing—are moved this way and that at the twitch of a
thread, held in a small hand already dyed red with the victim's blood.

For even as he swallowed his last oyster, even as he
munched his way resentfully through his cold meat, even
as he began on the peach, already Harold Caxton had been
a dying man. "Why couldn't we have had smoked salmon?"

he had asked angrily; and, after all, smoked salmon could have been sent down from Harrod's just as easily as oysters. But, "We got what was easiest," she had replied; and ultimately Inspector Cockrill had asked himself—*why*? Why should oysters have been easier than smoked salmon?

Answer: Because you cannot conceal a capsule of poison as easily in a plate of smoked salmon as you can in a plate of oysters.

A man who likes oysters will retain them in his mouth, will chumble them a little, gently, savouring their peculiar delight for him. A man who does not care for oysters—and Mr. Caxton was not one to make concessions—will swallow them down whole, and be done with it.

Harold Caxton had had a heavy cold—he was always having colds—and the house was full of specifics against the colds, though he would not touch any of them. Among the specifics would certainly be some bottles of small capsules made of slow-dissolving gelatine, filled with various compounds of drugs. A capsule, emptied out, could be filled with enough cyanide to kill a man. An oyster, slit open with a sharp knife, could offer just such a pocket as would accommodate the capsule and then close over it again, thus concealing the poison-filled capsule.

No time, of course, as she had truly said, to achieve it all in the brief period when she and Theo had visited the house. But an oyster bar would be found in London, if Cockie searched long enough—and he would search long enough—where a little, blue-eyed woman had yesterday treated herself to a dozen oysters, eaten only eleven, and left behind her only eleven shells. A small plastic bag, damp with fluid from the uneaten oyster, no doubt was also got rid of in the powder room. For the rest—it wouldn't take a moment to slip into the dining room (Theo having been sent off like a small boy to the loo) and substitute the poisoned oyster for an innocent one on Harold Caxton's plate.

Ten minutes later Elizabeth the virgin queen had given her hand to a man who within the hour, and by that same hand, would to her certain knowledge be dead; and had promised before God to love, cherish, and keep him till death did them part...

Well, if there was an afterlife, reflected Inspector Cockrill coming away from the Old Bailey a couple of months later, at least they would soon be reunited. Meanwhile, he must remember to look up hornets, and see whether the queens also have a sting.

If you've enjoyed *Guilty Creatures: A Menagerie of Mysteries,* you won't want to miss

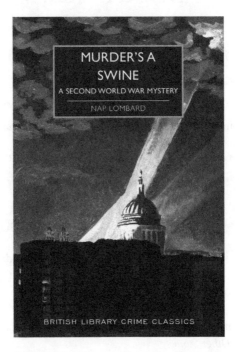

the most recent BRITISH LIBRARY CRIME CLASSIC published by Poisoned Pen Press, an imprint of Sourcebooks.

Don't miss these favorite British Library Crime Classics available from Poisoned Pen Press!

Mysteries written during the Golden Age of Detective Fiction, beloved by readers and reviewers

Antidote to Venom
by Freeman Wills Crofts

Bats in the Belfry
by E. C. R. Lorac

Blood on the Tracks:
Railway Mysteries
edited by Martin Edwards

Calamity in Kent
by John Rowland

Christmas Card Crime
and Other Stories
edited by Martin Edwards

Cornish Coast Murder
by John Bude

Continental Crimes
edited by Martin Edwards

Crimson Snow: Winter Mysteries
edited by Martin Edwards

Death in the Tunnel
by Miles Burton

Death of a Busybody
by George Bellairs

Death on the Riviera
by John Bude

Fell Murder
by E. C. R. Lorac

Incredible Crime
by Lois Austen-Leigh

Miraculous Mysteries
edited by Martin Edwards

Murder at the Manor
edited by Martin Edwards

Murder in the Museum
by John Rowland

Murder of a Lady
by Anthony Wynne

Mystery in the Channel
by Freeman Wills Crofts

Mystery in White
by J. Jefferson Farjeon

Portrait of a Murderer
by Anne Meredith

Santa Klaus Murder
by Mavis Doriel Hay

Secret of High Eldersham
by Miles Burton

Serpents in Eden
edited by Martin Edwards

Silent Nights
edited by Martin Edwards

Smallbone Deceased
by Michael Gilbert

Sussex Downs Murder
by John Bude

Thirteen Guests
by J. Jefferson Farjeon

Weekend at Thrackley
by Alan Melville

Z Murders
by J. Jefferson Farjeon

Praise for the
British Library Crime Classics

"Carr is at the top of his game in this taut whodunit... The British Library Crime Classics series has unearthed another worthy golden age puzzle."

—*Publishers Weekly*, STARRED Review,
for *The Lost Gallows*

"A wonderful rediscovery."

—*Booklist*, STARRED Review, for *The Sussex Downs Murder*

"First-rate mystery and an engrossing view
into a vanished world."

—*Booklist*, STARRED Review, for *Death of an Airman*

"A cunningly concocted locked-room mystery, a staple of Golden Age detective fiction."

—*Booklist*, STARRED Review, for *Murder of a Lady*

"The book is both utterly of its time and utterly ahead of it."

—*New York Times Book Review* for *The Notting Hill Mystery*

"As with the best of such compilations, readers of classic mysteries will relish discovering unfamiliar authors, along with old favorites such as Arthur Conan Doyle and G.K. Chesterton."

—*Publishers Weekly,* STARRED Review, for *Continental Crimes*

"In this imaginative anthology, Edwards—president of Britain's Detection Club—has gathered together overlooked criminous gems."

—*Washington Post* for *Crimson Snow*

"The degree of suspense Crofts achieves by showing the growing obsession and planning is worthy of Hitchcock. Another first-rate reissue from the British Library Crime Classics series."

—*Booklist*, STARRED Review, for *The 12.30 from Croydon*

"Not only is this a first-rate puzzler, but Crofts's outrage over the financial firm's betrayal of the public trust should resonate with today's readers."

—*Booklist,* STARRED Review, for *Mystery in the Channel*

"This reissue exemplifies the mission of the British Library Crime Classics series in making an outstanding and original mystery accessible to a modern audience."

—*Publishers Weekly*, STARRED Review, for *Excellent Intentions*

"A book to delight every puzzle-suspense enthusiast"

—*New York Times* for *The Colour of Murder*

"Edwards's outstanding third winter-themed anthology showcases 11 uniformly clever and entertaining stories, mostly from lesser known authors, providing further evidence of the editor's expertise...This entry in the British Library Crime Classics series will be a welcome holiday gift for fans of the golden age of detection."

—*Publishers Weekly,* STARRED Review, for *The Christmas Card Crime and Other Stories*

Poisoned Pen
PRESS

poisonedpenpress.com